85
3£

9

GW00986172

"So." Amusement bubbling inside, Aleytys tented her fingers, touching fingertip to fingertip. "If I take this Hunt, I should figure a way past a small armada, then set down on a world where electronic gear will work haphazardly or not at all. I have to outwit or outfight some of the most vicious and wily predators a hundred worlds could produce. I have to avoid local flora and fauna, which—if my luck runs as usual—will prove to be lethal. I have to pick up and transport a Queen who seems to be encased in a casket with life support mechanisms which together probably weigh a ton or two. Haul that out of whatever mess it's stuck in. Last, I have to take off somehow in a ship I probably don't have in the face of that armada I mentioned before, an armada probably doubled in size. Am I crazy?"

"There's a bonus, Lee." Head sighed. "The Haestavaada will buy you the best ship available if you can get the Queen to Duvaks."

"If." Aleytys moved to the door, stood with one hand on the cool wood, looking back at Head. "Think I can do it?"

"Yes."

Aleytys pushed the door open. "You better be right."

The Nowhere Hunt

Jo Clayton

DAW BOOKS, INC.
DONALD A. WOLLHEIM, PUBLISHER
1633 Broadway, New York, NY 10019

FIRST PRINTING, NOVEMBER 1981

1 2 3 4 5 6 7 8 9

DAW TRADEMARK REGISTERED
U.S. PAT. OFF. MARCA
REGISTRADA. HECHO EN U.S.A.

PRINTED IN U.S.A.

Prologue:

PROPOSING THE HUNT

WE WENT TOO NEAR THE ZANGAREE SINK. The translator's slow mechanical monotone drained the intensity from the agitated twitters and clicks of the dying vaad whose small form shuddered among the wires and tubes that were keeping it alive. As the air shrilled through the spiracles on its sides, as its eyes seemed to bulge from the immobile plating on its round head, it struggled to control the emotion that hurried disintegration nearer. For several minutes the only sounds in the sterile room were the flute wails of the vaad's breathing and the tick-tick of the instruments recording the pulses of its heart nodes. The vaad attendants watched the dying one closely, adjusting the flow of liquids to its needs, touching it, keeping it reassured by contact with its kind. This tactile presence—the three-fingered top-hand resting on the Y-cartilage in the center of its thorax—helped calm it until it could speak again.

TIKH'ASFOUR PACK CAME ON SHIP BY KHAKK'LAH SPUR. WAITING FOR QUEENSHIP (question). THIS VAAD KNOWS NOT. The chitin of the vaad's battered body was torn and cracked, flushing through pale iridescence as its strength faded. It lifted its head slightly, let it fall back, began talking again, slowly at first, then faster and faster, the monotonous drone of the translator conveying some of the intense emotion through the sheer speed with which it rattled out the words.

VALAAD CAPTAIN SEN'TATI BHUT FLED, DIPPING IN AND OUT OF FTL, CHANGING DIRECTION, LEAVING THE PLANE OF THE LENS, SPENDING FUEL WITHOUT STINT. THE PACK CAME ON, SANK TEETH IN SHIP TAIL. PACK CAME CLOSER AND CLOSER. STARTED RANGING SHIPS WITH QUILL MISSLES. SEN'TATI BHUT SAW ZANGAREE AHEAD. RAN, THIS VAAD THINKS, INTO SUDDEN BULGE WHEN BHUT SKIMMED ALONG EDGE OF SINK. SHIP WENT CRAZY. HAGGAR SUB-LIGHTS KICKED

ON, KNOCKING. GRAVITY WENT. VAADA SMASHED AGAINST
WALLS, STRUTS. SHIP IN GREAT TROUBLE. SUN AHEAD. ZOLDE-
VUUR. SEN'TATI BHUT SEE SMALL WORLD. WORLD CALLED
NOWHERE. AIR AND GREEN LIFE. CAN VAAD AND VALAAD LIVE
IN SINK(question). SEN'TATI BHUT KNEW NOT. SHIP BREAK-
ING UP AROUND VAAD AND VALAAD. TIKH'ASFOUR COMING AF-
TER. VAADA AFRAID. THIS VAAD CURLS INTO [noise] POSTURE
TO WAIT THE DYING. SEN'TATI BHUT FOUGHT SHIP DOWN.
CRASHED—NO, NOT CRASHED. CAME IN HARD. NOT VA-
PORIZED, ONLY BROKEN . VAADA DIED EVERYWHERE. BURNED.
CRUSHED. THIS VAAD'S ZESH, IT CURLED BESIDE THIS VAAD,
TOUCHED THIS VAAD. ITS HEAD . . . TORN OFF . . . THIS VAAD
UNCURLED WHEN IT KNEW IT WOULD LIVE. COULDN'T FEEL
ZESH. TOUCHED ROUND THING. ZESH'S HEAD. ROLLED AWAY.
BUMPING. ROLLED AWAY.

As the air whistled through the paired spiracles, the attendant stroked small top-hands over the Y, trying to quiet the
heaving body, while others fed more drugs into the tubes.

An elongated vaad stepped into view—a valaad, gaunt,
faded to the palest of blues, four eyes set in wrinkled yellow
rings, an iron chain thick with rust about its reed-thin neck,
an empty circle of the same metal dangling over its central
fissure, its chitin and cartilage stained with years of rust and
rubbing. The attendants parted hastily as the valaad moved to
the injured one's side. It placed its long, three-fingered top-
hand on the throbbing Y, then looked directly into the lens.
The image went dark.

Aleytys blinked into the shadows. "What do they want?"

As Head swung about to face her, her silver-gray hair
caught the window's faint glow with a shifting shine like
spilled mercury while the dim light touched her forehead,
nose and chin, drew shadows in black paint along hollows
and lines. When she spoke after her moment of silence, her
words came crisply, their restrained vigor so usual that
Aleytys was momentarily reassured. "They want you," Head
said. She lifted a hand. "Wait. The story's not finished."

The valaad moved away from the bed, frowned briefly at
the lens, then stepped out of the scene, leaving the injured
vaad lying quiet, barely breathing. After a moment it stirred.

A few harsh sounds came from the translator, then slow words.

THE VAADA STILL LIVING CAME TOGETHER, TWO VAADA BRINGING NEWS THAT THE QUEEN LIVED ALSO, HER LIFESUPPORT INTACT. HIVE BE BLESSED, THE QUEEN LIVED. SLEPT SAFE AND UNKNOWING. THE QUEEN'S GUARD, ALL ALIVE, TENDING HER. THE VAADA GATHERED, HAPPY IN THIS, TO THE ROOM OF IN-BEING. ONLY VAADA WERE LEFT. ONLY VAADA EXCEPT FOR THE QUEEN'S GUARD AND THESE WOULD NOT LEAVE QUEENSVAULT OR CONCERN THEMSELVES WITH VAADA SORROWS. NO ZESH PAIRS LEFT WHOLE. VAADA MOURNED THEIR ZESH. VAADA WISHED TO DIE, BUT THE QUEEN LIVED AND THEY COULD NOT DIE, NOT YET. The injured vaad lay silent, the other vaada mourned with it, clacking their mandibles in a slow sad rhythm. Then it spoke again.

OUTSIDE WAS TERRIBLE. HOT FOG. THINGS IN THE FOG. GRAY-WHITE BEASTS WITH MANY TEETH. THESE SWARMED INTO SHIP, DRAGGED OUT TWO VAADA. ATE THEM. *Nowhere* NOT YET IN THE SINK SO ENERGY GUNS STILL WORKED. VAADA DROVE OFF THE BEAST PACK. NATIVES CAME. ATTACKED WITH SPEARS AND POISON DARTS. SPEARS KILLED THREE VAADA, DARTS BOUNCED OFF. VAADA DROVE OFF NATIVES, KILLED SOME. IN SHIP SOME THINGS STILL WORKED. VAADA PUT DEAD THROUGH FOOD CONVERTERS, MADE MANY FOOD STICKS. THIS VAAD SECOND NAVIGATOR. WORKED SCANNER. SAW TIKH'ASFOUR ORBITING WORLD, SEARCHING FOR QUEENSHIP. TURNED SCANNER OFF BEFORE PACK FOUND SHIP. KSIYL THE HOOK, FIRST GUARD, CAME TO VAADA. SAID VAADA AND VALAADA WAITED ON DAVAKS FOR QUEEN. SAID THEY STOOD ON SHOULDERS OF THESE VAADA, THAT VAADA THERE DIED WITHOUT THE PRESENCE OF A QUEEN. SAID SEVERAL LIFEBOATS WERE WHOLE. SAID LIFESUPPORT IN BOAT NOT ENOUGH FOR TWO, NOT FOR THE LENGTH OF JOURNEY NEEDED. SAID ONE WOULD HAVE TO GO ALONE. THIS VAAD BEING THE SOLE NAVIGATOR AMONG THE LIVING, THIS VAAD TOOK THE LIFEBOAT AND CAME TO KAVAAKH. DAYS AND DAYS ALONE. DAYS WONDERING IF THE TIKH'ASFOUR WOULD FIND THIS VAAD OR FIND THE QUEENSHIP. THIS VAAD LANDED ON KAVAAKH. LANDED HARD. GOT MESSAGE THROUGH. The vaad suddenly pushed up, leaning its meager weight onto one trembling arm. Its face was chitin-plated and denied expression, its eyes dull, but the passion behind its words came through the lens. THE QUEEN, HUNTERS, GET HER OUT. GET HER OUT.

The attendant touched a hand to the Y-cartilage and the injured vaad collapsed. The screen went black.

"The vaad died a few minutes after that." Head punched the humming viewer off, stabbed a forefinger at the button that sent the shade flowing back from the window and let the cool white light from outside into the room, swung around in her chair, settled back, bright blue eyes fixed on Aleytys. "You look better." Her quick broad smile lit her face. "Not twitching any more."

"The Wild either soothes you or sends you crazy. You know that better than I." Aleytys rubbed her nose. "Gray and I—well, we came out of the snow at peace with ourselves and with each other." A corner of her mouth twisted up. "A change that. It's probably a good thing he went off on a Hunt before the euphoria wore off." She laced her fingers together in her lap and stared down at them. "How's he doing?"

"No word yet. And none expected for another month at least." Head pursed her lips. "You've had the first of the implants. Feel comfortable with it?"

"Comfortable enough." Aleytys looked down at her hands, smiled. "Five little forcefields. Handy."

Head winced. "That was feeble, Lee. Very feeble."

"Mmh!" Aleytys nodded at the wall where the screen had been. "I take it I won't be going back to University for a while?"

"You will sooner than you think. There's still time to finish the implants and check you out on them." Head leaned forward, pulled an untidy pile of fax sheets in front of her and squared them with a few brisk taps.

Aleytys moved her eyes from the fax sheets to the square, lined face. "You've got a Hunt for me."

"Obviously." The fax sheets rustled as the hands on them moved about. Head stared down at the sheets in silence, long enough for Aleytys to wonder what monsters waited for her in them. Finally the bright blue eyes lifted and fixed on her. "Background. The Haestavaada and the Tikh'asfour—rather similar as species go, physically at least—have been sniping at each other for the past two centuries, god knows what about, they surely don't. Neither species can afford the cost

of an all-out attack on the other so they have to be content
with pecking at each other. The Haestavaada are good at de-
fense, but hesitant and unimaginative when they attack. The
Tikh'asfour are brilliant fighters but spend nearly as much
time squabbling with each other as they do trying to fight the
Haestavaada. Not long ago, however, one of the Packs put
together a suicide squad and slipped it through the Haestavaada defenses on their colony world Duvaks. They managed
to kill the Haevstavaada Queen there and her three juvenile
Queens before they were shredded by the frantic vaada. Once
the news of the Queen's death got out, the vaada all over the
world went into shock. It was all the valaada could do to get
their defenses in place then send off an urgent message to
Kavaakh. The Haestavaada on the homeworld got one of
their juveniles ready, mated her, boxed her up and sent her to
Duvaks on Sen'tati Bhut's ship. You heard what happened to
that."

Aleytys frowned. "They can't send another queen—with a
fleet to protect her this time?"

"They don't have another the right age." Head tapped
slowly on the pile of fax sheets. "It would take them several
years to ripen one."

"Why is having a queen on Duvaks so . . ."

"So necessary?"

"They haven't lost the Queen on Kavaakh. If they need a
symbol?" She shrugged. "I don't see the problem."

"Right." Head sighed and settled back into her chair.
"Kavaakh is too far away. They need a Queen among them.
You can research this more, but this is the gist of the matter.
Interesting species, the Haestavaada. Got four separate kinds
of individuals—if a hive species can be said to have individuals. I suppose it can, looking at that poor damn vaad in the
tape sequence. Anyway. They've got true Neuters—the
vaada. They're the workers and the great bulk of the population. Next biggest section has the Neutered Females—the valaada. The leaders. They run the worlds. Intelligent and more
aggressive than the vaada. Then the Males. Very few of
those, maybe not more than ten at any one time on each
world, pampered pets, that's all. Finally the Queens—true females. Egg-layers. Only semi-intelligent, insanely aggressive
before they're mated, stone-lazy after, which is just as well
since they spend most of their time producing eggs. Very

short life-spans. After a little more than twenty years they start producing defective eggs. A Juvenile is mated and the old Queen killed. The Queen on Kavaakh is reaching her end. The Kavaakhi Haestavaada had only two Queens of the proper age. They sent one of these to Duvaks but they won't send away their only other properly aged Juvenile, not even to save the lives of their kin on Duvaks."

Aleytys frowned. "Save the lives?"

"Without their Queen it seems that vaada just curl up and wither away. The valaada are tougher but there aren't a lot of them and they can't keep a world going by themselves. If Duvaks doesn't get a Queen relatively soon, the Tikh'asfour will have hit the Haestavaada very hard indeed. So they want someone to get their Queen back for them."

"Since they don't just go in and lift her out themselves, this looks like one of the nasty ones you seem to save for me."

The bright blue eyes closed. "Council thinks I should turn the Hunt down."

"Well?"

"The Haestavaada asked for you specifically, Lee. Your reputation spreads."

"Go on."

"*Nowhere*—ridiculous name for a world, though appropriate from what I've heard—anyway, it's swung into the Zangaree Sink which effectively seals it off from the rest of us for another five or six months—why I said we had time to finish your implants. Far as I know, there's no way you can get to that world until it swings free of the Sink. You or anyone else." Head picked up the fax sheets and fanned herself with them. "The last report of a Haestavaada spy drone says that two Tikh'asfour Packs are hanging around on the edge of the Sink, passing the time by fighting with each other. There'll be more when *Nowhere's* due to emerge."

"So. I probably can't get past the Packs and I couldn't land on the world even if I did manage to slip past. Anything else?"

"Scavengers."

"You're joking."

"Sorry, Lee. Seems they were either hanging around behind the Pack or stumbled on them after the attack began. Bad luck either way. Three ships landed on *Nowhere* just before it slipped into the Sink. God knows what the Scavs are doing down there without workable electronics. Whatever it is, they've had three months to do it in."

"So." Amusement bubbling inside, Aleytys said, "If I take this Hunt, I should figure a way past a small armada, then set down on a world where electronic gear will work haphazardly or not at all, if I can think up a way to get down on *Nowhere* before it emerges. I have to outwit or outfight some of the most vicious and wily predators a hundred worlds could produce. I have to avoid local flora and fauna, which—if my luck runs as usual—will prove to be damned lethal. I have to pick up and transport a Queen who seems to be encased in a casket with life-support mechanisms which together probably weigh a ton or two. Haul that out of whatever mess it's stuck in. Last, I have to take off somehow in a ship I probably don't have in the face of that armada I mentioned before, an armada probably doubled in size. Am I crazy?"

"The Haestavaada have promised to give you anything you ask for." She met Aleytys's skeptical eyes and held up a hand. "There's a bonus, Lee."

"There damn well better be."

Head sighed. "The Haestavaada will buy you the best ship available if you can get the Queen to Duvaks."

"You really want me to take this on, don't you."

"I'm in a bind," Head said slowly. "The RMoahl keep hounding the Council. They want you bad and they're getting hostile about it. No one knows just what those spiders will do. Thing is, anyone who fools with them tends to disappear permanently." Her wide mouth tightened into a smile. "The reputation you're getting creates another problem for me. Hunters! Egos on two legs. The Watukuu seem to be grabbing onto everyone and gabbling out how you backed a Vryhh down when you Hunted for them on Sunguralingu. The tale's come back to me from a dozen sources, customers who've asked for you—like the Haestavaada. They grumble when I refuse but most end up taking another Hunter. Guess how the Hunters like it. Hunh! And they have friends on the Council. Fortunately, your first Hunt was such a long shot and the fee so big that you brought in more than enough to cover what we've spent on you so far. And—egos aside— you're a damn good advertisement for Hunters Inc. These two things have been enough to swing Council votes in your favor." Head moved her shoulders against the chair back, made an effort to smile. "As long as I can slap the fees down in front of them, there's no problem. And as long as you take Hunts no one else wants." She ran her fingers through her short silver hair. "If you can survive the next few years, the tightroping should be over. I don't say everyone will accept you, we're not that kind of society, but for most you'll belong to Wolff and we've learned through hard times to take care of our own." She was silent a moment, the bright blue eyes flicking nervously about the room until she fixed them on Aleytys. "Dammit, I want you to have that ship. I near busted my ass screwing it out of those bugs, and getting the bonus confirmed in Council and put into the contract."

"I go in alone this time?"

"Gray's on Hunt. You know that." Head rubbed at her nose. "Sybille's free." She grinned at Aleytys. "Want to partner with Sybille?"

"You can't be serious?" Aleytys chuckled. "Can you see that steel-clawed bitch sharing anything with me, especially a Hunt?" She flexed her fingers. "Small bloody shreds. You've made your point. Let me think about this. If I can come up with a reasonable attack on the difficulties, I'll take the Hunt." She stood. "Let you know tomorrow."

"Take these with you." Head shoved the pile of fax sheets across the desk. "Summaries of what we know about *Nowhere* and the Zangaree Sink. More about the Haestavaada and the Tikh'asfour. Schematics of Haestavaada and Tikh'asfour ships. Dossiers on the better known Scavs, lists of some other names. Anything else I could come up with to help you out."

Aleytys grimaced at the thick pile. "I'll let you know *late* tomorrow." She rolled the sheets into a compact cylinder. "Thanks. A ship?"

"If you get the Queen to Davaks."

"If." Aleytys moved to the door, looked back at Head. "Think I can do it?"

"Yes."

Aleytys pushed the door open. "You better be right."

Roha

CHAPTER I

Roha straddled the limb and scraped lines of sap into a resilient lump. She didn't like how sticky it made her hands but ignored that and popped the ball into her mouth. Wrapping her legs tighter about the limb, she licked her fingers clean, then wiped them across her thighs. As she chewed the juices from the sap, her head began to buzz. She worked back along the limb until she felt the trunk hard and cold against her skin, then let herself soften, felt her flesh begin to merge with the hardness between her thighs, against her back, with the whispering around her from the pendulant leaves. "Mat-akuat," she whispered. "Dream tree, tell me . . . tell me . . . tell me the day. When is the day? When do we pull the peace sapling from the earth? The day. The day. The day. Mambila eats the sky. When is the lucky day day day day? The day the day the day?"

She stopped her chant and looked up through the thin branches dropping like lines around her, knife-blade leaves, fluttering and whispering louder and louder. She strained, trying to hear what they said, then relaxed again and looked up. To the west the sky was filmed by a webbing of light, a misty cloud webbing, moving, creeping across the sky like a slime beast crawling over swamp water. She blinked. The sky hazed out before her eyes into an echoing silver mirror. The hanging branches were streaks of silver, shivering, shimmering silver, then an absence like an emptiness in the air. The leaves were tongues dark and light, then suddenly pierced with color glowing from within, a green-gold light. Nearby an imbo sang and the beauty of the song pierced her heart. She saw each individual note soaring at her, gold darts coming up and over, they pierced her and she rejoiced, the joy so terrible it was a pain.

The leaves whispered to her. The soft uncertain wind that

touched her skin was a wash of pale blue. The night bent into curves of dark and light, into patterns. Patterns, everything was pattern, was flat and stern, was dark and light, the patterns built and built, sound, touch, feel, all patterns, stern and dark; she was compressed, folded, held within, stretched out, a pattern herself, feeling the answer growing in her, the name of the day hovering over her tongue. About to savor it, to roll it on her tongue and know it, she was wrenched from her gentle contemplation. The sky broke over her, a terrible terrifying fireball shattered the dark and plunged down . . . came down . . . the sound tore her apart, the light burnt her to ash, the sound shook the world. She felt the agony of the earth as the terrible thing struck. A glow brighter than the sun burned the earth, burned her, fire crisped her skin, she screamed and when the pain died a little she cried into the dark, "Help me, cousins. Bright Twin, Dark Twin, the Earth-womb calls me. Mother Earth you call me, you tell me to find the thorn that has pierced you, struck you to the heart, you call me to find and burn the poison thorn."

Her voice seized in her throat and she could say no more; she sat with her back pressed against the trunk, feeling waves of evil coming from the burning thorn, waves that drowned her, made her gasp for breath. She clutched at the limb and wept, saw her tears like drops of fire falling, falling, drying against the cold earth, the earth stretching under her, turning strange, a mirror, a dark mirror. The tree pushed at her, rejected her, the bark pushed her away, the limb bucked under her, pushed her hands away.

"Roha!" The sound drove into her, a stone blade slicing through her. It flayed her. She looked in terror into darkness her eyes refused to pierce. "Roha." A sound, a tender sound. She loosed her hands from the limb, glancing uneasily at them. The dark green skin was smooth and tight against flesh and bone. She blinked, looked again. The haze of the sap was retreating, the darkness under the tree thinning. A shadow balanced on the high tangled roots. She breathed in the warm flow of affection and concern coming from the shadow. Retreating farther from her vision, she could breathe and speak and perceive again. "Rihon, did you see it? Wait, I'm coming down."

Shaking and weaker than she liked, the patterns breaking before her, the patterns lurking in the corners of her eyes, she groped through dream and dark for the climbing rope, swung down it, the knots her own fingers had made comforting to her, whispering comfort into her feet and fingers. Then she was down, balancing on the air-roots, facing her brother. She held out her hands. Brother and sister touched, palm to palm. More of the ache left her. "Did you see it?" For a cold moment she wondered if it was a dream; it was hard to know, sometimes, what was real and what the dream-sap conjured out of air.

"A great light like a seed of the sun falling." Behind the calm in his voice was a touch of awe.

Roha shivered. "I saw the mistlands take it." She grasped his hands and held them tight. "Rihon, we have to burn it. We have to go out there."

"Roha, no." He moved away from the trunk and jumped onto the hard-packed earth of the path. As he turned, the Web-light painted slick gleams on the tilted planes of his face, underlining the worry that wrinkled his forehead and thinned his lips. "We can't go there." He helped her down. "The mistlands?"

Roha hesitated, then hopped down beside him. Silent, thoughtful, she followed him as he turned away and began walking down the path toward the village, his skin again giving back gleams of Web-light.

With the sap still bubbling in her blood, she passed from the solid smells and touches of the forest into a heightened state where she saw/heard/smelled everything around her with a terrible clarity, everything around her, in front of her, in the layered leaves and soil beneath her feet, behind her back. She saw everything, and finally when all the intrusive sense impressions smoothed out, walked again through the black and white patterns, the sound—patterns imposed on patterns, slashes of violent color across the black and white.

Then Rihon took her hand again; the warm firmness of his skin pulled her back to reality.

She trotted beside him, circling a mat-achun that dripped silent acid in a mist about its trunk, avoiding a slow, creeping herd of many-legged tambi, bloodsuckers with miniature vines growing from their rubbery flesh, vines that jerked out and wrapped around prey, mostly small rodents; she brushed aside, a little later, several blundering pudsi, whose short broad wings whirred noisily as they wheeled about under the

trees chasing giant buzzers and other large insects. There
were thousands of insects making soup of the night air, filling
it with a vast hum; Roha's skin twitched constantly and she
tightened her nose slits against them.

She could hear the noise from the village before she stepped
from the tree shadow a little behind her brother. She caught
hold of Rihon's arm and stopped with him at the edge of the
village, hidden from the excited people by the shadow under
one of the many stilt houses. The night breeze was blowing
through the thatched roof, raising a whispery rustle a little
louder than the insect hum. "Everyone's out," she muttered.

Rihon nodded. "The noise."

"I suppose so." She scowled at the circling people. Through
the continually shifting groups she could see the Serk pacing
restlessly before a hastily assembled bonfire, circling about
the Niong, her long thin arms waving passionately while the
Wan watched the Lawgiver as she argued with the scarred
massive male who served the village as War-Leader. Mediator
and judge, the Wan was an old neutered male with a lined
gentle face and a skin paled to a green-tinged ocher. Roha
leaned against Rihon and smiled as she watched him; he was
the only father she and her brother had known. She didn't
even know which of the women was her mother. As soon as
living twins hatched from a double-yolked egg, they became
the village luck, belonging to everyone, passed from woman
to woman, fed the premasticated pap all babies got, given the
best of everything the village had, given everything but a
family of their own. Except for the Wan who loved them and
schooled them.

The Wan shifted the plaited kilt over his bony hips,
stepped forward quickly as the Niong raised a fist. With other
Amar circling behind him, hissing their shock and disap-
proval, the Wan placed a quiet hand on the Niong's bunched
muscle, met the glare of white-circled eyes with a calm resolution. The Niong backed off, dropped his hands and stood
waiting.

Roha glanced at the Mambila web. She sucked in a deep
breath, smoothed her hands down over the woven-grass kilt
tied around her slim hips, looked up at Rihon. He took her
hand and nodded.

Together they walked through the ring of their people. The
Amar were uneasy, moving about constantly, talking in low

short bursts, mothers stroking their infants in the birth slings
that kept the unformed hatchlings tight against the skin.
Other children ran about playing innumerable games of chase
and tag, disturbed by the fears they sensed without really
knowing what made them so restless, small yellow-green
forms wriggling through narrow openings in their parents'
groupings, giggling and shouting, wrestling, tumbling over
and over in frenetic contests that passed rapidly from play to
serious combat. When the noise got too bad, a few adult
males left their groups and cuffed the fighters apart.

A ringing in her ears, the fever back in her blood, clinging
to her brother's arm, Roha moved slowly as if against a current in a flooding river, moved slowly through the Amar
toward the fire.

Behind that fire by the Ghost House with its openwork
demon coiling over the door and its elaborately woven walls,
the Haur-Amar, the village elders, stood muttering together.
As Roha came up to the fire, they started throwing confused
questions at the Serk and the Niong, demanding to know
what the light was, what it meant, what they should do.

*Is the sun broke? Did it seed? Or did Mambila seed? The
pale one, did she break the sky? The floating ghosts, have
they spawned a demon? Tell us what to do, Serk. Is there
danger, Wan? Do we attack, Niong? What do we attack?*

The questions wove together in a hash of sound and the
Three didn't attempt to answer, only waited out the storm.
When the Elders saw Roha and Rihon they turned the spate
of noise on them.

*Roha, what saw you in the womb-tree? What was it struck
mother Earth? What does it mean? Is it dangerous, Rihon?
Dark twin, tell us what you know. Bright twin, what do we do?*

The Niong dived past the Serk and grabbed Roha's arm.
"The Day, Dark twin. You went to the womb-tree to speak
with Daughter Night, Earth's mother. What did she say?
When will uprooting the peace branch bring good fortune to
our war? The nuggar are swarming, the tubers pile up in the
storehouse. The Rum-Fieyl push at us. It's time. Time!"

Roha stared at him. His face blurred, twisted, before her
tearing eyes. The Falling Fire had pulled her away from the
Tree too soon, the drug-sap still running strong in her. The
words the Niong yelled in her face carried no meaning. They
slid off her like rain. His face spread and spread, his eyes

glared, were hot fires like the fire in the mistlands, the burning wound, the earth screaming to her of its pain, screaming so loud the sound drowned the other sounds, the words and the wind and the crackle of the fire behind her. She cried out in answer, the sound tearing her throat, screamed again and again, snatched her arm from the Niong's bruising grip, stumbled back from him until the heat from the fire brought her to a stop. Extending her pale horn claws, she began to lacerate her chest, her eyes turning up until only the whites showed, foam gathering at the corners of her mouth. Her screams deepened to howls.

Rihon bounded to her side, flung out his arms, joining his howls to hers. He began swaying, then danced around and around in a tight circle until he tripped and fell. Then he lay twitching on his back, repeating over and over the hoarse meaningless cries

The Wan whispered to the Serk, then the two of them pushed the babbling Elders and the crowding fearful people back from the Twins. The Wan murmured to the Niong, persuading him to back off, finding this easy enough because the Niong was badly shaken by the result of his words. He was staring slack-faced at Roha who swayed back and forth, the blood dripping down her slick green skin, over her prominent ribs, along the narrow waist to pool against the draw-cord of her kilt.

The Wan edged close to her, caught her arms, held them, his hands strong and gentle on her. Turning her till he was behind her, his arms crossed over her bleeding chest, he held her tight against him until the warmth of his body drove out the hysterical chill in hers. After several minutes of immobility, she blinked, sighed, then cried out as she felt the pain of her scored flesh for the first time. She collapsed against him.

The Wan lowered her until she was lying beside her brother. She caught hold of Rihon's shaking hand. He lay quietly, his eyes closed, his ragged breathing slowing to normal, recovering as she did, the link between them stronger than ever.

The Elders shuffled about in uneasy silence. That silence spread until even the screaming, jabbering children grew quiet, stopped their games and clung together.

Roha opened her eyes and sat up, wincing at the pain of her claw-wounds. As she looked around, the people and the dying fire were elongated streaks of black and silver, then reality came swimming back to her. The Wan helped her to her feet, then reached out a hand to Rihon. "Water," she muttered, rubbing at the streaks of drying blood on her chest. "I need water." Her tongue rasped over dry lips.

The Wan turned from Rihon and looked around, then he jabbed a forefinger at a small boy who edged unwillingly past his mother's legs and stood in front of her, scuffing one foot against the dusty, dry earth. "Tik-tik," the Wan said, smiling with affection at the boy. "Bring me a gourd of water. For the dark twin."

The boy grinned and ran off. He came back quickly with the water, thrust the gourd at the Wan and retreated hastily to his mother's side.

Roha washed off the blood, biting hard on her lower lip as air hit the tears in her flesh. She reached out and took Rihon's hand, then looked past the Wan at the scowling Niong. "No," she cried, her voice ringing out over the silent still crowd; she turned her head, looking over cousins and friends, age-mates, children, adults. "Forget the Fieyl." She knotted her hands into fists, feeling the power rising in her, feeling the exploding tension rising inside, feeling these molded into words that leaped from her mouth like stones flung at the fearful Amar. "Forget them. The pattern is broke." She flung out her arms. "A thorn poisons the Mother," she cried, stamped her foot on the ground, wheeled around twice to face them all. "I am your pachi-siku, the dark Twin. My womb lies in the earth. From my womb was the earth created. She calls to me, Mother Earth, Daughter Earth. She calls. She is wounded to the heart. The bright evil poison drips into her blood and bone." She beat her fist on her chest, not feeling the pain. Her eyes glared at them but she didn't see them; she saw only a great bright thorn hanging in front of her. Flecks of foam gathered at the corners of her mouth as she spoke. Beside her, Rihon's eyes had the same glare.

As soon as she stopped talking, Rihon raised fisted hands. Flame mirrored down his slick, sweating sides, fire in his eyes, leaping from him to the people, to the staring Rum-Amar, to his cousins and uncles and aunts; he gave a great bound and came down in front of Roha, his feet planted hard on the earth, a great hoarse wordless cry tearing from his throat.

They were all breathing together, young and old, even the newest and least-formed hatchling, breathing together until they merged into a many-mouthed, many-legged beast, Rihon's age-mates, male and female, slapping at their thighs and hooting in soft low pants as he roared, "I am your pachi-kilot the bright Twin, my seed is given to the earth, from my seed comes all that lives, from my seed in the beginning all was made. The living on the earth-womb cry out, heal the Mother, draw the thorn from her flesh. Take it out. Out. Out."

"Out! Out! Out!" the younglings chanted.

"Forget the Rum-Fieyl. Forget them. Forget them."

"Forget! Hunh! Forget! Hunh! Forget!"

"Into the mistlands!" Roha cried, linking her arm with her brother's. "Draw the thorn. The mistlands! The mistlands!"

The Wan stepped in front of Roha, placed a hand on her shoulder. "Hush, Twin, you don't know what you're saying." When she tried to push his hand away, he shook his head. "Quiet, little one," he murmured. His other hand closed about the water-worn greenstone hanging on a plaited cord about his neck.

Roha closed her eyes. Beside her, Rihon fell silent, stood shifting his weight from one foot to the other; she could hear the scrape-scrape of his feet, and hearing it, she shivered, the fever draining from her bones and blood as she swayed forward until she was clinging to the Wan, her cheek pressed against the dangling stone.

He patted her shoulder, then let her fold down until she knelt round-shouldered, her head hanging. Rihon dropped to his knees a little behind her. She could feel him there, almost feel the wet warmth of his breath on the back of her neck.

With the Serk grim and silent beside him, the Wan turned slowly, his eyes moving over the half-hypnotized Amar.

Out in the shadows cast by the dying fire, the beast of nose and mouth and hand broke apart, the chanting and the thigh clapping and chest beating died away until there was silence except for the buzzing night insects, the rustling of the breeze through the thatched roofs, the hissing and muted crackling of the fire. Blinking slowly, his worn gentle face turned stony, the Wan searched the dazed faces of the Amar until he saw the one he wanted. "Gawer Hith, come here."

The wiry old woman wriggled through the crowd and

stopped in front of him, five young girls clustering shyly behind her, her apprentices who went everywhere with her, chanting with her under their breath, intent on memorizing her words.

The Wan touched his talisman, leaned forward; his face close to hers, he murmured, "When the Serk is finished, sing."

The old Gawer nodded, understanding what he did not say. When the Wan stepped back into the shadows to stand beside the silent frowning Niong, she moved to one side, her cluster of apprentices hurrying to settle crosslegged about her feet.

"The Sacred Twins have said things to think about." The Serk's voice was resonant, produced from deep in her chest, a throaty music the Amar strained to hear. "The Haur-Amar will meet to speak about these things and touch the ghosts there." She flung an arm up, pointing at the structure rising on long stilts behind her. "With Serk, Niong, and Wan. And the ancestors still in the Dark Twin's womb. You, Rum-Amar, you stay and listen to the Gawer." She stepped back to join the Wan and the Niong, waving a hand at Hith.

As the Elders and the others climbed the ladder and moved around the openwork spirit that guarded the door, the Amar broke apart into family groupings and contested peacefully for seats around the Gawer. Gawer Hith settled herself on a chunk of wood, took the small drum from her neck and began tapping her fingers over the taut skin, drawing forth a muted rattle that called those sitting in a shallow arc in front of her to silence. Roha sighed and stretched out, her head on Rihon's knee.

Hith struck the drum more firmly, glanced up at the sky pursing her lips at the creeping glow-web obscuring more than half the black bowl. The notes of the drum slowed, took on a more compelling power.

> *In the beginning*
> *In the beginning*
> *There was Night,*

she chanted, her voice deep and rich, dark and rich, sonorous and filled with portent,

> *The night she was cold*
> *Black and cold*

The night she was alone
The night she was filled
With nothing, with pain
The pain it grew
The pain it broke the night
the pain it shone, it burned
The pain it grew, grew

The clamor of the drum was a creeping of the skin, a cry of
the terror that waited in the night, the powerful voice was a
shout of triumph, of joy

And it was a fire
And it was a sun
The sun he burned
Green and gold he burned
On the cool night he looked
The cool soft night he desired

The drumbeat slowed again; Hith chanted softly, so softly the
Amar held their breath to hear the words sighing like a whispering in the wind

Night lay with Sun
Night burned with desire
Sought the seed of the sun
The first seed it was weak
The seed blew Against Night
Clung to Night

The drumbeat clamored, demanded, tapped faster, faster, faster . . . then slowed

Sank into Nothing
Brought forth Nothing
Lay upon the Dark
Burning on the Dark
The second seed
Grew and grew, moved
Across the dark, reaching
Touching, lines of fire
Reaching seed to seed in
A great and spreading web

Hith threw her head back, stared up at the web that obscured half the sky. She crooned the evil name, then spat it out, hissed, growled,

> Mambila
> Mambila
> Mambila
> Sun shrunk small, small,
> Threw his fire into Night
> Night burned great with Twins
> Forth they came from Night's Womb
> Male and female they came forth
> Dark and Bright they were
> Full grown came they from the womb of Night
> Holy Twins, the Holy Two

Hith stopped the chant, let her fingers brush and tap slowly on the drum until she had them breathing in unison again—in-out, in-out the Rum-beast breathed. She broke the rhythm with a sudden high shout that brought answering cries from the Amar.

> Night saw the Two
> Night was pleased
> Night celebrated the great birth
> Night desired
> Night desired more
> from the Dark Twin she ripped the womb
> From the Dark womb Night made Earth
> Stone and water, soil and mist
> From the bright Twin
> From the shining one
> Drew she forth his seed
> Over the earth spread she the seed

The drumbeat was slower, the Gawer's voice crooned, caught up the Amar, sang to the Amar until the Amar sang to her:

> From seed and womb came
> Life that roots in the earth
> Life that moves in water
> Life that moves in air
> Life that runs on four legs or six
> From seed and womb came Rum
> In the image of the Twins

> *Night made all Rum*
> *Male and Female*
> *Made she Rum*
> *Bright and dark*
> *Dark Twin, bright Twin*
> *Amar's luck*
> *Amar Amar Rum-Amar*

With the Amar echoing her, Gawer Hith ended on a high triumphant note . . .

And fell into silence. The Amar began stirring, getting up, moving slowly, sleepily toward their high house for the few remaining hours of dark. Hith slipped the drum back on its sling, smiled across at Roha, let her apprentices help her up, then she also went off toward her house.

Roha lay with her head on Rihon's thigh, looking up at the sky where Mambila crept farther and farther across the star-dusted black, hearing distantly the voices in the Ghost House, knowing they were thinking up ways to keep her and Rihon out of the mistlands, knowing also what she had to do. No words were going to persuade her otherwise. *This is what we were hatched twins for,* she thought with a touch of complacence. Rihon bent over her, sensing her contentment. She smiled up into his dreaming eyes and lifted her hand. He closed his fingers around hers. *Nothing else matters,* she thought.

Roha

CHAPTER II

The Wan shook his head. "Not yet."

Roha fidgeted with her kilt. "Why not? You talk and talk and nothing comes of it." She threw back her head and stared up at the sun, its greenish round already floating above the treetops. "The morning's half gone." She leaned against Rihon, needing his strength and unquestioning support. "We're going to go. You can't stop us. We're going to go, even if we have to go alone."

"Roha, Roha." The Wan shook his head. "You shout too loud of what you *will* do. Niong wants the two of you put in a cage while he wars on the Fieyl. Serk hasn't made up her mind yet where she's going to come down. If you push her, it will be on you. The Haur-Amar have near started a war of their own over whether to follow the Niong or let you have your way."

Rihon spoke from behind her, his hands tightening on her shoulders. "And you? Where do you stand?"

Roha waited with her brother for the Wan's answer. Though she'd threatened to go without aid, the idea terrified her now that mornings had brought a cooling of her passion. Under her head she could feel the pound of Rihon's heart and knew he shared her fear. *We will go,* she thought. *We have to, but. . . .*

The Wan turned away to stare at the billowing clouds from the mistlands, smudgy domes of white against the blue of the sky. "There is nothing I can lean on, nothing like this has happened before. What do I do, children? I have to think what's best for the Amar." He spoke softly, slowly. Roha had to strain to catch his words. "I can't see my way." He passed a shaking hand over the back of his head. "Evil, you said, Roha. I think you're right. See how it's split us apart, that thorn." He turned to face them, a weary old man, stooped

25

under a burden almost too much for his strength. "One way or another, it will be decided by nightfall. Be patient a little longer, Roha. It might be better for the two of you to leave the village a while so you don't make the trouble worse." He waited for their nods, then walked toward the Ghost House, his shoulders bent, his feet dragging.

Rihon sighed. "Damn thorn." He caught Roha's hand and pulled her toward the trees. "Come on, Twin."

They ran through the tangle of trees, ducking under the twitching ends of the seeker tendrils on a mat-akul. Roha giggled, snatched up a dead limb, teasing the tree with it, poking at the tendrils, giggling again as they closed blindly about it and drew it toward the eating hole in the trunk. Rihon snorted and pulled her on.

They found a maza-circle and plucked several of the fruits, wandering farther into the forest sucking at the purple juice in the seed cells under the tough rind. They spat out the small white seeds, spraying them at wriggling yekkas and small klahts that moved like furry shadows through the underbrush, hunting in dirt, leaves and decaying wood for grubs and other crawlers.

Roha flung away the last of the husks. "Let's go see the Nafa. As long as we're back before sundown. . . ."

Rihon kicked at a klaht scrambling past his foot, watching gloomily as it tumbled over and over, then scurried off, squeaking with terror. He glanced at her, moved to her side and strolled along with her. "She makes me feel funny, long and skinny and pale. Like a mistlander without fur. And all that hair on her head. Who ever heard of a person with black hair? Black! Roha. I still think she could be a demon. Remember when she came? All those strange shiny beasts she had with her? Remember how they ate the stone? Like a man eats a boiled tuber they ate the rock for her. And she couldn't even talk right until you taught her. Worse than a new hatchling."

Roha grinned. "Big hatchling. Put me on your shoulders and I could look her in the eye."

"You know what I mean."

"I do and I think it's silly. Poor little klaht, scared of anything bigger'n you."

"Scared!" He grabbed for her.

Giggling, she ducked away, running from him through the

trees, heading for the clearing on the edge of the mistlands where the Nafa had dug a hole in the rock to live in instead of doing the sensible thing and living high and cool in a stilt house with sides of woven grass that could be rolled up to catch the wandering winds even in the hottest of days. Laughing, dancing ahead of Rihon, she circled the Nafa's wall like a green shadow, her brother a weaving green shadow behind her.

The Nafa climbed to the top of the wall and sat dangling her legs over the edge. She watched them quietly, waiting with the cool measuring patience that fascinated Roha and exasperated Rihon. Her long flat face was still, her mouth curved into a slight smile, her round dark eyes following them as they played in front of her, as she sat waiting, still as a carving, like the spirit figure Zuri carved for the Ghost House door.

Roha grew tired of running. She stopped in front of the Nafa, stood there panting, sweat running down the sides of her face. She fixed her eyes on the Nafa in both fascination and revulsion, aware of Rihon behind her, staring over her shoulder at the woman, wanting her to go away. Roha stirred. Eyes still fixed on the woman, she sidled three steps one way, arms swinging, three steps the other, arms swinging. Abruptly she dropped to the ground, sat cross-legged before the woman, tilting her head back, looking up at her.

The Nafa moved for the first time, restless under the intensity of Roha's gaze. Her eyes moved past Roha, rested a moment on stubborn, silent Rihon, then returned to Roha. She said nothing. She waited.

"Did you see the burning thorn?" Roha asked suddenly.

The Nafa looked blank, lifted her eyes to the sky with its tracing of Mambila web, frowned, shook her head. "I don't understand."

"There was a falling thing burning in the sky. It bedded in the mistlands last night. You didn't see it?"

"No." The Nafa rubbed a thumb along her too-thick, too-soft mouth. "I was inside. Busy. Tell me."

"A big light falling. A burning thorn. With a great, terrible noise, the screaming of a demon big enough to eat the world. Burning. Burning." Roha began to slip into a heightened state; she stopped thinking and only saw, felt, chanted, saw the patterns forming, patterns . . . Rihon knelt behind her, clasping her shoulders. "Burning," she whispered. She quieted, spat away the bits of foam clinging to her lips. "Evil."

"How can you know that?" The Nafa's voice was quiet; her eyes searched Roha's face. Roha had never seen her look so disturbed. Her long narrow hands were pleating the soft shimmering blue cloth she wore wrapped about her long thin body. "Wait till you look at it. Don't. . . ."

"It is *evil!*" Roha spat, the intensity of her belief vibrating in the word. "Evil," she repeated more quietly. "Evil."

"Think, Roha. How do you know, how . . ." The Nafa's voice grew wavery and distant like a humming in Roha's ears. For a moment those words had no meaning. The pale, flat face shimmered before Roha; she saw wavy gold lines undulating out from the Nafa's head, melting into the quivering air. Roha sucked in great gulps of the damp air, tasted the sweet-salt tang of blood in it, tasted death in it. The woman on the wall was a blue blur in her eyes. Something. . . . Something . . . what was she saying . . . wait . . . see . . . ask . . . ask why? ask what? . . . if it's not . . . not evil . . . not evil? *"No!"* She jumped to her feet, freeing herself from Rihon's hands. Wheeling about, she ran blindly to the trees, running because there was no way she could stand still, running from questions she didn't want to ask. Rihon ran behind her; his concern reached out and enveloped her, drawing away the pain, giving her back certainty and purpose. She ran until her sides ached with the pain of breathing, then threw herself, shaking and exhausted, on a patch of grass, not bothering to beat out the life that crawled among the roots.

"Roha, dammit." Rihon snatched her up and began slapping at the suckers that had already attached themselves to her. Then he held her away from him and stared. The suckers were curling up and falling away from her, dead. "What . . ."

Roha looked down at herself. She lifted a shaking hand and brushed it across her face. "The dream-sap," she murmured. "In my blood. It kills them. Hold me, Twin."

She leaned against him. Rihon was her anchor into the real world. He cooled her blood, brought her peace. Even when they ripped her womb from her and he felt her agony as his own, even then he stayed with her, given her strength when it seemed she'd drain away, melting back into the earth.

When she was calm again, she walked away from him, moving up the slope of the mountain, climbing until she was high above the trees. She stopped, looked vaguely about, sat down on a rock. Rihon settled beside her. He took her hand and held it between his. Once again the earth was solid under her.

She looked down and could see the garden clearings where the village women had burned away the trees to make their tuber plots. There were women and girls working among the tuber vines, others shooing off nuggar trying to get past the fences. She scowled. "Too many nuggar."

"You knew that."

She moved her shoulders irritably. "I mean the Niong wants the war with the Rum Fieyl. He'll use the nuggar swarm to push that."

"Maybe the Wan will say they can have the war-feast before we move against the Thorn. It's a kind of war, isn't it?"

"It's what Wan and Serk say it is." She looked away from the village and stared at the Nafa's clearing at the edge of the trees like a bald spot on a mangy beast. "I ran farther than I meant."

"Maybe you'll believe me now. About the Nafa, I mean."

"It wasn't her made me run off."

Rihon snorted and jumped up, looking down at her with disgust. "You just don't want to admit it. Why'd you run then, huh? Why'd you run?"

Roha sniffed. "I wanted to. That's why, brother. I'll run when I want to, if I want to. So?"

Rihon turned his back on her, sweeping his eyes over the trees below. Suddenly he gave a startled exclamation and pointed. "Look." He ran back to her and caught hold of her arm. "The village, Roha. Look."

Men and boys were gathering in the space before the Ghost House, milling around, waving spears.

Roha sucked in a breath. "The tree. Do you see the peace tree? Did they dig it up?"

"Wasn't time." Rihon squinted, trying to make out details. "No fire. I don't see it."

The milling throng broke apart, pouring from the village in small hunting bands.

Roha hugged her brother's arm. "Nuggar hunt, Twin.

We're going, I know it, we have to be going. They're going to hold a Karram for us, our own war-feast." Her eyes moved on to the rolling clouds that hid the floor of the distant basin and she shivered, her elation draining away. "The mistlands."

Roha

CHAPTER III

Roha cracked the bone and sucked out the marrow. Rihon was stretched out beside her, a gourd of pika-beer cradled in his hands, sitting upright between his ribs, rising and falling with each slow breath. His head was propped up on a chunk of wood; he was smiling drowsily at the dancing around the fire. Roha ran her tongue over the shards then dropped them on her brother's head. Laughing, he shook them off, then lifted the gourd, offering her a drink.

She swallowed a bit of the musty bitter liquid, felt the fermentation tingle a little in her blood. She was too tired, too sated with meat and drink for anything to stir her deeply, even the thought of tomorrow's leavetaking. She picked through the depleted pile of meat on the slab sitting on the ground by her knees, found a bone with meat left on it. She tore off a mouthful and offered the rest to Rihon. He yawned, grinned, began chewing at the bone.

A band of boys ran past, whooping, brandishing small bows with pointless arrows, short sticks with fire-hardened points, herding squealing giggling girls ahead of them, wrestling, breaking off to run some more, twisting in and out of the stilts holding up the houses. Across the dying fire small girls formed into a circle, stamping round and round, chanting out the sah-sah beat. Near them, larger girls were cross-dancing to a beat provided by others who clapped cupped hands on thighs as they squatted in a circle around the dancers. In front of the Ghost House, most of the adults were sitting around Gawer Hith, listening to her chant the old tales. When one was done, they called out the next they wanted, pressing gourds of pika-beer on the old woman until she was swaying, blinking, propped upright only by the young arms of her apprentices. Her voice was strong in spite of her age; she never missed a word, even though she was very

31

drunk. Late in the afternoon her voice finally hoarsened and
the Amar let her stop. She curled up on the ground where
she'd been sitting and went to sleep, snoring nearly as loudly
as she'd chanted.

The day wound its slow way around fire and dance, pika-
beer and burnt meat.

Toward sundown, when even the liveliest of the children
were drooping and the adults staring sleepily at coals flickering toward death, Churr jumped to his feet and fetched three
logs from the pile laid apart beneath the Ghost House. Holding them over his head, he ran with them to the dying fire
and cast them into the middle of the coals. Green and sappy,
the logs started smoldering, then crackling and popping, sending up gouts of smoke. Churr stood sucking in lungfuls of the
aromatic smoke. The somnolent Amar stirred, staggered to
their feet and joined him in the blue mist, snuffing up smoke
greedily, expelling it, sucking in more, till they all were
reeling, the sap-smoke sending them higher than the quanti-
ties of pika-beer in their bellies.

Churr shook his fists, howled. He was a tough man at the
height of his strength, veteran of a handful of Rum-wars, am-
bitious—he wanted to be the Rum-Amar's Niong—with more
skin patches than any other man in the village. He wore the
patches now, souvenirs of every man he'd downed, hand-sized
swatches of skin sliced off over the heart, dried over a fire,
threaded like dangles on cords. They hung around his neck,
were tied in rounds about his biceps and made a long skirt,
dangling to mid-thigh, slapping softly against his flesh with
every move he made. He howled again and the others howled
back, beat on their chests, danced up and down in one spot,
stamping against the earth, swaying back and forth.

Churr shook a fist in the direction of the mistlands.
"Floating ghosts," he roared. "Churr comes after you. Churr!
Churr will catch you by your tails and pull you from your
skins." He slapped at his chest. "I am Churr. With my spear
I'll pierce you, with my arrows I'll stick you, you can't hurt
me. I am Churr. I am fast as the wind. You won't touch me,
floating ghosts, you can't catch me. I'll take your skin and
make me a mat to sleep on. Come for me, I'll kick you into
the sun and you'll burn and drop your drippings on the mistlands and the mistlands will burn with you. I am Churr,

dancer of blood, I am Amar's Churr. There is no one like me. Look at me and be afraid. I am Churr."

One by one the twenty men chosen for the mistlands raid leaped to join Churr, adding their boast to his. The remaining Amar gave them a rhythmic background of grunts and hoots.

Floating ghosts can't eat me . . . I will walk over the thinnest crust, so light is my foot. . . . I will walk over bog and boil without sinking . . . I will eat the kinya-kin-kin, I will eat them before they can eat me . . . I will fool them. . . . I will walk on them. . . . I will crush them beneath my feet . . . I will feed Mother Earth with the blood of the kinya-kin-kin. . . . I will skin me a dozen mistlander demons. . . . I will bring their skin home with me and cut it up for thongs to tie my spears. . . . by myself I will kill the demon seed. . . . I will crush it . . . I will pull the thorn from the flesh of the Mother. . . .

No longer listening, Roha cracked a last bone and sucked lazily at the marrow. The smoke that eddied around her was beginning to dance in her blood. She let the bone shards drop to the ground, swallowed, yawned. Rihon was asleep, snoring a little. She wriggled down, rested her head on his thigh. Overhead, trails of mist crept from the trees, slipped past the roof peaks. The fire flickered, throwing red light on the mist, turning it to tongues of flame. The chanting and boasting from the fire flowed over her as she stared up at the widening Mambila web. "Mambila, Mambila, Mambila," she whispered. "Mambila. Mambila." She yawned, slid her hips back and forth over the ground until she was more comfortable, then drifted into a deep sleep.

The morning was crisp and cool, the sun still veiled behind the line of trees. Roha splashed water from the wooden tub over her head and chest, beginning to feel alive again. She scrubbed the grease off her skin and the stains of dried beer and tied on a new kilt. Stretching, yawning, content with herself, she looked up and saw Rihon easing down the ladder from their house. He stumbled toward her, yawning, grimacing, rubbing at his temples, wincing as morning light struck at his blood-shot eyes. With a grin, she stepped away from the tub. "Dunk your head, Twin. You look worse than the nuggar." She jerked a thumb at the bones heaped in a greasy pile near the black ash of the bonfire.

Rihon came wobbling toward her. "You don't need to yell."

"Wasn't." She flicked water into his face and ran off to the breakfast fire of the neighboring house.

She sniffed at the bubbling mush. "Is it done, Mama Zidli?" Slapping at her stomach, sliding her tongue along thin lips, she went on, "Got enough for Twin and me?"

The woman grunted, dipped a few dollops from her pot into a wooden bowl. "There," she said. "Need more, get it from another fire."

Roha looked into the bowl. It was about half full, more than enough for her but not for Rihon. She visited more of the fires, collecting another bowl of mush and two mugs of loochee. As she trotted back to her house, she sipped at the strong infusion of chima leaves, the warm liquid coiling through her body, washing out the last of the mists of sleep.

Rihon was sitting on the platform of the house, swinging his legs, waiting for her, his eyes fixed on the bowls tucked into the crook of her arm. She looked up at him, then moved slowly and carefully up the ladder, balancing her thin body without using her hands. With a whoosh of relief, she stepped onto the narrow ledge and thrust one of the mugs at her brother. "Lazy klaht."

He yawned and grinned up at her, reaching a long arm for one of the bowls of porridge; he took the mug after that and drank thirstily, gulping down the steaming liquid. As he dipped fingers into the thick white mush and stuffed it into his mouth, Roha settled herself beside him and began eating.

She was soon finished. After looking with disgust at the remaining mush, she dropped the bowl over the edge. She stretched, groaned, then drained the last of the loochee and tossed the mug after the bowl. Rihon was still eating. She glanced at him, sighed, then went inside, brushing past the woven mats that hung over the low opening.

Rihon's sleeping mats were crumpled in a heap in one corner. "He never. . . ." Shaking her head, she rolled them into a compact cylinder, tied them off and stowed them in a corner.

She looked around, wondering just what she should take

with her on the raid. The winter robes hung on a peg driven into one of the wall supports, jikkil skins glowing softly brown in the shadowed interior of the house; they were soft and supple, pounded and chewed until they were as flexible as living skin. She took the robes from their pegs and dropped them on the floor. Rihon's spear she dropped on his robe. Stone knives for both of them, one on each robe. Then she added two leather pouches to the piles. There wasn't much else in the house; everything the Twins needed the village provided.

She walked out of the house, wondering what the Web would bring this season. Working with Gawer Hith, she and Rihon kept the Amar sane while Mambila ruled the sky. Though the web teased at her mind it was no more upsetting for her than the drug-sap she swallowed continually; for the others, the time under the Mambila web was a time of madness, quiet or noisy madness. Fieyl and Zalish, Tandir and Dangal, all the tribes of the Rum, they lost many to the Mambila madness. But the Amar had the Twins. The Sacred Twins who seemed to absorb all the madness. She looked up at the wisps of the Mambila Web invading the day sky. Before long it would stretch across the whole sky, day and night. *Fifteen years*, she thought. *For fifteen Webs we've been Amar's luck*. She touched her brother's shoulder. When he looked up, she said, "Look inside, see if we should take anything else. I don't know."

He shrugged. "Why should we take anything?"

"This is different, Twin."

Rihon got reluctantly to his feet and ducked through the door. Roha sat on the platform, swinging her feet, watching the men gather in front of the Ghost House, moving about Churr.

She was still watching when Rihon came out and dropped a neatly tied roll in her lap. "Good enough," he said. "Pouches for food?"

"Yes." She smoothed her hand over the leather, surprised a little to see it shaking. Rihon knelt beside her, grasped her shoulder. She leaned her head against his arm and drew in a long shuddering breath.

Churr left the twenty at the Ghost House and marched across the ground to them. He stopped by the ladder and looked up. "It's time." His eyes shifted to the sun just rising over the trees, came back to Roha. "Where, Twin?"

"Past the Nafa's wall," Roha blurted. "Straight on into the mistlands from the Nafa's place."

Churr said, "Get trail food at the Ghost House."

Amar children trailed behind them, skirmishing in mock battles, whooping, dancing, giggling, excited to the point of incoherence. At the first garden patch Churr turned on them, snarling his annoyance, sending them yelling back to the village. In the roughly circular clearing women and girls rested on their stone hoes, watching them move past, calling out encouragement. They came to the edge of the clearing, staring after the raiding party until they passed out of sight among the trees.

When she came from under the trees, Roha glanced to her left. The Nafa was sitting on her wall, her long legs dangling over. The cloth she wore wound around her was red today, with a wide gold border that caught the sun and glittered, sending dazzles into Roha's eyes. She looked away, not liking the things she thought she saw in the woman's face.

At the edge of the downslope she stopped. Churr scowled; with an impatient jerk of his hand he urged her on. When she didn't move, he brushed past her and began picking his way down the easy slope. Roha stared at the tendrils of mist. Felt the fingers of mist touching her face, coiling around her ankles, spiraling around her body, beckoning her, whispering to her through the pores of her skin. She was frozen with terror. She couldn't take the first step down. She closed her eyes and stood shaking. She was afraid. She couldn't move.

Rihon moved up close behind her, pulled her back against his chest, held her until his warmth warmed the chill out of her. He was her anchor, he steadied her. When her trembling stopped, he took her hand and led her onto the slope into the mistlands.

Roha

CHAPTER IV

Roha rubbed slowly at her arm. The mist rolled about the gravelly open space of the camp area, thick and thin like smoke, changing until she saw beasts and demons form and dissipate as it blew past. She was tired. Hour on hour winding past stinging bushes, alert for things that could leap out at them, searching the mists for the floating ghosts, stretched, straining, all this had sapped body strength and nervous energy. In the center of the clearing, two of the men were turning over rocks and stirring through the gravel, killing whatever ran out. Rihon and the others were hunting for small game out in the mists somewhere. Roha rubbed harder at her forearm, began scratching at small bubbles in her skin where she'd brushed against a strange bush with leaves of a green so pale it was almost white and wide purple veins.

Her head jerked up as a fumerole beside her spat up spurts of sulphurated steam. She moved away a few steps, circling around a scraggly bush, moving nervously under the spreading limbs of an almost leafless tree, feeling alien here, feeling the animals and plants watching her, distrusting her. Her feet were noisy on the gravel, noisy even on the tufts of stiff, short grass growing up through the gravel, scattered haphazardly around the clearing, scratching her whenever she stepped on them. She circled the open space, too restless to sit, even to stand still. Mambila web was stronger in the sky and beginning to work in her. She watched the two Amar stirring the gravel a minute more, then wandered about a large pile of rock to stand beside the hot spring, watching purple bubbles pop and pale purple mists glide across the seething water. The pile of rock was thick with small tight clumps of poisonberry whose plump purple berries had been dropping into the water and cooking there for uncounted years, turning the water into a thick soup that sent up sweet

37

enticing odors which had trapped many of the mistland creatures. Bones were scattered thickly among the rocks and
several putrefying bodies lay half-in, half-out of the water.
She poked aimlessly around the pool, avoiding with some
care the drifting poisonous vapors. On the far side a patch of
bright green grass was ruffling softly in the slight breeze,
looking like a piece of her own forest. She stared at it,
wanting to step in the middle of the grass, to lie down in it,
to roll in it. A quiver in the bushes by her feet drew her eyes
away from the green and sent her back a step, dislodging a
stone that rolled toward the bush. A small furry beast burst
from cover and scrambled frantically away, blind to where it
was going, running at full speed into the patch of green.
About a foot from the edge he sank out of sight. Cautiously
Roha moved closer, leaning over a little so she could look
down on the place where the beast had disappeared. Strands
of grass had been shoved aside or torn loose to wave roots
like white worms in the air above a gray slime. Grass moved
to cover the open place; there was no sign at all of the beast,
not even a disturbance in the slime. When the smooth blanket
of green was intact once more, Roha swallowed, shivered,
turned her back on the grass and its harsh reminder of mistland's treachery. She stared into the mist, felt the eyes of the
life around her, waiting, watching, hostile, felt the poison in
the leaves reaching for her, stared into the mist and felt
Earth's pain calling to her, flowing up through the soles of
her feet into her legs. Behind her she could hear the bubbling
of the poison spring and the heavy *plop-plop-schloop* as the
larger bubbles burst and sank back into the thick liquid. The
voices of Amar reached her; the hunting party was back. She
heard Rihon laughing. Darkness was lowering through the
mist, drifting down with a strange slowness meeting an equal
darkness creeping up from the ground.

"Roha!" Rihon's voice broke her from her paralysis and
she hurried back toward the campsite, watching carefully
where she put each foot, hating this land, this treacherous
dangerous land.

The campfire was a cheerful crackling in the center of the
clearing. Several of the Amar were seated apart, skinning and
gutting the animals the hunters had brought back. Roha
glanced at these, wondering if anything in this place could be
wholesome. She was at once troubled and relieved to recog-

nize a scrawny nuggar and some kissuni, small succulent hoppers with round mobile ears and extravagant hind legs; she looked fearfully at the firm red meat, wondering if it too could conceal some trap beneath its familiarity. The hunters looked unconcerned; one was humming softly as his knife sliced the skin from a large kissun. She moved away slowly, went to Rihon who was standing by the fire, holding his spear, looking satisfied with himself.

"I got a nuggar." He showed her the bloodstains on the spear's stone point and on its shaft. "Sent it all the way through."

Roha touched the dark stain. "You're sure they're all right to eat?"

"Hunh, Twin, don't be a klaht." Grinning cheerfully, he turned her favorite epithet back on her. "Meat is meat."

She looked around. "Where's Churr?"

"Scouting around. Making sure no kinya-kin-kin are heading toward us. Or floating ghosts. They're supposed to come out with the dark."

"I know that," she muttered. "Everyone knows that."

Rihon butted his spear in the gravel then dropped a hand on her shoulder. She pressed her hand down on his, the pool of warmth steadying her. "What's wrong, Twin?" His voice dropped almost to a whisper. "Did you see something?"

"I don't like this place."

"Who does?" He hugged her, then pushed her away. "You'll feel better with some food in you."

Roha leaned against Rihon, taking strength from him as she had so many times before. The fire had burned down to a heap of coals, the living red forming image after image across the dead black. She followed these with dreamy eyes, hypnotized into a drowsy comfort by the shifting patterns. In the clearing around the Twins many of the Amar were already asleep, rolled tight into their sleeping leathers, their heads covered, their toes naked to the darkening night. Two guards strolled about the clearing talking briefly when they met, glancing now and then at the Twins.

Yawning, Roha shifted away from Rihon and lay back, her head resting on her own robe, still rolled in a tight cylinder. The knotted mist overhead was lit from below by the remnant of the fire and from above by the greenish light from the Mambila Web. Through the thinner stretches of the low ceiling she could make out the tracery of the Web. Scratching absently at the fading rash on her arm, she closed her eyes and turned her attention inward, trying to read the strength of the fever in her blood. Too tired to concentrate, she abandoned the effort and stretched her legs out, so that her soles were toasting by the fire. Yawning again, blinking slowly, she watched the mist thicken and thin as the breeze teased at it. Drifts of bubbles, a few at first, then more and more came bouncing past, things seen only by the emptiness they made in the thicker parts of the mist. For several minutes she watched those emptinesses bobble over her, then she poked Rihon in the side. "What's that? Up there." She pointed.

Rihon jerked, blinked, startled from a half-doze. "Wha . . ." He looked up, following the point of his sister's finger. The bubbles startled him; he jumped to his feet and poked his finger at one. "Cold." He dropped beside her, stretched out, moving his robe-roll until his head was comfortable. He took her hand. "Funny."

The mist over them continued to blow into knots and dissipate into fine veils. Roha's eyes grew heavy as she watched the bubbles gyrate.

A fireball arced suddenly across the sky, so bright it burned through the mist. Roha gasped and clutched at Rihon's hand. Another fireball appeared and went down. And another. Within a dozen heartbeats, all three were down and dark. Roha trembled, gasped, rolled over and pressed her face against Rihon's chest.

He lay still, smoothed his hand over the satin curve of her head, down her trembling back, over and over until she stopped shaking and lay heavily and silently on him. After a minute more she moved from under his arms and lay on her back staring up at the swarming spheres of nothingness clustering over her.

"Roha?"

"I don't know. I don't know. Maybe it's the same." She closed her eyes, pressed the heels of her hands against the lids, feeling the hard round under the skin. "I don't feel . . . no, not the pain, not. . . . I don't know." She dropped her hands to her sides.

"All right, Twin." He took her hand. "Never mind. We'll take care of the Thorn first, then we'll see about the Seeds."

He sat up, reached around behind him for the robe-roll. "Go to sleep, Twin. We got a long way to go tomorrow."

Roha sighed, sat up, winced. "My head aches."

"Sleep."

Roha sniffed. "Easy for you." She watched as he spread out the leather robe and began rolling himself in it. When he was still, breathing steadily, she sighed. Her head was throbbing and there was a sour taste in her mouth. She was exhausted, her body ached, her mind swam restlessly in deep fatigue, but she wasn't sleepy any longer. She watched the fire where most of the red had died, wondering if she should stir it up. Finally she lay back, her head pillowed on the roll, leaving the fire to finish dying.

The floating bubbles swam more thickly than ever. She found their constant erratic motion confusing. Unlike the fog they moved against the direction of the wind—as if clusters of soap-weed bubbles moved against a stream's current. She watched more closely to see if what she thought she saw was really happening. Two of the empty spheres bumped suddenly. Bumped and merged. The emptiness was larger and she saw threads hanging below it, hair-fine filaments almost as transparent as the bubble above. More of the bubbles bumped and merged. The sphere of nothing doubled and tripled in size, the dangling filaments longer and thicker until they were as big around as her fingers. She sat up. "Floating ghosts," she whispered. Shaking, she reached toward Rihon as the ghost drifted toward her, the dangling tendrils like the limbs of the mat-akul seeking her, twitching up at the tips, reaching for her. She closed her fingers hard on Rihon's arm, pulled at him frantically, terror closing her throat. Across the clearing the two guards were talking quietly, their backs to her. She tugged harder.

Rihon came muttering out of his leathers, angry at being disturbed from a deep sleep.

Roha was shaking and moaning, unable to move. A huge emptiness hung over her, tendrils falling down around her head. She sat open-mouthed, tears streaming down her face, feeling the ghost reaching into her head, drawing her out, sucking her out, peeling her out of her shell of flesh.

Rihon snatched up the spear lying by his side, slashed it through the emptiness hovering above his sister. He cut it in half. The two halves closed up unharmed, began to merge

once more. Roha cried out then, a terrible hoarse scream that
tore at her throat. He slashed again, whipping the stone point
of the spear through and through the emptiness until the
large sections of the ghost split into smaller and smaller
pieces, slashed again as they tried to merge. Roha screamed
and shuddered, plucked at herself, feeling as if her bones
were coming out of her skin, as if her skin was on fire. Whirl-
ing the spear through and through the space over her head,
Rihon forced the bobbling small ghosts back.

Roha lifted a hand, lifted the other; the burning passed
away from her. She looked around, gasping in great mouth-
fuls of the damp air, shaking so hard she couldn't talk. The
two guards were running toward her, spears held ready as
they sought the thing that had frightened the Twins. Rihon
was swinging his spear wildly through the fog, trying to drive
off the last of the empty spheres. Roha snatched up handfuls
of coarse gravel and flung them at the ghosts, not caring that
the stones struck the guards also. The bubbles retreated farther.

A guard's hand closed around her wrist. She looked up, her
eyes wide, a trace of foam at the corners of her mouth.
"Floating ghosts," she hissed and pointed at the tiny bubbles.
"They grow and grow and suck at you." She wrenched her
hand free and caught up another handful of gravel. With an
exclamation of horror, the guard ran to join Rihon, his com-
panion following, puzzled but willing to fight whatever was
attacking them. Together the three of them drove the ghosts
from the clearing.

Roha leaped to her feet and wheeled into an impromptu
dance of triumph to a wordless song of gladness. For the moment she was ecstatic with the joy of being alive and whole
within herself. Rihon and the guards joined her, laughing and
beating the butts of their spears against the ground. When she
spun breathlessly to a stop, Rihon slapped his palms on his
chest over and over, chanting, "Floating ghosts, floating
ghosts, we are the Twins, the Sacred Twins. You can't hurt
us, you can't swallow our spirits. Let your nothingness vanish
before us. We laugh at you. We spit at you. Ho!"

Ameb shifted his spear from hand to hand; he'd run to Rihon's aid without much thought, now he looked a bit sheepish
and puzzled. "Little bubbles in the mist?" He slid his eyes to
meet those of Dunun, the other guard. "Floating ghosts?"

Roha saw their disbelief. For the Amar, floating ghosts

were the most horrible of monsters, creatures unkillable that sucked the souls from the bodies of helpless, hapless warriors foolish enough to venture within the mists. For generations no one had seen them, no one really knew what they looked like. Ameb and Dunun could hardly believe that tiny emptinesses in the mist were those dead beasts, even when the Sacred Twins told them so.

Rihon slammed the butt of his spear impatiently against the ground. "They come together," he said loudly. "There was a bubble hanging over Roha. A bubble bigger than your two heads together, with roots like the seeker tendrils of the mat-akul wrapped around her head and shoulders."

Chilled and nauseated by the memory, Roha clasped her hands over the curve of her skull. "It was sucking." She swallowed and swallowed, shuddering until she could hardly stand. "It was sucking my spirit from my body."

Dunun glanced uneasily upwards, checking the mist for the small empty spheres. The horror in Roha's voice had convinced him more than Rihon's explanation. Ameb still looked skeptical but he too glanced up from time to time.

"Watch for them," Rihon said quietly. He rubbed his hand hard across his face. "When they're little, they can't hurt a Rum. If you let them get big. . . ."

The guards nodded, then moved off, dividing their attention now between the ground and the mist over their heads.

"You should sleep." Rihon touched Roha's arm. "The guards will watch better now."

"You think so?"

"I know they will. Come." He led her back to their abandoned robes. He untied hers, spreading it beside his own. Then he lay down, pulling her down with him until she was lying beside him, her head resting on his upper arm, her body fitting between the curve of his arm and his side.

In a few minutes she was warm and relaxed but still not sleepy. She heard his breathing even out, felt his muscles slacken as he slept, but she still could not follow him into sleep. She stared up at the mist-obscured sky. *Fireballs*, she thought. *Three of them, smaller and slower than the falling thorn. They came down . . . where? Behind us. By the Nafa's house. The Nafa. One morning she was there, suddenly there, out of nowhere she was there.* For the first time Roha thought to wonder where the Nafa had come from, this being who was so different from everything else she knew. *Where did she come from?* Roha ran the tip of her tongue over dry lips. *Did she ride fire down from the sky?* The thought came suddenly to her, striking her like a fist in the face. She gasped at the newness of it, the horror of it; it was a terribly upsetting thought. She screwed her eyes tight shut and turned her face into Rihon's side. *He doesn't like the Nafa. He never did.* She breathed deeply, taking pleasure in the strong salty smell of his body. *Maybe he's right; maybe she is a demon. She's always asking questions. Like she doesn't know how people live. Why doesn't she know how people live? When she came.* . . .

On the second day after the Nafa appeared, Roha crept from the shelter of the trees to stare at the new wall. The strange creature was sitting on the wall, watching her. It was soft, a pale brown like the weathered sandstone high on the mountain side. It had a thick mane of blue-black fur on its head, fur that moved lightly in the breeze. It was wrapped in a long thing like a strip cut from the sky. Roha was fascinated by the shimmering blue. She wanted to touch it to see if it was as smooth and soft as it looked. She walked slowly toward it though Rihon tried to hold her back. She jerked free and slowly approached it. It sat very still on the wall, waiting with a patience that soothed her pounding heart. It spoke and she knew it was a person. A quiet series of sounds came from its mouth. They had no meaning for Roha but they cooled the heat in her blood. She'd held hatchlings briefly when their mothers needed freedom for a moment; she'd felt the tiny humming of them against her skin, felt it enter into her so deep that she wept without knowing why; the stranger's sounds were like that for her.

Questions, always questions, Roha thought. *Why do you have wars when the nuggar swarm? How do you burn out new clearings when the old wear out? Why did they burn the houses each time they moved the village? Why did they build their houses on stilts? What did they think of the Mambila Web? Tell me your stories. How did the world begin? Questions. Questions. Questions.*

Roha sighed, then pulled the end of the leather robe over her head. In the warm darkness she let her eyes close. Words moving slower and slower through her weary mind, she drifted finally into a deep sleep.

Roha

CHAPTER V

For three days the Amar fought through the mistlands. The floating ghosts were more and more persistent in their swarming; the Amar got little sleep, spent their days swinging at bubbles, dodging away from seeking tendrils. One Amar dodged into a heavy bush and died with a hundred tiny darts in his skin. Another stepped onto a patch of bright green grass and sank before he could be pulled out.

On the morning of the third day, Roha rounded a clump of rain-trees and saw a great round egg looming through the mist. A grey egg higher than a hill. . . . or a seed. . . . Roha stared, a pulse drumming so loud in her ears she didn't at first hear Churr speak.

"Is that it?" he repeated, pulling at her arm. "Is that what we're after?"

She licked her lips, stared at him blankly until the meaning of his words finally reached her. "Yes," she whispered. "Yes!" she cried. "Yes, yes, yes."

The Amar fighters spread out in an arc on either side of the Twins. Churr nodded briskly to Roha, then whistled a double note. The warriors started moving cautiously forward, keeping the arc as smooth as possible, using brush and rock piles as cover, watching at the same time for the many dangers from plants and the earth itself. Pushing Roha behind him and ordering her to stay there with Rihon, Churr ran forward and took his place in the center of the line. Drifting like shadows across the ground the Amar crept toward the Egg.

Roha clutched Rihon's hand, staring at the Egg. She took a step forward. Rihon tried to pull her back. She looked at him. "I have to."

"Roha, you've got no business interfering with Churr."

"I won't. Rihon, come on, we can't see anything back here."

He shrugged and let her go, following quietly along behind, ready, she knew, to catch her if he thought she went too far. She ran ahead on quiet feet until she was close behind Churr.

He knelt in the shade of a liggabush, similar enough to the healthy ones outside to seem safe. The Amar knelt beside him in their circle lying hidden outside a broad clearing. Roha stopped, excited and afraid. She looked about and saw billows of stone cast up beside a steaming pool. She touched her hands to her face, wondering if she dared. Behind her Rihon grunted. He set her to one side and marched past her. After kicking lightly at the glassy stone, he started climbing until he lay stretched out on the top. For a moment he looked down the far side, then beckoned to her.

Roha scrambled up beside him and looked down.

The Egg was laid on its long axis, part buried in a cast-up mound of earth. Behind it a geyser was sending up gouts of steam and sulphur vapor that spilled over the bulge of the Egg, condensing on the shell, staining the matte gray surface yellow and green and brown in long uneven streaks. The wind shifted a little, carrying to Roha's nose the stench of sulphur and another odor, acrid and abominable; it clogged her throat, brought her claws arching out of her fingertips. Her ears flickered and her nose flattened. A cold rage rose in her. She could hear breath snorting in and out of Rihon's nose and feel the same rage cold in him. She growled deep in her throat, heard the same purring growl from Rihon.

There was a gaping round hole in the shell, somewhere around the middle, and in that hole stood a demon. It moved its head slowly from side to side, round black eyes glittering even in the dim diffused light coming through the mist. Hard bulges at the bottom of the face moved and clicked, then it came out of the hole, balancing awkwardly down the planks slanting from the lip of the hole to the ground. Its middle two arms were folded tight against its bulky hard chest, the upper two arms stretched out for balance. It walked bent forward, moving with an unseemly bouncing gait. Several others came from the hold behind it. One stayed behind, standing in the hold, watching its fellows, clutching a long snaky tube in its lower pair of arms. One of its upper arms was braced against the edge of the hole.

As the demons spread out and started gathering leaves from the bushes outlining the clearing, a last demon came scuttling from the inside of the Egg. It looked frantically about then crouched at the feet of the standing demon. It seemed to be trembling as it pressed back against the stander's legs. Roha felt a blast of anguish and was momentarily confused, but the feeling didn't last and she went back to glaring angrily at the creatures.

The demons moving around the clearing were picking up grubs from the earth dam thrown up around the ship, stripping leaves from bushes that clung to life though most of their roots had been pulled loose from the earth by the bulk of the Egg. The demons didn't seem to care what they took. They plucked leaves and berries from poisonberry bushes, brushed casually past the darters ignoring the poppings and the darts that spanged onto their hard skins and glanced off harmlessly. Roha watched, tense with expectation, waiting for the demons to discover the crouching Amar, but that didn't happen. The glittering black orbs never seemed to look beyond the stripping pincers at the end of their middle arms. She stared at the demons, hating them, refusing to accept the life signals she was getting from them. She dragged her claws over the rock. Hideous, evil; Mother Earth was crying out to be relieved of them. She shivered with the pain of that cry, refusing to admit that the great cry came from within the Egg instead of the earth beneath.

A thrice-repeated whistle shrilled across the clearing.

Churr leaped from cover, whooping, "Mar! Mar! Amar! Mar!" The warriors followed him, running at the demons. Roha grabbed Rihon before he could move, held him beside her. He was angry, hissed at her. She cried out as his claws raked the skin on the back of her hand, drawing blood.

"Roha." Anguish filled his voice, but he pulled free anyway and started down the rock.

"Don't leave me." He ignored her cry and jumped down, then ran for the clearing. Roha scrambled after him.

In the clearing Churr planted his feet, threw the spear. A demon went down, pierced through the soft Y on its chest where the hard plates met. It swayed, then fell with a clashing of limbs, air whistling loudly through the holes on both sides of its chest.

Yelling, screaming, releasing her rage and confusion in a furious but useless series of actions, Roha ran through the conflict, striking at hard bodies, pulling at multi-jointed arms, pushing, going round and round the open space.

More demons fell. They seemed curiously helpless, stunned by the attack. Many of them froze. Others struck clumsily at the spears or at the Amar warriors.

There was a chittering, excited and shrill from the figure in the hole. The demons broke away as best they could and ran stiffly but with surprising speed toward the hole. When they were near the Egg, they went suddenly down on their bulging faces. Before the Amar could react, the demon in the hold pointed the end of the tube at them.

Fire streamed from the end of the pipe. The demon moved the fire-stream across the front of the attackers. Amar fell without a sound, the flesh burned from their bones. Behind them, other warriors shrieked as they caught the wash of the fire. They fell to the earth, rolling over and over, trying to smother the searing pain. The demon began to swing the tube back.

Churr snatched at the spear quivering in a demon body beside him. He twisted it loose and flung it at the demon in the hole. The spear caught one of the upper arms at the joint between arm and shoulder, carrying the arm away into the blackness of the hole. With a hissing cry, the demon fell back. The tube was wrenched from its pincers and fell flat, its fireflow stopping.

Again before the Amar, even Churr, could react, the fallen demons scrambled to their feet and ran up the planks into the Egg, carrying the injured demon with them. leaving the crouching trembling demon behind. It snatched at the tube.

Churr whistled. The Amar who could still walk or crawl ran back into the mistwall and out of sight among the bushes. For a moment, the stream of fire followed them, then it was gone. Running wildly, whimpering and hysterical, seeing the black and white patterns again, running heedless of where her feet landed, Roha fled the clearing.

Rihon caught her and held her while she struggled and cried out, foam gathering on her lips. When she quieted a little, he led her back to a spring and sat her down beside the hot, clear water. The damp heat seeped into her, relaxed her, leached away the excitement which softened into grief. She began crying quietly, mourning the dead and the dying.

Churr came to them. "Twins, the dead wait you. And the dying."

Roha looked up at him. She closed her eyes, reached out blindly. Rihon took her hand, held it tight in his. "We have to do this, Twin." He hugged her. "We have to."

"Yes." She opened her eyes, extended her hand to Churr. He lifted her to her feet, took the stone knife from the sling by her side and presented it to her. Roha grasped the hilt. This was her business, this was something she owed her people. Gravely she raised the hilt of the knife to touch her lips. She'd done this mercy before. Done it in every war since she was old enough to walk on her own.

With Rihon following her, his hand on her shoulder, she walked to the place where the dead and wounded waited her. Those in a haze of pain lay twisting on the earth, moaning, screaming. One was crying out repeatedly, not loudly, but without ceasing. The sound broke through her hard-won calm; she started trembling, nearly dropped the knife. Rihon's fingers tightened on her shoulder and strength flowed into her from him. She sucked in a deep breath and knelt beside the whimpering man, sickened by the stench of charred flesh. His face was burnt terribly, the white bone of his cheek showing through. She spread her hand out just above his heart, not able to touch him because of the burns there. Rihon dropped beside her and touched the fingers that held the hilt of the knife. With her brother echoing her, Roha cried, "Bright Twin, Dark Twin, Earth receive!" She drew her knife quickly across the suffering man's throat, leaning back to avoid the brief spurt of blood.

They moved on and knelt by each of the other dying Amar, giving their quick surcease from pain, sending the Amar souls back to the Dark Twin's womb to await rebirth.

Five of the raiders were burnt beyond recognition, their bodies hauled at some risk from the clearing; six men died under the mercy knife, four had scattered burns and two more had bones broken by demon blows. Roha touched the living, drew their pain into herself, then she went away from them, back to the bubbling pool. She sat on the warm earth and let that warmth draw the pain from her.

Rihon came quietly to her and sat beside her to stare with her into the bubbling water and watch the lines of steam dancing up off the surface. Roha reached out. Rihon closed his fingers around hers. They sat in silence, letting the horror of the day slide away from them. Behind them the sounds of digging went on and on.

Roha

Xs Clayton

CHAPTER VI

Roha lay beside Churr behind a thin screen of scraggly brush, the mist circulating sluggishly above them, watching the barricaded hole in the side of the Egg. Churr's face was drawn into grim lines, the scar that ran from the corner of his eye to the edge of a nostril was pulsing pale and dark. Roha wriggled uneasily in the slight hollow her body had pressed in the moss, making the leaves above her shake with a papery whispering.

Churr's hand fell heavily on her shoulder; he hissed a warning. She pointed and he snapped his head around. A demon form showed dimly behind the barricade. Its bulging eyes moved slowly over the silent brush and wall of mist, then it drew back into the darkness. For several minutes nothing happened, then part of the barricade was pulled aside and more of the demons appeared in the opening. They came bouncing down the planks, heads turning warily. In the long narrow three-fingered hands of their upper arms, two of the demons carried spears salvaged from the Amar and the bodies of fallen demons. Two more carried gathering bags. Their stubby antennas twitched constantly, their round bulgy heads turned and turned, the bulges below their four eyes chewed continually, producing clicks and chitterings that grated on Roha's ears. Her claws came out again as their biting acrid scent clogged her nostrils. They trotted across the clearing to a group of bushes that still had most of their leaves and small sour fruits.

Churr reached out, touched Duagin, the warrior next to him, on the shoulder, then moved his finger in a short arc along the line of brush, jabbing it finally at the cluster of demons. Duagin nodded and rose to his feet. He darted silently through mist and brush, disappearing before he'd gone more than a dozen steps.

A moment later Duagin burst from the brush, took three quick steps, cast his spear at one of the foraging demons, then ran back into the brush.

Churr cursed under his breath. One of the guard demons moved with surprising speed, thrust the spear it held into the path of the flying spear and deflected it just enough so that it only scraped along the hard skin on the shoulder of the gathering demon. There was some excited clicking and chittering, then the demons returned to the collection of leaves and fruit. One of the guards creaked over and picked up the deflected spear, held it in the pincers of its lower pair of arms. Several minutes later the demons hefted their filled bags and retreated warily to the Egg. The barricade was shoved back into place and the Egg settled into silence.

Churr rose, cursing, went trotting off after Duagin. Roha looked after him, then sat up, her eyes fixing again on the gray bulge of the Egg. The spear count was falling fast. Since the demons had taken to collecting them, the Amar were losing two or three spears a day. Her claws extended then resheathed themselves, repeated this again and again. *It has to be killed; the Egg has to be killed,* she thought. *They have to be killed, those demons.*

Churr came back and stood beside her, looking at the Egg. She could see the knots at the angle of his jaw, could see the scar on the side of his face paling and darkening. She knew the determination was hardening in him to break off this attack. When their eyes met, she knew what he was going to say and she didn't know how to stop him. She even knew he was right, but she knew, too, that she was right and the two rights confused and troubled her. Food was scarce; the Amar had to spend much of their time and strength in the hunt, going farther and farther each day into the treacherous mist. Here, at the Egg, this dragging, futile, endless fighting was exacerbating the madness from Mambila. One Amar, Dunun, sat hunched over his knees, staring at the ground, muttering incoherently. Several others were scarred and battered by fighting with each other, some look or comment setting off hair-trigger tempers. She looked away from Churr, hugging her knees tighter against her chest.

Rihon came out of the mist, three scrawny kissuni dangling on a game string slapping forlornly against his leg. Behind him the two other hunters had equally meager catches. He held up the skinny bodies. "Look at this; waste of a lot of time."

Roha's claws came out again. She started rocking on her buttocks. There was a knot in her throat. She had to speak, but she couldn't talk; she knew if she tried to talk, her voice would quaver and break.

Rihon gave his string to Pitic, one of the hunters, and went to sit beside Roha. He worked her hand loose from its grip on her leg and held it between both of his.

Pitic flattened his nose at the Twins, then turned to Churr. "There's something out there." He thrust his fist back the way they'd come, the two game strings and their burden swaying with the movement of his arm. "Following us, it was."

"Big?" Churr continued to watch the Egg.

"Big enough. I never saw 'em, if that's what you mean, just smelled their stink."

"Stink? Demon?" Churr rubbed at his scar. "Or animal?"

"Not animal." Pitic glanced at Ameb, who nodded his agreement. "Stalking us too good. Didn't feel like animal. Not demon. Smell was wrong."

The third hunter, Fulz, scratched at his head. "I got a good whiff of 'em twice. Sure not demon. More like kinya-kin-kin. Us and the Twin we talked it over. Think it's Mistlanders."

Churr snorted. "Mistlanders, hunh! Scare-tale for kids."

Pitic looked stubborn. "Something's out there. No animal, neither."

Churr glanced up at the ceiling of mist, mist that glowed with the faint green light of the Mambila Web, then examined the faces of the hunters. Finally, he turned to Rihon. "Twin."

Rihon looked up. "Think I saw one when the mist blew thin for a minute. Taller than a Rum, covered with stiff white fur, running along bent over. Mistlander for sure."

Churr nodded slowly. "That's it, then." Before continuing to speak, he glanced down at Roha, his wrinkled eyelids drooping over his eyes.

She waited for him to speak, waited for the words that would send them back. She tried to stare him out of his intention.

He shrugged and turned away. "Get that miserable catch skinned and cooked. We start back tomorrow at first light." Then he stalked off into the mist.

"We have to destroy the seed." Roha shivered and began weeping, blinked desperately, then opened her eyes wide. She pushed against Rihon's knee and staggered to her feet. Before she could burst through the brush and rush toward the Egg, Rihon was up beside her, holding her shoulders.

"No!" He pulled her back against him. "You can't do anything alone."

She struggled, twisted about, trying to break away from him. "Help me, brother. We have to destroy it."

"We can come back." He wrapped his arms around her narrow chest and held her tightly. "Roha, we can't stay here any longer. Pitic is right about the Mistlanders. They're out there, going to attack soon. They don't want us here. Roha, Roha." He rested his head on hers, his cheek warm against the smooth skin. "Let the Mistlanders fight the demons for a while; when we come back, we can finish the seed."

"Come back?" Roha sighed. "I know . . . I know all sorts of things. They won't come back with us, Twin. Or let us come back if they can help it." She curved her hands over the hands that held her. "Oh, Rihon, I'm tired and I'm hungry and I just don't know what to do. Things pull one way, pull another."

"We'll be eating in a little while. Maybe things'll be better then."

Roha patted her hands lightly on Rihon's. "What would I do without you, Twin?"

Day was merging with night, the mist thickening, sounds taking on an eerie echoing quality. Whiffs of a sour, musty smell drifted into the clearing as an abrupt wind change caught the circling Mistlanders before they could move. None of the Amar tried to sleep even though the sentries were alert and prowling about the camp. Tension was thick enough to breathe in with the mist. The Floating ghosts were swarming but the Amar were afraid of them no longer, only cautious, keeping limber switches at hand to break up any ghosts that tried to merge.

Without warning, stones were hurled into the clearing, thicker than hail and thrown a great deal harder. Churr knocked Roha flat, fell beside her. Rihon threw himself on top of his sister to protect her from the stones. The Mistlanders followed the stones, swarming over the Amar, whining

and spitting, flinging themselves on the Amar warriors.
Besides their crude slings, they had no weapons, but they
were larger than the Amar, with terrible tearing canines,
hooked claws on their four fingers. They raged through the
clearing with such ferocity that they drove the Amar into a
hollow circle. The warriors who still had spears stood jabbing
at the attackers. Below the level of the spears, Amar moved
on hands and knees, slashing at hamstrings or any other tar-
get offered.

The attack broke off as abruptly as it started; those Mistlanders who could still move faded into the mist and were
gone.

Churr broke from the circle and walked among the fallen
Mistlanders, slashing throats of any who still moved or
breathed. Pitic thrust a toe into the ribs of one Mistlander,
kicked it over. The Mistlander was a long, lean monster with
six limbs instead of four, almost no neck, a small, ball-shaped
head set on narrow upper shoulders. Two curved tearing
teeth protruded from a black upper lip, fitting in a groove in
lower jaw. Large black eyes stared sightlessly up into the
mist; mobile ears were pressed back against the round skull.
It was covered completely by stiff white hair.

Wrinkling his nose at their stench, Pitic caught hold of a
wrist and started pulling the body from the clearing. With a
snort of disgust, Fulz grabbed another. "Let's get this mess
outta here, before those stinking kin-kin come back."

They pulled the dead Mistlanders to a spot downwind of
the camp, piled firebush over them and set it burning, retreating hastily as the appalling stench of burnt hair was
added to the sickening odors drifting around the bodies. Roha
stared at the flames, ignoring the smell, unaware that she was
being left behind. The flames danced around her, writhing
around her, wreathing around her. She gasped as a hand
touched her arm, for the briefest instant the hand seared her
skin, then the burning was gone. Rihon pulled at her. "Come
on. You can't stay alone. They'll kill you."

Roha blinked at the fire, resisting Rihon's tug. "Fire," she
murmured.

"Yes," Rihon said patiently. "It's fire, Roha. Come on."
Underscoring his urgency, a stone came whuffling past Roha's
head, startling her from her haze. With a gasp of horror, she
ran toward the camp, Rihon close beside her.

The night passed slowly, stones falling among the Amar with dulling regularity. When dawn lightened the mist and the sun began to heat it into retreating, Churr stood warily, stretched, his eyes searching the surrounding bushes. The weary Amar came from their shielding leathers stiff and grainy-eyed. He waited until all the sane were gathered around him. "No hunting this morning. We go hungry. Done it before. Pitic, scout ahead. Keep your sniffer working to warn us about the Mistlanders. Rest of you, watch out for rocks. Those stinking monsters are too damn good with those slings."

Roha wriggled through the Amar and stopped, facing Churr, her hands fisted on her hips. "Wait."

"Why?"

"One last try. We used firebush to burn the Mistlanders; why not burn the Egg?"

Churr stared at her a moment, then rubbed his chin as he turned slowly and examined the Egg. "Stone don't burn."

"Is that stone?" She indicated the great curve of the Egg. "Ever seen stone like that?" She tugged at his arm. "How do you know it won't burn?"

"Didn't when it fell." Churr started to turn away.

Roha stepped in front of him again. "We could try. It wouldn't take long," she said softly, fixing her eyes on his, willing him to agree.

Churr looked down at her for a long moment, then he lifted his head and contemplated the Egg. Finally he shrugged. "We'll try it."

Working in pairs, one guarding while the other gathered fireweed, they cut great armloads of the pitchy brush and piled it around the Egg, keeping out of sight as much as they could. When they were finished, they retreated while Churr, Roha and Rihon stayed close to the Egg.

"I had a dream," Roha said softly, her eyes bright with tears. "I saw the Egg burning with a great white fire that filled the sky."

Churr looked skeptical but took the firepot and pulled the moss off the coal inside. He tilted the coal onto a torch of twisted withes and blew it into flame, then shoved the torch into the firebrush. He backed off hastily as the weed caught and flames leaped six feet into the air. He retreated to Roha and Rihon; the three of them stood watching as flame tore through the piled-up brush.

The fire burned out, adding streaks of soot to the sulphur yellows and copper greens. It did no other damage. Roha's shoulders slumped. She was suddenly too tired to argue any longer. She trudged along behind Churr, her feelings numb, her passion temporarily burned to ash.

Paced by the Mistlanders, the tired, dispirited Amar began heading back to their village, leading the passive Dunun, leaving behind only a few dead demons. The Egg was untouched, still poisoning Mother Earth.

Roha

CHAPTER VII

Days slipped by, each day a thorn in Roha's heart. Twenty Amar warriors had marched into the Mistlands with Churr and the Twins; seven had staggered out—with one of the seven a Lost Child. Half the families of the village mourned a dead brother, mate or son. Roha trembled continually under the impact of their blame. She let Rihon collect food for her from the family fires because she couldn't face any longer the hostile stares of the women.

And there were the other demons. The three fireseeds that came from the sky had lice on them, sky-demons that swarmed from the cooled husks of the seeds, killing anything that moved around them until they found the Nafa's House and moved in on her, leaving behind them more Amar dead, women this time, garden workers drawn to them by a curiosity that overcame their fear. Day and night the warriors watched them, killing them when they could, being killed or wounded by the noisy flinging sticks of the demons, sticks that threw very small stones with such force they tore through Rum flesh more destructively than any spear. More dead to pile on Roha's aching shoulders—more pain until she bowed under it, wondering if she could endure this burden.

And day on day on day, the Mambila Web hung over them and the madness spread among the Amar in spite of all the Twins could do. Night after night, they chanted with Gawer Hith, sought to draw the madness from the people into themselves and through themselves, to let it dissipate in the forgiving heart of Mother Earth. But the failure with the demons and the death of the warriors undermined the faith the Amar had in the Luck of the Twins and they could do much less.

Roha crept from the village early one morning, afraid of the sky-demons but even more afraid of the anger and frustration she felt in the village; she was near the limit of her endurance; another day of reproaches and silent blame was more than she could stand. She wound through the familiar trees, touching the friendlies, avoiding the hungries, her mind running round and round on the old aching themes, the poison Egg, the demons, the poison that was killing the Amar. She started running, trying to escape the anger and frustration inside her, running wildly, without watching where she was going, a soft whining deep in her throat, drops of sweat dripping from her face.

Her hand struck the trunk of a tree. Gasping, shaking with the force of the emotions raging through her, she wrapped her arms about the trunk and sank down until she was sitting on the earth, the damp, cool mother whose coolness crept into her heated body and soothed her. She pressed her cheek against the leathery bark, sucking in the cool spicy scent of its sap. "Mat-lizine," she whispered, feeling her breath creep hot along the bark. "Comfort me, comforter." She sighed and dug a claw into the bark beside her face, sniffing avidly at the pungent droplets spraying past her nose. Closing her eyes, she let the tart smell flood through her, cleaning out the tangle of emotion. After a minute she held her forefinger beneath the tear her claw had made, catching the thick white ooze as it trickled down.

At first it was cool, then it warmed as it solidified into a hard mass wrapped around her finger. She sniffed at it, then sucked at her knuckle until the sap was gone.

It slipped into her blood and her racing body slowed. The things that tormented her drifted away until they were less important than the distant song of an imbo that reached her ears and shivered there like reified delight. She sighed with pleasure, rubbed her cheek against the bark.

Finally she grew restless, could sit no longer. She pushed onto her feet, patted the tree with sisterly affection, then drifted along a shade-mottled path, not caring much where she was going. She danced now and then with a friendly tree, hands slipping around-around the trunk, body swaying with the rhythms of the wind-stirred branches.

Humming to herself, running with the breeze, she wound through the trees, circling the village, circling the garden patches burned into the forest, edging around the Nafa's clearing, turning back at the rim of the Mistlands, circling along this route again and again, feet making new prints on top of old on the soft earth beneath the trees.

When the effect of the sap wore off, she began to feel hungry but she shivered at the thought of returning to the village and sought through the forest until she found a patch of zimber bushes. She plucked a few of the red-purple fruits, sank her teeth into the tight-grained flesh. Thick purple-red juice escaped from the corners of her mouth. She wiped it away with the back of her hand and went on tearing the resistant flesh from the pits.

She threw the last of the pits away, rubbed with disgust at the juice stains on her hands and body, then she trotted up the mountainside to the pool at the base of a waterfall.

She moved warily through the brush and trees, eyeing the pool, sweeping her gaze over the mountain around it until she was sure no devils lurked in ambush. She emerged from her shelter, untied her kilt, dropped it on a rock, then ran at the stream and plunged into the icy water. Sputtering, splashing about, shuddering at the shock of the cold against her skin, laughing, she played in the pool then stood with the water murmuring past her and scrubbed off the lingering juice stains.

With a yawn and a last stretch, she waded up the bank, feeling the weight of her body coming back to her and with that weight, some of the trouble to her spirit. She lay down on a flat rock to let the sun dry her. Succumbing at last to a bone-deep weariness, she slept.

When she woke, the sun was low in the west, sparking a ripple of exploding color in the Web that dazzled her. She jumped to her feet, crossing her arms over her flat narrow chest. The spray from the waterfall drifted past her, settling in large beads on her skin. Still tired, she felt the euphoria of the earlier part of the day dissipate; she knotted her kilt back around her hips, her eyes on the Web as she wondered what new troubles the coming night would bring.

The dark seed fell out of the sun, cutting a great arc across the sky. It spat out a trail of light that lost itself in the shimmer of the Web for a few seconds then was gone. White cups, three of them, bloomed behind it. They caught the wind and came down slowly, holding fistfuls of air in their hollows, the black seed swaying below them. Roha stared until the seed was close, dipping toward the trees where the other fireseeds pointed sharp noses at the sky.

Growling deep in her throat, Roha fled down the mountainside, running recklessly, giving no thought to footing or other dangers. The sound of the seed whumping down shook the air around her. She stopped her plunging run at the edge of the new-made clearing by catching hold of a mat-izar, a spice tree.

The slim silver-gray tree shook with the force of her hurtling body, showering down a mist of pale pollen, covering her with the fine golden grains. She brushed impatiently at her face, pinching her nose-slits at the overpowering stench of the spice, fighting off its dream-call. Pressed against the smooth bark, she peered through the bell-curve of the hanging branches at the great round seed sitting in the ashes of its fire-fall, half buried in thrown-up earth, draped by the stiff folds of the cups that had slowed its descent.

For several minutes nothing happened, then a piece of the side blew away and a creature wriggled out of the small hole left behind. Roha's claws came out. "Demon," she hissed, then pressed her lips together.

The creature was tall and thick-bodied, hard to see against the background of stone and tree. It stretched, oddly like a hatchling newly come from the shell. Roha hugged the trunk of her sheltering tree, shivering with fear and anger and a furious curiosity that held her in place, watching intently as the demon began to move around.

Reaching up, it fumbled with the skin on its head, then pulled it off. Roha stifled a gasp as she realized that the stiff grayish substance was clothing, not skin at all. It tossed the head covering back into the hole then ran five-fingered hands like the Nafa's through long thick hair the color of fire, long hair like the Nafa's except for its color. The demon had a pointed nose like the Nafa and a wide, soft mouth like the Nafa's. Roha closed her eyes, dizzy with the spice and this suggestion that the Nafa had come from the sky like the other demons. *No,* she thought, claws extending and retracting, extending and retracting as she fought to deal with the feeling she still had for the Nafa. *She isn't like them,* she thought. *She never tried to hurt us. She isn't like the other demons . . . but this one looks like her. . . .*

A flight of crevla fluttered into the clearing and began cir-

cling over the demon's head. It looked up, startled. Then
Roha felt a terrible force slamming at her, clawing at her,
drawing her soul forth from her body. When she could see
again, the crevla were fleeing, leaving behind several dead.
Roha blinked. The demon was kneeling beside the dead, filled
with an anguish that left Roha gaping. She settled back and
tried to puzzle out the meaning of these things as the demon
crawled back into the seed.

When it came out, it wore different clothing, looser and
softer and even harder to see in the gathering darkness.

Her fear gone for the moment, Roha watched without
comprehending as the demon locked shining rods together to
make a long thin thing with many wheels. It went briskly to
the pile and broke open several more of the pods it had
thrown from the seed and pulled out a lot of cloth like the
cloth it wore. It used this to make a small shelter which it set
up on the thing it had built. Finally it wove a web of trip-
wires about the thing, then crawled inside the shelter and
didn't come out again.

Glancing continually at the silent shelter, Roha edged
through the curtain of dangling limbs and moved across the
clearing toward the seed with exaggerated care to avoid scattered branches and clusters of leaves. As she spread her
hands on the seed, it sang to her of great cold and great heat,
of distance and shock, of strangeness beyond her comprehending. It confused her, frightened her, oppressed her spirits.
Wheeling, she fled from the clearing, panting and weeping as
fear took hold of her again. She plunged into the thicker
darkness under the trees, fleeing along familiar paths toward
her village.

Gawer Hith was sitting cross-legged in front of the Twins'
house. Wisps of smoke from smoldering torches lying scattered on the ground mingled with the lines of drifting mist.

Roha came slowly toward her, a sick feeling in her stomach. She stood silent in front of Hith, pushing her toes
through a drift of ash on the ground, reluctant to ask what
she knew she had to ask. She glanced around the village, but
the other houses were silent; none of the Amar were stirring.
Unhappy, worried, tired, she hugged her arms across her
chest. "What happened?"

Gawer Hith grunted. Fingers moving over her drum, she
said, "Mambila madness took Dunun's brothers. They tried to

burn your house." She jerked a thumb up and back. "Niong stopped them and I got them calmed down after a while with Rihon's help. He's not hurt," she added swiftly as Roha cried out, reaching toward her with shaking hands. Gawer Hith tapped her fingers idly on the drumhead. "Things getting bad, girl. Could be you'd better go live up the mountain for a while." Her voice was calm, without blame, but Roha shivered anyway. Hith nodded slowly. "Get some sleep, girl. I'll stay here so you don't need to bother yourself about another attack, least, not this night."

Roha shifted from foot to foot as she tried to decide what to do. Abruptly, she dropped to her knees and knocked her forehead to the ground in formal acknowledgment of her debt, then she jumped to her feet and scrambled up the ladder.

Rihon was sleeping, curled up on his mat, his leather robe spread loosely over his head and shoulders. Roha dropped beside him and edged as close as she could, pressing her back against his side. Rihon muttered and dropped his arm over her. Warmed by the strength of her brother, Roha calmed and drifted off to sleep.

THE HUNT

CHAPTER I   Aleytys

"Five days." Taggert swung the pilot's chair around and frowned at her. "Long time to drift in that thing. Closed in like that."

Aleytys tripped the catches on her crash web and crawled out of her chair. "Head guaranteed it was detection-proof, that's all I care about. Got the Tikh'asfour on the screen?"

"Will." He swung back, thumbed a viewscreen to life. She came up behind him and watched over his shoulder as he pointed to three sets of dots standing a little way out from a fuzzy darkness inside a paler blur. "Looks like they've spotted the place where *Nowhere*'s coming out of the Sink. Sitting on it."

"Just as well. Makes getting in easier."

He rubbed at a long, off-center nose, glanced up at her, his pale blue eyes measuring her. "Getting out could be a heller, Lee."

"Haestavaada have set up a diversion. They're supposed to have a fleet hanging back out of detection range waiting for my signal." She shrugged. "That's a couple weeks away, Taeg. Now, you just get me in close enough for the drop."

"Easy enough." He flashed her a lopsided grin, then moved his hands over the board, the lights flickering on his dreamy intent face. He was the best of the Hunter pilots, working as much from the feel of the ship as from the constant flow of data in front of him. Aleytys watched, smiling, her hands resting on the back of his chair. She knew she should go back to her place, that what she was doing was dangerous, but she took a great pleasure in watching his work and in knowing he was Head's gift to her, Head's blessing on her attempt to secure independence for herself.

Using the convolutions of the Sink to shield his ship from detection, Taggert eased closer and closer to the smudge that represented the world *Nowhere*, winding through the splayed-out web of forces that was almost a living thing, pulsating in space, trapped in one spot, trapping within itself one small worthless world with no heavy metals to make fighting the Sink cost-effective. Poison plants, hostile natives, and a difficult location. Nothing to lure anyone here. *Nowhere*.

Sweating and uneasy as the instrumentation began to be unreliable, looking a little wild as if his senses were betraying him rather than the instruments, Taggert slowed until they were creeping along. Without taking his eyes from the board, he murmured, "Crawl into your rubber womb, Lee. This is as close as we get. Damn if I stay here a minute longer than I have to."

After an interminable wait the chemical rockets fired, then the three chutes bloomed above the capsule. In her cocoon, Aleytys snapped awake, the haze of boredom blown away. Five days in that cramped womb where movement alternated between a wriggle and a crawl, five days of mostly sleeping as she dropped into the sink, five days a thousand times worse than all the simulations she'd played preparing for this—no, she thought, not preparing. There was no preparation for this dark compression that went on and on, the noise hammering at her, on and on. The sharp jerk as the chutes deployed slammed her against the web and padding. The slow swaying that followed was worse; her stomach protested and her mind flickered. The Sink reached for her again. Sometimes she could hold within herself the nearest stars as well as the whole of the Zangaree Sink, visualizing the fuzzy wavelets of electrons as well as all life that walked the worlds circling these stars; other times she was locked within the bony curve of her skull more effectively than any inhibitor had managed.

The swaying ended in a jarring impact; her body jounced about the cocoon until she was afraid of breaking bones and pulling ligaments. Then there was silence. Stillness. The steady pull of gravity. She sucked in a deep breath, then let it trickle out again as her fingers fumbled at the catches of the cocoon. When the interlocking leaves of protection had slipped away, she crawled out of the hollow, wriggled to the hatch and shifted the guard plate of the puzzle latch that locked the hatch in place. She pushed and pulled in the sequence she'd memorized, then slammed her hands against the hatch, popping it loose.

Stiff and sore, she pulled herself awkwardly from the capsule and dropped to the earth. She stretched, groaning with the pleasure of straightening her body, then stripped off the hood of her support-suit. After shaking her head and running her fingers through her hair, she turned slowly, her eyes sweeping over the silent round of trees.

A breeze wandered over the ash and shattered tree crowns in the small clearing, blowing strong spicy scents into her face, teasing her hair out from her head. She turned farther, slapped her hands against her sides and laughed, blessing her luck and the efficiency of Hunter computers. Rising over a skim of trees, the setting sun red and gold behind them, the tops of three ships caught the light and sent dazzling glimmers into her eyes. Scav ships. She brushed the hair back from her face, rubbed at tearing eyes, then turned to the half-buried capsule, forced for the moment to wait for the appearance of the Scavs. She crawled back inside and began tossing out the supply cells that lined the walls.

When all of them were out, she came crawling through the hatch, jumped down and began stacking the cells beside the earth mound. Now and then she glanced at the ships, wondering if any Scav had been alert enough to notice her arrival. She finished her pile and walked away from it, stopped in the center of the clearing, stood kicking at clods of earth, watching ashes rise and settle as her boot toe disturbed them. Restless and impatient, anxious to get her plan moving, she cursed the laziness of the Scavs, fell silent as the futility of that struck her, opened the fastenings of her suit and pulled it away from her neck to let air flow in onto her sweating skin.

A slow hooting brought her head up. Several blunt-faced creatures flew over her, beating the air with leathery wings. Tufts of gray fur humped energetically on the scrawny bodies, large eyes glowed like black stones, small sucker mouths worked continually. The fliers circled clumsily above her head, positioning themselves for attack.

Aleytys stared at them. *Bloodsuckers*, she thought, then looked beyond them at the tracery of the Zangaree Sink, felt the uncertain beat in her head, shrugged. Gathering a mind-warning, she projected it at the bobbling fliers.

When it hit them, they fluttered in distress. Several

dropped to the ground and writhed at her feet. Others struggled away from her, booming loud pain-filled cries. Dismayed, she let the warning collapse. "Damn Sink," she muttered, then knelt by the fliers on the ground, wondering if she dared try her healing. She poked a finger into the side of the nearest creature, felt the cold flaccidity of the body. "Dead." One by one she touched them. All dead. She sighed. "Have to be careful until I can control this better. Damn Sink."

Depressed by this inauspicious beginning, she came heavily to her feet, looked around once more at the empty clearing, then climbed back through the hatch.

Standing hunched over in the small cabin, she stripped off the support suit, wrinkling her nose at her own smell. After five days without bathing—though the suit was supposed to cope with this as it did with her other functions—she felt grimy and disheartened over the Hunt. Using a trickle of water from her limited supply, she scrubbed herself as clean as she could, sighing for the luxury of a full bath. As she dried off, she fixed her eyes on the ghost round of the hatch. "No!" Air exploded from her lungs. She straightened without thinking and slammed her head against the low ceiling, shocking tears into her eyes. "I've had this place. No more. Not a minute more." Brushing at her eyes, she groped for her hunting clothes and pulled on a mottled gray tunic and trousers.

Outside, the air was getting cooler. Wisps of fog crawled from under the trees, puddling in hollows and stringing out in thin lines along the ground. Aleytys twisted her body about, working out the cramps and stiffness of her long confinement. Finally she stretched her arms as high as she could reach, rising onto her toes, stretching until her bones cracked, then dropped her heels down, yawned, scrubbed her hands hard across her face, her head beginning to feel stuffed, the things she looked at flattening out or distorting their shapes. She closed her eyes and the dizziness left her. With a feeling of uncertainty she moved back to the capsule and began to break open certain marked cells, the distortion of her vision continuing to come and go. Frowning and anxious, she straightened, rubbed at her eyes, then sniffed the air, realizing with sudden relief that this distortion occurred whenever a particular spicy scent came to her on the strengthening wind. *Not the Sink*, she thought.

Working with the contents of the special cells, she assembled the carrier on the far side of the clearing where the breeze was strongest. It was a construct of rods and wheels, that carrier, broad in the bed, flexible enough to bend to the vagaries of the surface, the wheels high enough to let the carrier straddle large rocks and most of the brush it would encounter. It could carry over a ton, be pulled along by two or three people, and winched up slopes too steep for human muscle. Hunter technicians had built it for her to cope with the uncertainties of the Zangaree Sink.

As she labored, the fog crept around her, merging and breaking, carrying with it the exotic odor of the forest. She swam in a film of sweat that clung to her like a second skin, each breath a struggle in the heavy humid air that made her feel as if she drowned, air with no life in it however much she gulped it. Her disorientation grew worse. At times she could reach out, her sensing range tremendously enhanced, brief flashes when she came close to foundering. Much of the time her skull was an iron round locking her inside. When the carrier was at last assembled, she straightened, stretched. Then she broke out the shelter and set it up on the bed of the carrier.

The shelter was constructed of spider silk from Heggistril, one of the strongest and lightest materials available. Each piece was woven to order, since cutting it was out of the question. Her tunic and trousers were made of the same substance and her boots soaked in the spider's poison to keep the leather supple as it made it impervious to most liquids.

Once the shelter was up, she set out a guard fence around the carrier, a series of trip wires attached to small but noisy charges. While she wasn't particularly enthusiastic about explosions going off around her, she didn't want some of the larger predators creeping up on her while she slept. Or any hostile natives.

The sky was a web of glowing and shifting light and the wind was booming against the spider silk when she crawled into the shelter, tugged off her boots and stretched out on the comforter, her aching muscles slowly loosening, her weary mind beginning to adjust to the demands of the Sink.

She woke feeling considerably better. The sun was just poking its head above the undulating line of mountains, the

web of the Zangaree Sink a curdled scum around its greenish
half-circle. She jumped down from the carrier, ran her fingers
through oily hair and thought ruefully of a hot and soapy
bath. Still, the air was crisp and fresh against her face, the
circle of trees a pleasing medley of greens, yesterday's humid-
ity blown away.

After kicking though ash and shattered trees to gather
wood, she built a fire, watched the flames grow, smiled at the
crackle of the burning sap that was perfuming the air around
her with a heady mixture of scents.

Knowing that she shouldn't do it, that Gray and Head
would take her hide off, she scored one of the branches with
her thumbnail, rubbed the sap that oozed from the cut between her thumb and forefinger. She felt a faint tingling on
her skin, a creeping coldness. Hastily she *reached* for her
power source, her black river winding among the stars—and
knew a moment of panic when it seemed hazy, unreal, too
far to reach. The effort causing a low wail from her, she
lunged for the black water, relaxed, let it flow into her body,
washing away the effects of the drug in the sap.

She was leaning against a carrier wheel, sipping at a last
cup of cha when the Scavengers came bursting into the clearing.

THE HUNT

CHAPTER II   Aleytys

Aleytys continued to sip at the lukewarm cha, watching them as they left the shelter of the trees.

The first was a big, dark man with a spectacular blaze cutting through his thick black hair, a strip of white which extended the line of a scar that touched his black eyebrow with a point of white, skimmed past the end of his eye and swept down to the corner of his mouth. After a rapid glance around and a low word to the two men behind him, he shifted his pellet rifle to the curve of his arm, stepped over a section of tree, and came toward her, moving with the alert poise of a hunting cat.

The two men—both smaller than he, both heavily armed—dropped behind a thicket of branches and wilting leaves, keeping their eyes moving along the line of trees, guns ready, bodies taut with readiness to move at the slightest warning. Aleytys began to understand why she'd had her respite. The Scavengers must have stirred up the natives and didn't relish moving about after dark.

Ignoring Aleytys for the moment, the big man strolled to the capsule, poked for a short while among the cells piled beside it, breaking open a few to inspect their contents. He smoothed his hand over his short beard, glanced at her, speculation glinting in his pale eyes. He moved past her and walked around the carrier, lifted the tongue, tugged at it, raising an eyebrow at the ease with which he started the carrier rolling. He jumped up onto the broad bed, fingered the spider-silk shelter, thrust his head inside, pulled it out. Jumping down, he landed lightly beside her, nudged her with the toe of his boot. "Who're you?"

Aleytys stared down at the leaf-laden cha pooling in the bottom of the cup, then moved to one side away from the pressure of the boot. *Here we go*, she thought. Leaning back,

she emptied the dregs of cha over his boot, smiled, looked up
at him, smiled again, saying nothing.

"Who sent you here?" His gray-green eyes narrowed; he
scowled at her, ignoring the cha leaves mixing with the dust
on his boot. She looked away from him, ran her fingers
through her hair. And said nothing. "Bitch!" he grunted. Face
flushing with anger, he grabbed at her.

Moving away from him, she said, "You tell me." In the
center of the clearing, the wind ruffling the hair at the back
of her head, she faced him and waited.

He shifted his hold on the pellet rifle. "Come here."

She glanced from his face to the rifle as the front sight
dropped until it was pointing at her left knee. "You hit what
you aim at?"

"This close who could miss? Come here."

Feet rustling through the scattered leaves and small
branches, she walked slowly toward him and stopped when
she was about three feet from him. "Aleytys," she said. "My
name."

The name touched some wisp of memory but apparently
he couldn't bring it up. "Who sent you?" he snapped.

"Nobody sends me anywhere. Who sent you?" Her eyes on
the hands holding the rifle, she tried to gauge just how far she
could go in establishing her independence without driving
him into a fury; she didn't want to have to cope with a shattered ankle or knee.

He stepped close suddenly, caught hold of her arm, his fingers cutting into her flesh, his strength greater than she'd expected. With one hand he lifted her, swung her around and
threw her onto the carrier, adjusting his grip as it rocked under her.

She kicked at him, missed as he slid aside; he slapped her
hard across the face, pushed her head back, his other hand
heavy on her throat. She started strangling, tried to dislocate
one of his fingers. He pushed down harder, brushed her hand
away with his free hand as easily as he would a pesty fly. She
let herself go limp.

With a grunt of triumph he pulled his hand away, slapped
her a final time, then released her, stepped back, stood looking down at her.

Struggling to show surrender despite the rage nearly consuming her, Aleytys slid off the carrier and crouched on the

ground, her head hanging, gasping and choking as she fought for breath. When she heard him step toward her again, she gasped, "Haestavaada. They sent me."

"Why you?"

The spitting crack of a pellet rifle interrupted him. He swung around as one of the other Scavs yelled his name. "Quale!"

"What?" Jumping a bit of trunk, he loped to them, eyes moving warily along the line of trees. "Greenies?"

The smaller of the two Scavs nodded, pointed. "Bunch of them in there."

"Wing any?"

"Don't think so." He shrugged, settled himself and squeezed off another shot, then leaned forward peering into the shadows under the trees. "Hard to tell."

Quale squatted beside him, dropped a hand on his shoulder. "We got to get out of here. Szor, you and Huut get that stuff loaded. I'll keep the greenies off your backs."

"Sure, Quale." Szor rose, followed by the silent Huut. Both men's faces were sullen and discontented as they moved toward the pile of cells; they paid no attention to Quale or Aleytys as they trotted from capsule to carrier and back, throwing the cells onto the carrier with unnecessary violence out of their resentment at being used as common laborers.

Aleytys flinched as an arrow sang from the trees, skimmed past Quale—just missing as he ducked away—and thunked quivering into the damp soil by her feet. Quale began shooting slowly, his targets half-seen shadows darting among the trees. Aleytys snatched the arrow free and scrambled on hands and knees to the carrier. Crouching beneath it close to one of the wheels, she examined the arrow. It was about eight inches long with three flights on one end, a stone point on the other, the stone coated with a dark gummy substance. *Poison,* she thought. *No wonder they don't go out at night. Fools.* With a snort of disgust she tossed the arrow aside. *Damn them, making my job harder.*

She gasped as a wild wail burst from the shadows under the trees. Edging her head around the wheel, she saw Quale lower his rifle and stand up. She chewed her lip a minute then crawled from under the carrier and stood. "What was that?"

"Got one of them." He looked around, then came toward

her, his gray-green eyes glinting with triumph. "From the noise, we hit a chief, someone important." He drew his hand down the side of her face, closed his fingers around her throat, moved her slowly from side to side, his thumb stroking her neck. "Soft. I could break you in half with a snap of my fingers." Abruptly, he shifted his grip to her arm and dragged her to the front of the carrier. "Grab hold." He kicked at the tongue. "Huut!"

Shrugging, Aleytys moved past him and caught hold of the tongue near the front, setting her side of the short crossbar against her stomach. Behind her she heard the Scav come shuffling up, his feet dragging through the leaves and ash. She eyes and the hand holding his rifle was white-knuckled with glanced around. There was a glazed unsteadiness about his strain. Aleytys shifted her grip on the crossbar. *He's about to blow*, she thought. *The Sink's got to him. If that's what Quale picks to guard him, I wonder what the others are like.*

- "Get up there and grab hold. We got to get this thing undercover before the greenies get their nerve up again."

Huut kicked at a section of shattered branch. "Ain't no horse."

Quale reached across the tongue, grabbed the little man's battlejacket at the throat and twisted. "I say you're a horse, you whinny. Hear?"

Huut's eyes widened until they were ringed with white; his mouth stretched open, the hairs of his ratty moustache fluttering as he strained for air. When the hate on his face intensified, draining away the last trace of humanity, Aleytys thought he was going to attack Quale, but he did nothing except stare at the big man, then lower his eyes. Quale shoved him away and stepped back. Settling his battlejacket around his shoulders, Huut slung his rifle across his back and tramped silently to join Aleytys, taking hold of the other side of the crossbar.

With Quale and Szor prowling along on either side, their eyes roving constantly over the silent trees, Aleytys and Huut hauled the carrier toward, then past, the Scav ships, breaking from the trees onto a wide path trodden deep into the soft damp earth.

After another fifteen minutes the soil underfoot grew thinner and stonier, the trees sparser and scrubbier. Wisps of fog snaked along the ground, drifting toward them from cloud

domes hugging the earth some distance ahead, intermittently
visible through brush and trees. Then they broke through into
a clearing.

The walled square in the clearing's center was seven feet
high, stone blocks set in a running bond, held together by
concrete that shone dazzling white against the dirty reds and
browns of the stone. Startled, not expecting any such structure on this primitive world, Aleytys let go of the crossbar
and stood staring until a hard blow between her shoulders
and an angry growl from Quale sent her stumbling forward
again. She sneaked a look back at him as she caught hold of
the crossbar. His head was turning constantly as he swept the
brush and scrubby trees around the clearing; the feral taut-
ness in his body and the intent concentration on his set face
spoke more strongly than any words of the danger that lay
around them. Feeling a coldness between her shoulderblades
at the thought of those poison arrows, Aleytys began to push
more enthusiastically. They circled the wall and stopped in
front of a gate whose porous wood had been treated with a
dark substance that hardened it and left it attractively
mottled.

Quale brushed past her and banged on the gate. "Blaur,
open up," he roared. "You asleep, I'll skin you cold." He
banged again. Behind them in the mist there was a sudden
scream and an arrow skimmed past his arm to skitter over
the wood and fall to the ground. "Haul ass, man. Greenies."

When Aleytys saw the arrow bouncing off the wood to fall
with its point punching into the soil, she dropped to hands
and knees and scurried under the carrier. Behind her she
heard a thumping and scraping and spared a moment to hope
the men inside the wall would waste no time getting that gate
open. She could see Quale and Szor sheltering behind the carrier, firing slowly at dark figures that popped up and down,
appearing and vanishing in the mist, insubstantial as ghosts.

Behind her she heard Huut's feet scrape against the hard
soil. She glanced around, wondering why he'd taken so long
to start firing. He was lifting his rifle, his eyes fixed on
Quale's back, white-ringed and staring, the hate in his face
startling in its intensity. Without stopping to think, she threw
herself at his legs before he could pull the trigger.

As the two of them rolled on the ground, wrestling for the
weapon, a flight of arrows hissed down around them. Aleytys

heard a meaty thunk and felt Huut convulse beneath her. She rolled desperately away trying to reach the carrier but a last arrow pierced the palm of her left hand, pinning her to the ground.

There was a roaring in her blood, an agony burning in her brain. Terrified, she arched her back, thrusting with her body and reaching with her mind for the safety of her black river; her *reach* was a frantic leap into nothingness that almost failed as the poison claimed her, then she collapsed flat with relief as she tapped into her power and the healing water came flooding into her, washing away the poison, rebuilding the destroyed nerve cells. When the burning was gone, she lay panting until her panic subsided also, then she pulled the arrow from her hand and flung it away. Drawing back a few wisps of the water, she healed the cut in her palm, rolled over, pushed onto her hands and knees and looked around.

Huut lay beside the carrier tongue, an arrow through his throat. The gate was open. Men were running toward the carrier, crouched over, wary. Behind her she could hear someone—Quale or Szor—still shooting at half-seen shadows in mist. She got shakily to her feet and stumbled toward the gate, her mind in turmoil.

Ignoring the startled looks that followed her, she moved through the opening, turned aside and sat on a plank propped up on several chunks of wood. She leaned her head against the stone and closed her eyes, shuddering, a belated reaction to her close brush with death—if the poison had acted a fraction faster, she wouldn't have had time or strength to nullify it. Her knowledge that she could heal just about any injury to herself, that she was faster and stronger and provided with more resources than the ordinary man or woman, this knowledge had made her careless, had tempted her into taking chances that a person more conscious of his or her mortality would have avoided. *I could have yelled*, she thought. *Could have called Quale, warned him, let him handle it. I didn't even think of that. Think! I didn't bother to think.* With a shaky laugh, she opened her eyes and looked around.

The carrier was inside and the gate was shut. Quale and the other Scavs were standing on improvised walkways like the plank she was sitting on; they were firing at irregular intervals at targets she couldn't see. More arrows were coming into the square, some of them sticking in the ground, others bouncing off the low structure in the center of the enclosure. Beside her, a lanky avian Otaz with dulled and ruffled vestigial feathers crouched awkwardly behind the wall and squeezed off a steady stream of shots. Three steps farther on four Ortels scratched at patches of parasitical lichens on their exoskeletons and took turns popping their bulbous heads over the wall to touch off an occasional shot, spending the rest of the time clicking and creaking at each other. Beyond these, three Tiks were chattering shrilly, half their speech outside her range of hearing, their huge eyes protected from the glare of the sun by special goggles, the short gray fur that covered their squat bodies ruffled and stained. On the far side of the gate, the humanoid Scavs were as raveled, nervous and battered as the nonhumans. Aleytys noted the separation of the kinds and their physical deterioration. *A lot of friction,* she thought. *And not more than a double dozen of them left. Three ships. Probably more than a hundred of them when they landed. And three Captains. Only Quale left. The Sink and the natives have been hard on them.* As she watched, one of the humanoid Scavs yelled and collapsed, an arrow through his shoulder. He was dead before he hit the ground. The others ignored him and continued as before. Aleytys shivered.

Outside the walls, the cries rose in a crescendo then died away. A last arrow came over the wall, hit the squat structure in the center of the enclosure, bounced up into the air and fell again to lie rocking on the earth. Quale straightened, let his rifle rest a moment on the wall as he drew his sleeve across his sweaty face. He scowled at the corpse. "Blaur."

A one-eyed black man with caste scars slashing his cheeks stood rubbing at his back, his blue-tinged skin shining with sweat. "Yeah?"

Quale jerked a thumb at the dead man. "Get rid of that. And keep thieving hands off that. It's mine." He stabbed a finger at the carrier then jerked his head toward the wall. "Put someone up there. Greenies've run off but I'll kick ass if I come up and none of you bastards is standing watch." As he turned away the Scavs came down from the walkways, separating into small clots that milled about until there was a maximum amount of space between them. Szor tapped the avian on the side to send the creature shuffling back to the wall.

Aleytys rose to her feet as Quale came toward her. Before she could say anything, he caught hold of her arm, thrust her ahead of him toward the stone hutch in the middle of the enclosure. He pulled her to a stop, dropped her arm and dug an intricately scrolled bit of metal from a pocket in his battle-jacket. Aleytys jumped, startled, as he stepped back and thrust the slip of metal at her. "Unlock it." He pointed to a heavy lock set in the top of the hutch.

She stared at the thing in her hand, looked back at him.

"Stick it in the slit and turn," he snarled, irritation at having to explain the obvious unsettling his less than stable temper. He turned away to scan the scattered groups of men and non-men, his back to her, making a point of his contempt for her.

She smiled down at the key in her hand, fitted it into the slot and turned. In spite of his pose of indifference, he heard the soft thunk of the bolt. He reached past her, took the key from the lock and stuffed it in his pocket. "Pull the hatch up."

A ladder was screwed into the stone, dipping into a pool of opaline light instead of the darkness she expected. Quale's hand was rough and hot against the small of her back. "Down," he grunted, pushing at her, sending her over the edge and scrambling down the ladder.

When she hit bottom, she stepped into a short tunnel, turned a corner and found herself in a comfortable and surprisingly large room. Several oil lamps hung from brackets screwed into the stone, throwing out circles of pale light on a gray-green carpet, on bookshelves sliced into the walls with their burden of books, notebooks, neatly arranged stone points, baskets, small wooden carvings. One table was backed against the far wall with a single chair pushed under it. A candlestick with a half-melted candle, an open notebook and a stylus were bunched together in the middle of the table. She started toward them, her feet whispering over the carpet, but stopped as Quale stomped in behind her. "Drij!" he roared. "Drij!"

A tapestry hanging on the wall to her left fluttered, then was pulled aside and a slender, dark-haired woman stepped into the room. "Yes, radi-Quale." Her voice was soft and submissive; she bowed her smooth dark head, touched long slender fingers to her brow.

Aleytys turned farther, caught the glint of satisfaction in Quale's eyes. She lifted her head and glared at him.

Ignoring her, Quale watched the dark woman begin to tremble as she waited for him to make his wants known. He smiled, glanced at Aleytys to see if she was absorbing the lesson in female behavior, the smile turning to a scowl when he met her defiant eyes. "Scrub the bitch down," he snapped to the dark woman. "See she's ready for me when I get back."

"Yes, radi-Quale," the woman murmured, speaking to Quale's back as he stalked from the room. Brushing back a wisp of hair, she turned her large dark eyes on Aleytys. "You'd better come with me." With a quick, nervous smile, she gestured at the arch where Quale had passed. "Save your strength for surviving." She touched lightly, quickly, at faint yellow and green marks on her face, old bruises almost faded away. "Don't waste it in futile rebellion."

"Not in futile rebellion," Aleytys retorted, then felt vaguely juvenile, like a child sassing its mother. She grimaced.

Drij shook her head, sighed and smoothed shaking hands over the folds of the long strip of cloth she wore wound around her slender body. "You'll learn," she said softly, a dull hopelessness weighing down the words. "Come. You'll enjoy a hot bath."

"Bath!" Aleytys sighed. "Magic word." She stretched, walked toward the tapestry, paused with her hand on the heavy material. "Behind here?"

Drij closed her eyes, pressed one of her long narrow hands against her diaphragm, her reaction startling Aleytys. After a moment, the dark woman murmured, "Yes. Wait. I'll show you." The shimmering silk she wore whispering an accompaniment to her graceful movements, she brushed past Aleytys into what once had been a small neat bedroom. Now the bed was a tangled mess of sweat-stained blankets and dirty sheets. Clothing was scattered over the floor. In spite of the soft fall of air through the ventilation ducts in the ceiling, the whole smelled of stale sex and dirt. Drij glided across the room, her back very straight. She pulled another hanging aside, clutched at her dignity and turned to wait for Aleytys.

Ignoring everything around her, her face a smiling mask that covered her growing anger and her comprehension of the shame that put faint spots of color in Drij's cheeks, she moved quickly through the room and stepped past her into an absurdly luxurious bathroom.

A lamp charged with scented oil cast a soft golden light over a wide, deep bath, a toilet, a dressing table, its mirror cracked across the middle. The perfume drifted in waves through the room, crisp and pungent pine scent. Drij placed a hand on Aleytys's arm. Aleytys stepped aside and let her slip past.

The dark woman knelt beside the bath. She reached out and swung the tap handles over, holding her fingers repeatedly in the gush of water then moving the handles until she had the degree of heat she wanted. With a soft grunt from the effort, she stood up, smoothing wisps of fine black hair back from her face, beads of steam like dew on her dark amber skin. "I tapped into a hot spring when I had this shelter built. Have to be careful I don't get the water scalding hot." She looked around. "One minute." Brushing by Aleytys, she pushed past the curtain and could be heard rummaging about in the bedroom. Aleytys smoothed her hair down, took a step, winced as her dusty soles grated against the pale green tiles; the sound made her teeth hurt. She dropped onto the side of the tub, yawned, sat watching the water come roaring in. After a moment she began rubbing at her throat where the marks of Quale's fingers were dark sore lines on her flesh. She looked up as Drij stepped into the room, a clean towel over one arm and a cake of soap in her hand. Giving these to Aleytys, she braced herself again, reached over the wide expanse of water and wound the taps shut.

Trailing her fingers in the water, Aleytys sighed with pleasure. Drij laughed and turned to leave. At the doorway she stopped, one hand light on the curtain, her wide mouth open in the first genuine smile Aleytys had seen on her worn face. "It wasn't so bad. He's not the lover he'd like them to think he is." She fluttered her fingers at the ceiling. "Sometimes he wouldn't bother me for weeks." Stroking the back of her hand over her bruised cheek, she spoke again, her intent to reassure obvious though the words weren't quite the right ones. "When he . . . he failed, he'd get drunk, beat on me to feel like a man. You're new. He probably won't have difficulties but, for your own sake, help him as much as you can. . . ." She hesitated. "For my sake." The long hand on the curtain began to tremble, the curtain rings to knock against the rod. "Make him feel like the greatest thing that ever . . . be careful. He's not stupid." She stared at the tiles, reluctant to leave the room. "Are you hungry? I can fix something. I'll bring a robe. He hasn't let me do a wash for a while so clean things are getting low. Ah, I know. I'll fix a pot of cha." She started to step through the doorway, then turned again. "He's Farou." Her mouth twitched up. "Any sign of female intelligence or competence is a challenge. He considers it a threat to his masculinity." Her mouth stretched into a sudden grin. "You're going to give him fits. My name is Drij Patin, by the way. I'm supposed to be a cultural zenologist. Dropped in here to study the Rum—the people on this planet. My god, it's good to *talk* to someone again." She pushed past the curtain and was gone.

Shaking her head, Aleytys stripped off the spider silk and eased herself into the hot water. As she scrubbed at her sweaty body, she frowned at the spreading islands of suds. Drij was a complication she hadn't expected. *I can't leave her here,* she thought.

When Drij came back with a tray of sandwiches and a steaming pot of cha, Aleytys was washing her hair, her head a mass of lather. She waved a hand as Drij set the tray on the dressing table and began pouring the steaming amber liquid into a pair of cups. Aleytys slid her body down in the tub, rinsed her hair. She came up again, wiping the water from her face, squeezing it from her hair. Smiling, Drij brought her a cup.

Aleytys sipped at the cha, feeling warm and oddly content. "The natives—you said Rum?—how hostile are they?"

Holding her cup, Drij lowered herself to the floor until she was resting with her back braced against the tub's side, her long legs drawn up, one hand curled loosely on her knee, the other lifting her cup to her lips. She sipped at the cha, her face troubled. "At least they have the Sink on their side. It'd be a slaughter up there if the Scavs could use their energy weapons. The Rum . . . the Scavs have killed a lot of them. Even the first day, they bragged about sighting in their rifles on greenies. The Rum keep coming, though. How many did they get this time?"

"Two." Aleytys pulled her knees up and leaned against the tap handles. "How many Scavs have the Rum taken out? I saw three ships. There should be a lot more men up there."

Drij tapped long nails against the cup, making the ceramic ring. "Hard to say. I never got a chance to count them when they first got here. Only time Quale lets me up is when I have wash to hang out or when he makes me haul up supplies for the men." She was silent a minute, staring down into the steaming amber liquid in her cup. "He won't let any of them down here and he wasn't about to lower himself by toting loads." She sighed. "But that's not what you need to hear. I think they fought among themselves before they got here. Even with that, I . . . as a guess, from things I heard, they've lost a man or two most days since they landed. That poison is fast and fatal."

"Poison." Aleytys wrinkled her nose. "Think you could hand me some of those sandwiches?" When Drij was settled again, Aleytys bit into the bread and meat paste, chewed thoughtfully, swallowed. The bread was a bit stale, but the paste inside was thick and juicy. She finished the sandwich and reached for another. "Know what the Scavs are after?"

"Same thing you are, I presume."

Aleytys laughed. She straightened her legs, watching the bubble islets rock precariously around her torso. "You might be right." She emptied the mug and set it on the floor beside the tub. There was silence except for the gentle lapping of water against the sides of the tub and the soft hiss of the flame in the oil lamps. Aleytys shifted position, sliding down until her head was resting on one of the tap handles. "Tell me about the Rum," she said drowsily.

Drij's dark head bent over her cup, her hair falling forward to curtain her face. "What do you want to know?"

"Hmmm?" Aleytys yawned. "What they look like, how do they fight? Why do they fight? How dangerous are they? Anything that could be useful." She yawned again, sliding lower still in the water, half asleep as the warmth eased away her tensions. She closed her eyes, half-listening to Drij's soft voice, half-wandering among thoughts drifting haphazardly through her head.

"Rum weapons are stone. They're expert at turning out different kinds of points. Also expert in the properties of poisonous plants. This world abounds in poison. . . ."

Harskari, Aleytys thought, *you hearing this? Dammit, talk to me. Swardheld, old growler, where are you? I need you. Shadith? Talk to me. Haven't you left me alone long enough?*

She touched her temples, sighing when the diadem was silent and her mind empty.

"They've worked out a complex system of intertribal warring that maintains itself because it acts to keep the population within manageable limits and lets used-up land lie fallow long enough to regain its fertility. Slash and burn agriculture would otherwise turn the forest into grassland and many species of animals would die. Without the trees the Rum would die also. . . ."

Quale, Aleytys thought. She moved her toes and waves of the cooling water swirled around her body. *He'll want to know where the Queen is. Won't believe me if I give in too fast, damn him. Not looking forward to letting him slap me around. I need him. He controls the men I need to pull the carrier.*

"Roha says the nuggar swarm and when they do, the Amar—her tribe—war. Nuggar are six-legged rooting beasts. Egg layers. When the clutches hatch the forest crawls with the little beasts. They are near full-size when this world dips into the Sink. The tribes pick a lucky day. The Amar leave this choice to their Twin Roha. They take the men out and slaughter as many of the nuggar as they can and bring them back for a feast that can last for as many as four days." The soft voice pattered on drifting in and out of Aleytys's consciousness.

Quale has to have the ships' keys hidden down here somewhere. He wouldn't let those get away from him. That's power. No way he'd let power slip through his fingers. I wonder if Drij knows anything about where he hid them. She built this place. Better not say anything now, he's got her whipped. No, not whipped, not exactly, but. . . .

"The Rum seldom get much meat. It seems to give them an overabundance of energy that they use up in elaborate and very bloody battles. The losers are pushed off their land, most of the men dead and the women taken as slaves to work more garden patches. They don't add to the birthrate because they are ritually unclean for several years. . . ."

I wonder if the natives will keep after us once we start for the Queen. Probably. Poison. I hate it. It's their home ground. The vaad talked about fog. Continual fog. They could sneak up close and massacre us. Unless my head works. We'll come out of the Sink in little over a week. She scrubbed her hand across her face. *Madar! too many complications. . . . Still, a ship . . . I can take a lot to get me a ship.*

"The Sink exacerbates the violence of the Rum-wars. Many of the warriors become berserkers. Their thinking becomes tracked. Once they're locked in on some course of action, they keep going over the same round until they reach some kind of resolution." Aleytys opened her eyes and met Drij's grave, sad glance. The dark woman stroked long fingers absently over the green and blue splotches on her face. "They aren't going to stop attacking us, not as long as there are any of us left. I'm one of the demons now. You too." She looked down at her cup, ran the tip of her forefinger around and around the rim. "They'll keep coming until we're dead or they are." She dropped into silence for several minutes then sighed and began murmuring again. "They're egg-layers, reptilian in ancestry. The hatchlings are undeveloped, they need constant care by their mothers. Since they don't lactate, the mothers regurgitate for the infants, feeding them semi-digested food. Mother-child bonds are very strong, which balances the warrior society to give women far more status than they ordinarily would have in such a culture. . . .

Aleytys closed her eyes again, letting the soft voice flow over her unheeded. *Harskari,* she thought. *Listen. A ship. Once I have a ship, I'm not planet-bound any more. I won't have to depend on chance and persuasion any more. I'll be free. We'll be free. I can find my mother, I can find Vrythian. Help me! Harskari! Swardheld! Shadith! If you care anything about me, help me!* She sat up, slapped her palms against her temples. *Help me!* When she opened her eyes, she saw Drij staring at her, startled and anxious, heard the whispered words echoing in her ears, winced at her self-betrayal. "I'm sorry," she said. She scooped a handful of water and splashed it across her face. "How do you let the water out? I'd better get ready for Quale."

"It's for me to apologize." Drij stood up. "Under the taps. Pull the lever. I'll get you a robe. I am sorry, it's been so long since I could talk about my work. Quale didn't like it; it reminded him. . . ." She shrugged and moved quickly out of the room.

Aleytys rose onto her knees, feeling under the tap for the lever. As the water swirled away, she stepped from the tub, snatched the towel and began drying herself. "Dumb. Ask her

to talk then make it obvious I'm not listening." She wrapped
the towel around herself and padded to the chapot. Lifting
the lid, she peered inside, then shrugged as she saw that it
was nearly empty. As she replaced the lid, she heard Quale's
voice in the bedroom.

"Where is she?"

There was silence a moment. Aleytys turned to face the
curtain as Drij said dully, "Bath."

Aleytys grimaced. "First time I'm a whore by choice. Dammit, Harskari, I'm not asking you to do anything, just talk to
me."

The big man shoved the curtain aside and stood in the
doorway his eyes running insolently over her.

She stood without moving as he crossed to her. He cupped
his hand under her chin and turned her head from side to
side. "The Haestavaada must've been outta their bug heads.
Sending a woman. You're pretty enough, but not to a Bug.
How the hell you got around them . . . . ." He pulled the
towel away.

THE HUNT

CHAPTER III   Roha

Roha saw the mat-izar through the tangled branches of an acid-tree. The bell-shaped spice tree stood like a pale shadow among the darker foliage, its wide, flat flowers trembling on desiccated stems, one by one snapping loose to float tipping and wheeling on the brisk morning breeze that stirred a golden mist of pollen about the izar. She stopped, so suddenly that Rihon bumped into her. The Niong closed hard callused hands over her arms, pulled her around. "Where?" he hissed.

Confused, swallowing repeatedly, Roha avoided his eyes; she wanted to go back to her house and curl up on her sleeping mat. The Niong tugged at her. He was crowding her. She still hadn't made up her mind about the new demon. Letting her body yield to his pull, she kept her eyes on the mist pooling in long strings along the ground. She could smell the bitter scent of the demons, the crazy killing demons. Rihon pulled her back against him. "All right," she murmured, "all right." She closed her eyes tight. "There. Just past the mat-izar. The dark seed came down there."

The Niong loosed her arms; he sucked in a long hissing breath and blew out the song of an imbo. Three times he warbled the rising trill, then he faded into shadow, silent as a shadow himself.

Roha trembled, quieted as Rihon patted her shoulders and murmured comfort to her. She turned her head so that her ear and cheek were pressed against Rihon's chest while she gazed into the shadows after the Niong. Though she saw nothing but the whispering trees, she knew what was happening around the dark seed's clearing. The Amar warriors were spread in a short arc around it, creeping closer, bows strung, arrows ready to dip in the poison pots. She burned with an anguish she didn't understand. In all her short life she had never faced such uncertainty. She had only her feelings to guide her and these were so confused that she moved in a fog thicker than any in the mistlands.

Rihon tugged at her shoulder. She tilted her head, staring up past his chin. He turned her toward the village. "Let's go, Twin," he whispered. "Niong don't want us here." He brushed past her and trotted off, circling wide around a stirring mat-akul, slapping away a questing tendril. She didn't try to follow. He came back a few steps. "Roha." The word was a breath against her ears. He beckoned impatiently. "Come on."

"I have to see," she hissed, speaking more to the wind that pressed against her than to her brother. "I have to."

Rihon came slowly back. Before he reached her, she wheeled and ran toward the mat-izar. She slipped under the dangling branches, holding her breath against the pollen, and stretched out on her stomach, precariously concealed behind stiff tufts of dead dry grass. There was a rustle behind her and a shower of pollen grains. She held her hand over her nose, glanced back, saw Rihon settling behind her. He grinned, then flattened his nose further with the ball of his thumb. She felt a sudden rush of affection, clasped his hand, then turned her attention to the clearing.

As she peered through the grass, the biggest demon started throwing the red-haired one about. Shaking with fear and confusion, she dropped her face into the grass until she could trust her reactions again. They were enemies, the firehair and the sky-devils. Enemies! Rihon's hand rubbed along her spine, calming her yet more. He knew, her brother, he knew what she was feeling and he did his best to help her.

She heard a shout. The demons had seen someone. *Not me, please,* she thought. *Mother Earth, let it not be me.* She looked again into the clearing. The firehair was under the long thing, the little demons were running back and forth carrying white eggs from the dark seed and throwing them on the long thing, and the big demon was casting the small deadly stones from his spitting stick. He wasn't looking toward her, so she relaxed a little, frowning, as Amar arrows glanced from his clothes. His luck stirred her blood to a rage that brought her claws out and digging convulsively in the soft damp earth. "Die, demon. Die," she hissed.

"Shhh." Rihon's warning was a thread of sound but she heard and controlled herself. He patted her twice then moved back a little. She could hear the grass rustling, then it was still. When she looked again into the clearing, she flinched, then pressed herself closer to the ground. The big demon was glaring straight at her. She held her breath, heard the stick spit and the tiny zing as the pellet sang over her taut body. When she looked again, he was facing another way. She felt a fierce triumph. "Twin's luck," she whispered.

Rihon lay with a terrible neatness, his face nestling in the grass. Forgetting everything else she pushed onto hands and knees and scrambled around. She stretched out a hand to touch him. "Rihon?" His flesh was warm. His head rolled limply until he was facing her. The eye she could see was half-closed. His mouth was a little open. She lifted his arm. It bent easily and, when she let loose, dropped to the ground beside his still body. She spread her hand over his back. "Rihon?" She felt nothing . . . didn't know what she felt . . . disbelief? Her hand pressing down hard, she shook him again. There was no resistance in him, no thing that leapt to the touch and said in this skin there is life. His back was warm, intact, under her hand. She slid her hand up along his spine, pressed it down on the resilient ridges climbing the middle of his skull. She felt a wetness and pulled her hand away, stared down at the red stain on her dark green skin. With the same slow disbelief, she turned his head farther so she was looking into his face. Between dull, half-open eyes there was a small black hole. She reached out to touch the hole, stopped her hand an inch from it. Her hand shaking, she stared at the hole. "So small," she said, then was quiet, the sound of her voice startling her. Outrage and grief hovered around her but she couldn't accept them yet. So fast, it happened so fast. Her brother was dead. She'd talked to him, turned, and he was dead. Her claws came out and she ripped at herself, drawing blood from her cheeks and chest. "Rihon." The golden pollen drifted down around her, clotting in her blood. "Rihon," she whimpered. Then she shrieked the name, a raw wail tearing from her throat.

THE HUNT

CHAPTER IV   Aleytys

Aleytys woke in darkness. The man beside her in the bed was snoring a little, his body radiating heat. She pushed the covers back, feeling sticky and unclean. After slipping from the bed, she stood for a moment looking down at him. *You make my skin crawl,* she thought. *I didn't know how I would feel . . . it seemed so simple.* She shuddered. *You want me again, you're going to have to chunk me on the head first.* She moved quietly to the bathroom.

As the water ran shuddering into the tub, she stared down at its ghost-glimmer. The towel lay on the tiles in a crumpled heap where Quale had dropped it. She shook it out and hung it on a hook by the tub, remembering Drij's words about clean things being in short supply.

"Clean!" she whispered. Sick and unhappy, she smoothed her hands down her sides, feeling the stickiness of sweat induced by her struggles and his heat. "Damn, damn. . . ." Holding down her nausea, she stepped into the tub and turned off the tap, then eased herself cautiously into the steaming water, feeling the heat bite into the tension as she stretched out, her head resting on the end of the tub. After a few minutes, she groped for the soap and began scrubbing herself.

Later, she lay half asleep, the cooling water lapping at her sides. She'd settled into a measure of calm. Her mind and body had adjusted to the interference of the Sink. No more inundations of data—images, feelings, events pouring into her head until she was dizzy with them. No more smothering in the prison of her skull. She yawned, her head slipped from the tub end, and she was suddenly submerged.

Sputtering and splashing, she managed to sit up, chuckling at the sudden disruption of her dignified self-pity.

Purple eyes opened in the back of her mind. "Hi, Lee."

Shadith's face developed out of the darkness. "Another bath?"

Aleytys edged cautiously toward the side of the wide tub. "So you decided to talk to me again." She caught the corner of the towel and jerked it down.

The singer-poet's pixie face smoothed into a wide grin. "You know why we went away. And we were right. You needed to be on your own." She sobered. "Some mess."

"You going to help or complain?"

"Going to watch more than anything. Talk to you some. You don't need help."

"Thanks." Aleytys started rubbing at her hair. "I think. One thing I've found out. I make a lousy whore."

Amber eyes opened. Shadith moved hastily aside and let Harskari come forward. "Aleytys," she said quietly.

For a moment Aleytys felt like a child under that measuring cool gaze, then she rebelled. "Harskari," she said, her voice a murmur in the dark room, as noncommittal as she could make it.

The sorceress smiled, her eyes twinkling, turning Aleytys limp with surprise. Harskari's rare low laugh filled her head momentarily with liquid music. "As Shadith implied, Lee, now that you don't need us, we can talk to you again."

"You didn't call me child," Aleytys murmured, feeling a gentle melancholy at this change in her relationship with the concatenation of forces that produced the images in her head. For her, Harskari had been as much a mother as any she'd known.

"Should I?" The sorceress raised a white eyebrow.

"No." Aleytys sighed, smiling as she saw black eyes open behind Harskari. Swardheld grinned, winked at her and went away again.

Aleytys found it hard to remember that these figures were phantoms in her mind, collections of forces imprisoned in the jewel traps of the RMoahl diadem, the trap that held her, too, once she'd put the circle of golden flowers on her head and found she couldn't take it off. These were her friends, in a way her closest friends. They lived in her and shared everything she felt and did. Harskari, the first victim, sorceress and psi-master. Shadith, the second victim, poet and singer, member of a long-vanished high-tech civilization. Swardheld, swordsman and mercenary, with all the hand and mind skills

needed for survival as a soldier in a feudal society. In an important way they were part of her, had shaped what she had
now, both her uncertainties and her competencies.

Shadith was reduced to sketched violet eyes while Harskari's form had developed until she stood in a tunic and long
skirt, her white hair blowing around her dark brown face.
She stood with an awkward grace, a slight smile on her face,
relaxed as Aleytys had never seen her. She tilted her white
head slightly as if she were looking into Aleytys's face.
"Friends stand on level ground, Lee."

Aleytys stirred in the water, feeling a flush of warmth that
had nothing to do with the warmth around her. "Well. . . ."
She stepped out of the tub, wrapped the towel around her, re-
gretting briefly the robe Drij had never brought, then stepped
into the bedroom. The mirrors coaxed enough light into the
small room to show her Quale's sprawled bulk. He'd moved a
little, kicked off the blanket. In the faint light, his profile
against the pillow was clean-cut, his scarred cheek was down,
sweat had nudged his thick fine hair into loose curls. *Too bad
you won't stay asleep*, she thought. He stirred, mumbled a
few blurred syllables, then was snoring again. Holding her
breath, she slid away from the bed, respecting his animal sen-
sitivity enough to make no unnecessary noises. The fading
bruises on Drij's face were sufficient warning.

She slipped through into the outer room, which was filled
with peace and a pulsing gray twilight, the stillness broken
only by Drij's soft breathing. The dark woman lay in one
corner, a blanket pulled over her, leaving only her face visible. Aleytys moved to the center of the room, stretched.
Yawning, blinking, she moved her feet sensuously across the
soft fibers of the rug, feeling at home again in her body,
happy at the feeling, delighted that the break between her
and her mind-friends had been healed, almost equally happy
that the Hunt had really begun. She trotted across the room
and went up the ladder, unbarred the hatch, then leaned
against the opening, her crossed arms resting on the narrow
ledge that supported the hatch.

The Sink was a web of light, pulsing and ominous. Bright
spots oozed from place to place along lines of light that continually shifted position. The packed earth inside the wall was
littered with bodies of the sleeping men and non-men. Nearby
one man was muttering in his sleep—no distinct words, but

anxiety made him twitch, his gnarled fingers scrabbling at his blanket. She heard the scrape of a foot and looked up. A man was walking slowly along the top of the wall, his rifle slung across his back. He strolled along, snapping his fingers now and then, glancing occasionally at the trees, radiating more complacency than alertness.

Swardheld's eyes opened, glinting with disgust. "Shithead," he growled. "If he was one of mine. . . ."

"You'd have his skin," Aleytys finished, struggling to suppress an attack of giggling that took her by surprise. "Well!" Scratching at her nose, she looked around again at the sleepers. "Probably the natives don't attack at night. Remember, old growler, the Scavs have been here the better part of a year."

"Don't matter. Things could change in a flicker." He snorted. "Strolling along on top that damn wall!"

Aleytys smothered a chuckle behind one hand, her eyes moving over the Web; its changes fascinated her. There was a sliver of blackness hugging the western horizon, a bit of sky no longer covered by the web. "Hah!" she whispered. "Look, friend. *Nowhere*'s starting to leave the Sink. Our timing is just about right." Suddenly sleepy, she hitched up the towel, then caught the loop on the hatch and pulled it shut.

In Drij's workroom, she stood moving her feet slowly over the padded carpet, her eyes fixed on the curtained doorway. "No," she said softly. "I won't." She pulled off the towel, curled up on the rug, and pulled the towel over her. In minutes she was asleep.

"Who sent you?" He held her by the hair, struck her face with an open-handed slap that produced more noise than hurt. He dropped her to the rug, stood over her. "Why you?"

Aleytys sat up, one hand rubbing slowly at her abused face. "I told you," she muttered. "Haestavaada; tall skinny valaad called Maladra Shayl. I'm supposed to be good at getting things out of tight places." She gasped as he wound his hand in her hair and jerked hard. He let her go again and she bounced a little on her buttocks. She stared up at him, cowering a little.

"Stinkin Bugs sending in a woman." He grinned. "They get what they deserve. You know where that ship is?"

"Yes."

"Hah!" He strode away from her, striking his fist repeatedly into his palm. "Quale's luck. I knew it!" He paced around the room, laughing and repeating, "I knew it! I knew it!" Finally he came back to stand in front of her. "Where?"

"In the mistlands," she muttered. "Near the middle. It's down permanent, not broken up. Queen's still alive."

The sounds of yells and the spitting of rifles came down the ventilation tubes to them. His grin widened. "Quale's luck again. I want half a dozen of those little green bastards. We need horses to pull that wagon."

In the doorway he turned. "Get some clothes on. We're going after the Queen soon's I collect some greenies. Drij too. Ain't leaving her behind to think up female tricks on me."

Shadith's purple eyes opened. "Toad." She watched him leave.

Aleytys grinned. "Don't insult the poor beast. The toad, I mean."

"What now?"

"A bath. Won't get another for a long time."

"You'll turn into a prune."

Chuckling, Aleytys jumped up and moved toward the tapestry.

Aleytys stepped from the bathtub and stood rubbing vigorously at herself. The battle was still going on up top; she could hear the blurred shouts and shots over the gurgle of the draining water. She winced. Too many dead and the count wasn't finished yet.

Drij pushed the curtain aside and came in. Her face was tired and unhappy and there were dark smudges under her eyes. She glanced nervously over her shoulder. "He's still up top. You all right?"

"No sweat." Aleytys began pulling on her hunting trousers. The spider silk clung to her damp body and was uncomfortably warm in the steamy room, but these were her working clothes and they gave her a feeling of competence and control. "You were right about that . . . that toad. A lover he isn't."

"Hush!" Drij spun around, her hand to her lips, her eyes wide and frightened. "Don't trust him. Ever."

Aleytys pushed her head through the tunic and began smoothing it down over her torso. "Relax." She picked up a comb Drij had left on the dressing table and began working out the tangles in her wet hair. Drij fidgeted by the doorway. "I'm an empath," Aleytys said impatiently. "I'd know it if he was hanging around." She frowned at the soft shimmering material Drij wore wrapped around her body. "You have working clothes? Something for trail wear?"

"Yes, of course." Drij ran trembling fingers over the curtain. "We're going into the mistlands?"

Aleytys twisted her hair into a knot on top of her head, driving long hairpins in to hold it there. She turned to face Drij. "What do you know?"

Drij looked down. "The few times Quale let me up. . . ." She shivered. "I heard some men talking. Something about a ship going down somewhere on this side of the world. Before that, before the Scavs came, Roha came to see me." Drij looked up, frowning. "She's the female half of a pair of twins belonging to the village near here. She was on the point of hysteria. Drug taking is a part of the native religion. This planet is rich in hallucinogens and other consciousness-altering drugs. Since she was hatched, Roha has been fed on these; she's saturated with them to the point that she has a hard time separating hallucination from reality. Her male twin, Rihon, is an anchor when he isn't caught up in her seizures." Drij stopped as Aleytys shifted impatiently. "Sorry, seems I can't stop lecturing. You did ask what I knew, remember?" She smiled nervously. "Roha's an intelligent little thing in spite of the drugs, hungry for knowledge in a way that shuts her off from the rest of her people, even her brother. That hunger brought her to me, overriding fear and cultural conditioning. Before the Scavs came, we were close to being friends. Damn them. Damn them. . . ." The whisper trailed away as Drij rubbed at her eyes. "I think she came to me for reassurance the day after the ship came down and I didn't give it to her. I tried to . . . she said a burning thorn had plunged from the sky into the mistlands, an evil thing carrying demons. Her mind was tracked. I tried to shift her in another direction for the sake of any that might have survived the crash. It was a mistake. She ran." Drij stared at the wall, her face sad.

Aleytys swung her foot slowly. "Did you tell Quale about the thorn?"

"Certainly not." Drij moved her hand in a jerky impatient

gesture. "He'd have gone in after that ship and dragged me
with him. Even the natives are wary of that hell. I wasn't
quite ready to die." Her tired eyes twinkled. "Not then and
not now. But I don't have much choice, do I."

"Afraid not."

Drij gazed thoughtfully at Aleytys. "I wish I knew whether
you've got a plan or simply don't see the danger out there."

Aleytys swung her dangling foot a bit faster. "I know what
I'm doing. I'm damn good at surviving, Drij. You'd better get
dressed. We'll be leaving sometime soon, whenever he thinks
he's ready."

The sun had drifted past zenith as Aleytys emerged from
the shelter, Drij behind her. The supplies she'd brought were
neatly packed on the carrier. As she moved nearer to it she
could see six struggling natives trussed in harness to the carrier tongue, hands and legs tied, eyes wild, mouths working,
foam spattering with each gasping breath. The Scavs were
circling restlessly, divided into two groups—a small tight group
of men standing behind Blaur and a bigger, noisier group,
including all the non-men, clustered around the carrier.

Quale brushed past Aleytys and strode to the gate. He
stood glaring at the Scavs, fists on hips, his pale eyes moving
over the restless beings as he waited for them to stop walking
about and talking to each other. When this didn't happen, he
roared out a string of obscenities, then a series of crisp com-
mands that prodded the Scavs into ragged lines on each side
of the carrier. He circled the men and non-men, inspecting
their arms, snarling at some, noncommittal with others. Back
at the gate he beckoned to Aleytys and Drij, then jabbed a
thumb at the carrier. "Get on," he snapped. "Keep your fool
heads down. Once we get out there, we ain't stopping. If the
greenies get you, too damn bad." He unslung his rifle.
"Blaur!"

The one-eyed black man gestured quickly to the men
around him, sending them onto the planks beside the gate.
They squatted with their backs to the wall, rifles on knees,
watching the rest of the Scavs with a cool detachment—in
some cases with wide grins—knowing they weren't going to
have to leave the protection of the walls and face the poison
arrows of the natives. Keeping two men with him, Blaur
trotted to meet Quale.

"We'll be back in a week, maybe nine, ten days." Quale frowned up at the pale lines of the Sink. "Should be coming out of this shit by then. Be ready to shift when you see us."

Blaur grunted. "You want the gate open?"

Quale looked past him at the Scavs. "Szor," he called. "Cut those greenies loose and get 'em on their feet. Rest of you . . ." He paused, watching their sullen faces. "When we go out, I don't want no stopping. Keep together. Watch your mate's back. You go down, you're on your own, so keep on your feet. We got a prize waiting bigger'n any of you bastards ever saw."

Szor slapped a taller man on the shoulder. "Gollez, you keep them standing once I cut their feet loose." He grinned at the whip in the big man's hand. "Tickle them if they sit down on us. We got no time to train these horses."

On the carrier, Drij sucked in a breath, pressing her face against the white supply cells. Aleytys grasped her shoulder, cursing softly at her helplessness, wincing each time she heard the crack of the whip, feeling Drij shudder with her.

As Gollez and Szor slashed the bonds around the legs of the small wiry natives and used a many-thonged whip on legs and back until they were on their feet, Blaur and his helpers were shoving the gate open.

A native leaped into the opening, bow raised. He fell, a dozen shots in his body. Quale roared with disgust at the waste of ammunition and ran back along the Scav lines thumping and slapping at his guards. Swearing, raging, he ran back to the gate. "Kleyt, Cran, get up here. The rest of you, first man who shoots before I tell him gets a bullet in the belly." He ran through the gate with the two men, stood alert, watching the trees, then the gusts of steam coming from the edge of the mistlands.

After some confusion the native males, bound, began moving toward the gate, awkwardly, jerkily, one stumbling into another until the carrier shuddered to a stop.

Szor glanced at Quale's back, his round face wrinkled with worry, then he hissed at Gollez. The big man turned slowly. Szor pointed his knife at the bound hands. "We gotta cut them loose, tie them to those crossbars so they don't walk all over each other."

Gollez rubbed a battered hand over his face. "Better hurry. He ain't feeling too sweet."

They cut the natives' hands loose and bound them to the crossbars, then urged them into a trot. Cowed temporarily by the whips, the green males leaned into the harness and began pulling effectively enough to get the carrier rolling at a slow trot. As they passed through the gate, Aleytys tapped Drij on the shoulder. "Stretch out," she murmured. Drij nodded, flattened herself on the bed of the carrier. Aleytys waited until she was settled, then did the same. The line of Scavs on their side of the carrier were moving at a fast walk, rifles ready, nervous and deadly, scanning the silent trees and scrub brush and the mist clouds in front of them. She watched them, hoping the natives wouldn't attack and be slaughtered, feeling obscurely guilty about the ones already dead. *Too many, and more coming*, she thought, then wrenched her mind from the small green corpses, trying to concentrate on the reason she was here, the vaada dying on Davaks, falling like leaves in autumn because they had no Queen, the Queen she was going to return to them.

Shadith's purple eyes opened in the gloom inside her head. "And a ship. Your own ship."

"I'd rather not think of that right now." The carrier lurched, then one of the captives screamed as Gollez used his whip. Aleytys shivered. "Not now."

"Don't be an idiot, Lee."

"Devil's advocate?" She dropped her head on her crossed arms, glad to shut out the prowling Scavs. "Leave me my little attempts at morality."

"At morbidity. All this is just because you aren't doing anything. Too much time to fuss."

"Shadith!"

"Well, think about it." The singer shook her aureole of red-gold curls. "You take yourself too seriously." She grinned. "Poor little she-Atlas with the universe on her shoulders." Her laugh was a dance of clear pure notes. Her face faded until only the eyes were left. One eye winked then both were gone.

After a moment Aleytys smiled, the world pulled back into perspective by Shadith's teasing. She sat up as the carrier jolted to a stop.

They were perched on the edge of a long incline. The six captives had balked when they realized where they were being driven. They were sitting on their haunches, their bound hands pulling the tongue down until its nose dug into the rocky soil. Aleytys caught hold of the carrier's edge and closed her eyes, trying to insulate herself from the sounds she knew would come. She couldn't shut out the snick-hiss-splat of the whips and the hoarse cries of the natives. Then the carrier tilted and started rattling down a steepish slope. Aleytys opened her eyes and looked around.

The grey-white mist was closing around her, limiting her vision to a dozen feet in all directions. As the carrier picked up speed, she started sweating freely. She hung onto the bumping carrier while sweat ran in rivers between her breasts. There was no trail, but the plant growth was short and scrubby and the rocks were small, little more than pebbles. The multiple wheels rattled over them throwing them up to patter against the underside of the carrier, striking through the interstices in the woven webbing of its bed, thwacking against her buttocks and legs. As the ride grew rougher, she began to worry about the natives pulling the carrier. She peered past Drij, who was hunched over clutching the webbing of the bed. The natives were running full out, glancing back repeatedly at the monster that threatened to roll over them.

Quale loomed through the mist. "You at the end," he roared. "Grab hold and slow this thing down." He waited until the carrier slowed to a man's long lope, then faded into the mist again.

Drij looked back, her face strained. "Lot of places I'd rather be." She pushed back hair that was straying across her face, swung her legs over the edge. The stiff short brush slapped against her boots and scraped beneath them, making small staccato sounds that lost themselves in the louder rumble and clatter of the carrier. She waved a hand at the mist. "How far into this do we have to go?" She snatched at a strap in the bed to keep from falling off as the carrier lurched over a nest of larger rocks. When the ride steadied, she waved a hand at the men moving beside the carrier, half-seen shadows in the thinning, thickening, drifting mist. "A lot of them will soon be dead."

Aleytys crossed her legs and tried balancing against the jarring of the carrier. She glanced at Drij. "Tell me about the mistlands." She grinned. "I don't mind a lecture this time." She shrugged. "If this place is so deadly?"

Drij stared down at the brush still slapping against her boots. "I probably shouldn't do this." She drew her legs up on the bed of the carrier. "The sap in most of these plants is a powerful drug of one kind or another. Many are poisons. Irritant fibers on leaves and branches, corrosive exudations, pollen, they've got a number of ways of attacking anyone who interferes with them. Be very, very careful about touching anything with your bare skin." She grimaced at her boots. "I'll have to wash these down before I take them off. Only way to be really safe would be self-contained airsuits." She smiled at Aleytys. "Or avoid breathing."

"Great!" Aleytys sniffed. "If that's all . . ."

Drij frowned at the curtain of mist undulating a few feet in front of her, at the half-seen figures of the Scavs, slipping and sliding clumsily along with the carrier as they rumbled and clattered down the slope. "The Amar," she murmured. "They'll follow us. Those fumble-feet. . . ." She indicated the line of men. "They don't know anything about this kind of fighting; they've got no feel for this land. They might be deadly with power-weapons but they're sitting targets here." She paused. "Us too. One arrow out of that. One scratch. And we're dead."

The carrier trundled over a bare spot then plunged into brush that wrapped tendrils around the wheels. Aleytys heard a thrashing out in the mist, then a startled yell, then rattling noises as one of the Scavs lost his footing and went rolling down the slope, followed by an avalanche of small stones. There were curses and, ahead of them, Gollez or Szor started whipping the captives, forcing them to pull harder and free the carrier from the tangled thorny mess.

As the carrier bounded from the brush patch and bounced over water-eaten washboarded stone, Aleytys swore. She looked thoughtfully at Drij. "I make a lively corpse," she said suddenly.

"What?" Drij lifted her head, startled, then suspicious.

Aleytys held out her left hand, palm up. "Look."

"So?"

"What do you see?"

"A hand." Drij tilted her head. "With dirty fingernails."

"Damn. Already." Aleytys sighed. "No, friend. See any wounds or scars of wounds?"

"Get to the point." Drij leaned forward. "These wheels are making too much noise. Scavs can't hear you."

"The natives attacked us before we could get through the gate. One of the Scavs was killed and I took an arrow through the palm." She waved her hand up and down. "That poison is a heller. Thing is, I'm a psi-healer. If I catch it fast enough, I can neutralize any poison they throw at me."

"Oh." The word was carefully noncommittal. "How useful." Drij leaned out and peered into the mist, keeping her balance. "They're out there, I know it. Only a matter of time. . . ."

Stones came out of the fog and rained around the men, some of them reaching as far as the carrier, with enough momentum left to sting the women. Drij curled up, her arms protecting her head. Her voice muffled, she called out, "Don't let them hit your skin."

Aleytys didn't move. She gave an exasperated sniff. "If you'd let yourself believe me, xenologist, you'd save yourself a lot of worry. Why aren't your Amar using their bows?"

No more stones were hitting the carrier. Out in the mist Aleytys saw several Scavs go down, heard shots, saw indistinct figures bending momentarily over the downed intruders, then fading into the mist. There was more shooting, more scrabbling and rattling of stones as Scavs chased after small elusive targets and went silent under the attackers' stone knives. A roar from Quale called the survivors back. He trotted along the lines of Scavs, cursing them for their stupidity and telling them he'd shoot them himself if they allowed themselves to be tricked away from the carrier again. Drij sat up, watched him for a moment, then relaxed, leaning against the pile of supply cells. "They don't seem to need them, do they? As a guess, I'd say they don't want to waste arrows in the uncertainty of this fog. Takes quite a bit of effort to flake out the stone tips and prepare the poison. Why waste work when all this free ammunition is available?" She gestured at the rocky surface of the flattening slope, then smiled at Aleytys. "This world is full of illusions, Lee. I've learned to believe very little of what I see. Or hear."

The carrier rattled down and down, the Scavs loping along close to it, shooting occasionally at thickenings in the mist that might have been a native or could have been only a shadow of a taller bush. The last half-mile of slope was so gradual it might have been taken as level except for the hurrying of the carrier that still needed the retarding weight of the Scavs at the rear.

The native males pulling the carrier stumbled along, walking head down and dull-eyed, apparently thoroughly cowed. Aleytys watched them as they neared a stand of tall spindly trees whose sparsely leafed crowns were lost in the mist. Something wasn't right. The feelings she got from the captives didn't match their appearance. She leaned over and poked Drij. "They're up to something," she muttered, nodding her head at the captives.

Drij studied the Amar for a moment. "They know this place." She wiped off some of the sweat that rolled down every crease in her face. Drops of moisture clung to the cloth of her tunic and trousers, the leather of her boots. The heat down here on the floor of the basin was claustrophobic; there was no wind, not even a wind of passage since they were moving too slowly to stir up a breeze. The mist hung close around them, draining away color, turning the landscape to patterns in black, white, and gray. Drij rubbed her eyes. The carrier was beginning to swing wide around the trees. She watched the ground ahead unreeling from under the fog, then turned to Aleytys. "You want to warn the Scavs?"

"Not especially. What abou. . . ."

A Scav ahead and to the right lurched, then shrieked with agony as his boots crunched through paper-thin stone into boiling water. Whimpering, screaming, pleading, his legs cooked to the bone, he writhed on the ground where two Scavs had put him after pulling him out. The carrier rolled to a stop, the natives watching with bodies tense, ears quivering. The other Scavs began crowding around.

Quale came out of the mist. The Scavs separated in front of him as he marched to stand over the moaning man. He looked down at him, then at the others, dropped the muzzle of his rifle against the injured man's skull and pulled the trigger. Then he kicked the body into the pool beyond the shell of stone. Before he straightened, the other Scavs had melted away and Szor was whipping the captives into motion. Quale stood silent and ominous, watching the carrier roll past, then he turned and loped ahead, a dark animal form in the mist. Aleytys followed him with her eyes, impressed in spite of herself, beginning to understand how he managed to survive and maintain his hold on the other Scavs. "He's different with men," she said.

Drij looked back. "He knows where he is with them. No threats he can't handle. With women. . . ." She shrugged. "Like I said, he's Farou."

"Mmm. Those Amar look frisky." The natives males were holding their heads higher, their large ears standing erect.

"They're starting to use the land. That was a setup. They didn't need to swing that wide around those trees." She laughed very softly. Then she stopped and stared ahead.

Aleytys searched the ground ahead, trying to pick out what Drij had seen but she didn't know enough to guess which of the innocuous-looking bushes or rock piles hid a stinger. "What is it?"

Drij crawled toward the front of the carrier, where she stretched out flat, her head toward Aleytys. "Watch the Amar. When they drop, you drop. Thank God the toka's on the other side. These cells should protect us." She was breathing hard as she thought about what was waiting for the Scavs. Her face was flushed, her eyes shining; she was filled with a suppressed excitement and an intense expectation—an expectation of death. Scav death.

Aleytys began to realize how terrible the past months had been for Drij. She was Indarishi, coming from a people deeply committed to reverence for all life. She knew violence and oppression and destruction, all the horrors intelligent beings can inflict on their brothers, but this was academic knowledge that could be contemplated at a distance, classified and dissected for motivation and outcome; the violence done to her was immediate and personal, affecting her in ways she couldn't yet begin to deal with. Aleytys backed up a little then stretched out flat, her face close to Drij's. "Toka? What's that? Plant, animal, or rock."

"Can you see a dark bush up ahead? Squat with lots of reddish leaves? We should be getting close to it."

Aleytys stared past bobbing Amar heads. "Right. Maybe six feet ahead. Hunh! Those little bastards are edging toward it. What've they got in mind?"

Drij's smile widened. "Roha brought me a sample once, showed me how it works. If you were close enough, you'd see round, hard fruits about the size of a fist dangling from thin tough stems. When they're ripe, they explode at the lightest touch, shattering into hundreds of tiny slivers, each with an attached seed and a bit of crystallized sap. Very, very poisonous, but slower working than the arrow poison the Amar use." She was panting in her eagerness, blinking repeatedly as sweat poured from her scalp. "One of the Scavs is bound to brush against it," she breathed. She licked away the salty drops gathering on her upper lip. "The small explosions will make them jump, they'll feel a few stings, maybe itch a little. They'll walk on . . . five, six, seven steps. They'll start feeling dizzy. They'll drop, dead before they reach the ground. Dead. . . ." Her voice trailed off and she lifted her head, listening intently.

When the sounds came, Aleytys almost missed them, but the jerking of Drij's body alerted her. Over the crunch and rattle from the carrier, she heard a series of small squeaks and sounds like rapid exhalations, then exclamations from several Scavs. She ventured a quick glance over the cells, dropped back instantly as she saw a Scav launch a kick at the offending bush while he pawed at a face bristling with small dark slivers. The Rum were flat on their faces now and several of the Scavs were brushing at battlejackets or pulling the slivers from faces and hands. Aleytys heard the sound of a whip and cursing from the drivers, then the carrier lurched forward. There was some disgruntled muttering from the Scavs but they seemed to view the dart bush as annoying, not dangerous. Aleytys sat up, her back against the cells. Drij lay where she was, listening again, her body taut with expectation.

The seconds ticked away, each stretched out and interminable. Nothing happened. Nothing . . . then Aleytys saw a Scav—no more than a shadow in the mist—stagger and drop. Then more were down. The captives slowed their trot, stopped as the other Scavs came running toward the downed men. Several of them were squeezing off shots at shadows in the mist, cursing the elusive greenies. Drij sat up, the shine gone out of her. "They think the Amar did it," she said dully. "They're right, but not like they think. How . . . how many dead?" Aleytys caught hold of her hands as she twisted them about each other and tried to warm away the chill she felt in them. Abruptly Drij was sobbing, great dry tearing sobs that shook her frail body. Aleytys eased her down until the dark woman's face was pressed against her thighs. She smoothed

the sweat-sodden hair off Drij's face, then patted Drij gently.
"Hush now," she murmured. "It's not so bad, not so bad, not
so bad." She continued to soothe the distraught woman with
hands and words, keeping her own anger and distress from
her voice until the storm had passed.

Drij pulled away and sat up again, recovered. "I don't
know why I did that."

"Strain." Aleytys knew it was inadequate, but it offered
something for Drij to catch hold of. "Riding along like this,
part and not part of what happens, it's hard for people like
us. We want to be in control of our lives." In her head purple
eyes opened, winked at her, vanished again. Aleytys
suppressed an appreciative grin. "Be better if we got off and
walked; at least we'd be doing something."

During Drij's nerve crisis Aleytys had heard—but paid no
attention to—a growing disturbance among the Scavs. They
milled about the corpses, glaring at the six Amar in harness,
muttering and cursing, their words getting louder and more
daring as Quale remained away. The Amar served as a focus
of their hatred. If they couldn't reach the natives out in the
mist, at least they could take out their frustrations on these.
One Scav prodded an Amar with the muzzle of his rifle,
slapped him with the barrel as he hissed his fury. Another
one used the point of a long knife to jab at a greenie. Aleytys
rose to her knees, wondering where Quale was, ready to
move at an instant's notice to protect herself and Drij if the
Scavs remembered the women.

A man kneeling by one of the bodies jumped to his feet,
screaming, "My brother, you killed him. Fucking greenies,
you killed him. My brother!" He flipped his rifle over,
gripped the barrel and brought the stock down on the head of
the nearest Amar. As that one dropped, his head split open,
the Scav whirled the rifle over his head and started to bring it
down again, the other Scavs yelling encouragement. There
was a sharp crack. A dark hole appeared between his eyes,
the hatred on his face turned to astonishment. He dropped
without a sound. The other Scavs backed away from him,
then turned to glower at the man watching them.

Quale stood on an outcropping of rock, a great dark preda-
tor ready to take out the next one to move. For a moment
they stared at each other, then one by one the Scavs lowered
their eyes, let the muzzles of their rifles drop. Aleytys

relaxed; as the Scavs moved away from the captive Amar, taking their places once again in the guard ring, she sat as before with her back against the supply cells. "Wonder how far he can push them."

Drij looked up; there were dark stains under her eyes. "He's the only way they have of getting off this world." Her fingers pleating the thin, loose material of her trousers, she went on, "Long as he doesn't let the pressure build until they forget that, he's safe." She sucked in a long ragged breath, let it out. "He's good. He'll maneuver small explosions. You'll see. They know he manipulates them, but they still dance when he pulls the strings."

With Quale looming above them on his rostrum, Gollez cut the dead Amar out of the harness. Grabbing an arm and a leg, he sent the body flying toward a barren section that looked like an upthrust of bedrock. The body broke through a thin skin of stone and released a powerful stench from a sulphur spring that began bubbling out over the rock. Cursing and gagging, Szor whipped the Amar onto their feet and started them moving again. Gollez trotted up, scarred face twisted with disgust. "This fucking hell-hole," he muttered as he swung up and settled himself beside Szor. "Queen better be there." He scowled back at Aleytys, then sat hunched over watching the Amar trot along. "Gonna watch them greenies; they been looking frisky."

Szor grunted. He watched Quale trot ahead and disappear into the mist. "The more they buy it," he muttered, "the more we scoop in. One ship's crew, all we need." He turned to Gollez. "I can navigate; you're a pilot. Couple of engineers. . . ."

Gollez grinned then shook his head. "Catch our rabbit first." He rubbed at his nose. "Tiks," he said dreamily. "Engineers. Thick up here." He tapped his temple. "Think about it."

Behind them as they dropped into silence, Aleytys lifted an eyebrow.

Drij shook her head. "Not a chance."

Aleytys looked over the edge of the bed at the ground below. They were traveling over rubble, pebbles and coarse sand with a few patches of grass usually smaller than a man's fist. She straightened cramped legs and let them hang over the side. "What next? Anything else around we should worry about?"

"As long as they avoid the bushes, nothing much. There's the patches of quag, of course, you can tell them by the thick grass growing over them; more hot springs, not good to step in. Poison water . . . kinya-kin-kin . . . mistlanders . . . floating ghosts. . . ." Her voice was slow, her eyes focused on the curtain of mist pulsating lazily, swallowing the landscape as the carrier moved along. After a while, she settled against the supply cells, closed her eyes, and drifted off to sleep.

Aleytys stretched out on her back, lay staring up at the unsteady ceiling. She was drifting. There was nothing to do, nothing but lie on her back and contemplate the changing knots of mist. Nothing to do. . . .

The cessation of movement and a growing confusion around the carrier awoke her from a too heavy sleep. Head throbbing, she pushed stiffly onto her knees, winced as her head threatened to vibrate into pieces. Palm heels pressing hard on her temples, she closed her eyes, then opened them wide as Quale loped from the fog, yelling for Drij. Aleytys caught hold of Drij's shoulder, shook her awake before Quale reached her, then settled herself with her hands folded in her lap. Beyond Quale she could see the Amar crouching, shuddering but stubborn under the ships and boots of Szor and Gollez. Out in the mist the other Scavs stood silent and nervously alert, half-seen, this time hardly seeming connected with the carrier and the warning of the Amar.

Drij waited for Quale to reach her. Sweat beaded on her forehead and upper lip. She drew the back of her hand across her face, then stared down at the smear of mud on her skin.

"You talk greenie?"

Drij jerked her head up, her dark eyes wide with fear. "Yes, radi-Quale," she breathed and had to repeat the words when Quale caught hold of her arm and dragged her off the carrier.

He shoved her toward the Amar, strolled beside her as she stumbled along. "Something got into them," he grumbled. "If there's trouble ahead I want to know it. Get it out of them."

"Yes, radi-Quale."

Aleytys slipped off the carrier and followed them. Szor and

Gollez were sitting on the front of the carrier, flicking idly at their legs with the thongs of their whips, making the metal tips skitter about like dancing bugs. She glanced at them as she moved past, met Gollez's cool interested gaze with a shrug and walked on, ending up beside Drij, looking down at the cowering Amar.

Quale nudged an Amar in the ribs with the toe of his boot. "They're scared shitless of something." He reached down, caught hold of the floppy crest on a male's bare skull and jerked his head up, ignoring his hissing and bared canines. "Ask him what it is."

Drij pressed her lips together. Her hands moved aimlessly, then drifted together at her waist, one pressed over the other. Angry at Quale for reducing Drij to a quivering mess, angry at Drij for letting him do it to her, Aleytys caught hold of her shoulder and shook her. Drij looked around, blushed with shame as she met Aleytys's eyes. She closed her own eyes and, with considerable effort, managed to control her shaking. She ignored Quale's impatient growl and said, "Ni-hat palle, Rum-Amar? Nadeleaa." She glanced nervously at Quale, said rapidly, "I asked what he's afraid of."

The Amar twisted, trying to free himself from Quale's punishing grip. Blood trailed down skin torn and savaged by the whips, dripping onto coarse sand. Quale jerked again on his floppy crest. "Tell him he'd better answer you," he snarled. "Or I'll dump him in the first hot spring we can find."

Drij flushed; her hands closed into fists. She looked down into the native's glaring eyes. "Ku jaila-le, Ras Amar. Niukuua ha ye." She paused then said quickly, "I told him what you said."

The native cried out as Quale jerked him to his feet, pulling with him the tongue of the carrier and the other Amar. Quale kicked the male's feet from under him and shook him until his eyes were ringed with white. Then he dropped him. "Ask him."

Drij sucked in a breath, glanced from Quale to the Amar. "Ni-hat palle, Rum-Amar?"

The Amar's tongue moved over his thin lips. "Kinya-kin-kin. Beh. Tenashar." Unable to use hands bound to a crossbar, he pointed with an elbow ahead and to the right.

"What's he say?"

"There's a swarm of Kinya-kin-kin coming past ahead of

us about . . . about . . ." Counting on her fingers, she translated Rum distances into measures that Quale would understand. "About a hundred feet ahead." She turned back to the native. "Ih-Rum. Yadwe, Rum. Nadeleaa yad'we. Nadeleaa. Amsivo yeniak-tupa ati-ati Kinya-kin-kin?" She straightened her narrow shoulders. "I just asked him what direction they're moving in, how long they will take to pass and how close they have to be before they're dangerous."

The Amar's ears folded back against his head. "Tak puan," he muttered. "A-a-tua didi telathea."

"They are crossing our path, not coming toward us."

The Amar shifted position a little, his broad feet scraping over the coarse soil. "Pinja keunedede. Kuen kehwa."

"He thinks it's a fairly small swarm. No danger to us if we don't get closer."

"Bastard's probably lying his ass off." He scratched at his short beard, scowled at the native. "What the hell's a Kinya-kin-kin?"

Drij shoved impatiently at a strand of black hair falling across her face. Standing aside and behind them, Aleytys watched Drij revert unconsciously to lecturing and with that regain a measure of self respect. *Knowledge is her touchstone for worth now,* Aleytys thought. *It's what she has left to cling to. He doesn't like it.* She glanced at Quale, then moved a step closer to Drij. *He'll punish her for this,* she thought. *For making him need her.*

"Kinya-kin-kin. . . ." Drij stared over the Amar's head into the mist until Aleytys touched her elbow. She looked around, saw Quale's glower and started speaking. "Kinya-kin-kin is the name of a swarm of small vicious predators. Six legs. Short, stiff white hair. Mouth half the length of the body. They could strip the meat from your bones in about thirty seconds. They kill and eat everything that moves ahead of them; in a pinch they'll strip bushes and grass, even lichens from the ground in their path. Individuals are kin, the swarm itself is Kinya-kin-kin. The swarm moves in a straight line from side to side in the mistlands; they're blind, don't let anything shunt them aside." She looked down, saw the Amar leaning forward still in a crouch, ears twitching. In the sudden stillness as she fell silent, she heard a low crackling sound punctuated by random squeals. "Kinya gongole-si, Rum-Amar?"

The Amar shrugged. "Nam."

Quale shouldered Aleytys aside and grabbed Drij's arm. "What's that?" His temper was evident. *It won't take much more to start him slapping Drij around,* Aleytys thought. *He can't take it when he can't understand what people around him are saying.* She rubbed at her nose. *What the hell am I going to do? I can't let him. . . . .*

Drij lowered her eyes. When she spoke, her voice was soft and submissive. "Radi-Quale, I asked him if that sound belonged to the swarm. He said it did."

"Hunh." He turned her loose, his rancor soothed somewhat by her attitude. "How long we got to wait for that mess to pass?"

"Rum-Amar." She waited until the native was looking up at her. "Jin-refu zim au gari wae-ne?"

The Amar thought a minute, glanced up at the sky then down at his bound hands. He rattled the crosspiece he was tied to, stuck out two fingers. "Lib kidole."

"Radi-Quale." Drij turned away from the Amar and stood in front of the big man, her head down, her hands clasped in front of her. "He says two fingers. That means the time it takes for the sun to move the width of two fingers. Roughly an hour and a half."

"Must be a hell of a lot of them."

"They don't move fast. Several thousand kin probably. Little bigger than mice." Drij edged away from him, bumped into Aleytys. She glanced around, flushing again with the shame that filled her whenever she had to grovel to keep Quale from hurting her. Aleytys patted her shoulder. Quale was already stomping off, yelling at the Scavs to come in close, alternating orders with strings of curses. Aleytys led Drij to the carrier.

She settled herself with her back against the cells, turned to smile at Drij. "You handled him beautifully; he was getting restive with all that gibberish."

After a long silence Drij said, "I've had a lot of practice."

Aleytys forced a chuckle. "Sad to think of such effort wasted. Soon enough you won't need it."

Drij stiffened. "What are you going to do?"

"You wouldn't believe me if I told you." With a grimace of disgust, Aleytys swung around and lay on her back staring up into the mist. "I'm getting very bored with this fog. This damn day is lasting forever."

Drij leaned over her and smoothed the small hairs off her face. "You can't say nothing has been happening."

"Can't I?" Aleytys closed her eyes. "Nothing has been happening to me, doctorli, just around me."

"And you regret that?" Drij tugged at a strand of sweat-sodden red hair. "The Sink is getting to you."

The time passed slowly. Most of the men sat in small groups around the carrier, some smoking tuumba, others chewing gra'll—both mild euphorics from the Singanor system. Some were drowsing, others prowling about carefully avoiding all vegetation. The Amar crouched in their harness, silent and stolid, waiting. The two Scavs Quale put on guard circled the carrier slowly, eyes nervously on the fog that rolled with a rising breeze, thickening and thinning until it was easy to imagine forms out there, watching and waiting.

While Drij dozed and brushed at crawling insects, Aleytys lay with her eyes closed, probing into the mist. Moving about out of sight of the circling guards, she felt other centers of life. One of these burned hot and strong, radiating hate and grief. She pulled away quickly whenever she touched this one. It was hard to be certain how many were out there because the foci kept moving about, but after a while she grew reasonably sure that they numbered about a dozen, twelve Amar out there, circling and circling, waiting . . . to attack, to rescue or kill their fellows, to kill the demons. Her own nerves began knotting up in response until she could not remain stretched out. She sat up, looking around, frowning.

"What is it?" Drij jerked erect when she saw Aleytys move. She looked past Aleytys to Quale, sitting near the wall of mist, his figure indistinct. He was lighting a tuumba roll from the hot end of one he held clinched between his teeth. He looked restless. She could see his head turning constantly, the red end of the tuumba roll like a small beacon in the growing darkness.

Aleytys started kicking her feet back and forth, watched her boot toes swing. "We're being watched. Out there. About a dozen of them. Amar, I think. Feels like that."

"Tonight. . . ." Drij began, then glanced over her shoulder at the crouching Amar still tied to the crossbars of the tongue. "You and I. We'd better take turns staying awake."

She flashed a sly grin at Aleytys. "Unless Quale decides to keep you busy."

"Phhah!" Aleytys wrinkled her nose. "He's not such a fool. You really think they're going to attack at night?"

"I know they didn't at the Shelter. But this is different; more a rescue than an attack. I think they'll come in and try to cut the captives loose first before they start trying to kill us. Males simply aren't taken captive in their culture." Drij's mouth widened into a sudden brief smile. "It's probably an insult, treating men as if they're women."

"You want to warn Quale?"

"God, no. I hope the Amar get their people out. I just don't want to be killed."

Once the swarm had passed and moved on enough to be no danger to them, Quale got the carrier moving again, then loped ahead, scouting for good water and a defensible campsite. When they crossed the ravaged track of the Kinya-kinkin, a Scav kicked loose a dead kin. He picked it up, held it by a short stubby leg and waved it around. It was about two inches long, shaped like an egg, the mouth at the pointed end filled with several rows of tearing teeth. It had large round ears and no eyes, was covered by short coarse gray-white hair, had a short tufted tail, six legs, and a nauseating odor.

A Scav held his nose. "Get rid of that fuckin' rat, Herz, or you'll be eatin' it."

Herz grinned and waved the kin about some more.

"Hell, that ain't rat you smellin', that's Herz." A wiry dark-skinned Scav with long greasy braids sneered at the paler and taller man. "Hang it round you neck, jaka, till it get ripe enough for you to eat."

With a curse, Herz swung the dead kin around his head and flung it at the taunter. When it splatted on his tunic, the man leaped at Herz.

Other Scavs came running, muscled the two of them apart. "Damn fools." "If Quale comes back, he'll kill both of you." "You got that much energy, go find some greenies and play with them." Sullen and still pushing angrily at the men holding them, the two Scavs were shoved to different sides of the carrier. The procession started on again.

"They're getting edgy." Drij wiped at her face, looked at

the mud and moisture. "It's hot enough; at least there's a little breeze now."

"And this is only the first day." Aleytys pulled her tunic away from her skin. "Nobody told me it'd be like this. Wish I'd packed a bathtub." She swiped at her neck. "Or a towel."

The ground started to dip again as the basin began to slope toward the central and lowest point. The atmosphere grew murkier. The breeze was stirring more and more strongly through the mist knots. The sun's wide blur was touching the western rim, the mist around it shimmering with bands of muted color. Aleytys felt more uneasy as visibility decreased and the fog drew in around them. The Amar were trotting along out of sight on the upwind side. There was something else, something that bothered her more. She felt a cloud of things . . . shapeless things, swirling around and above them like motes caught in a slow eddy. She felt hunger in them, a craving that scratched at her like bug feet.

She shifted uneasily on the mesh. "Drij?"

"What is it?"

"You said something about floating ghosts?"

"They're one of the things Roha mentioned when she talked about the mistlands. I don't know if they're real or myth."

Aleytys shivered. Her eyes scanning the mist around her, she muttered, "Real. Something's hanging close by and it's hungry."

Drij pointed toward a number of dim red glows bobbing about. "That?"

Frowning, Aleytys probed at the shifting blurs almost too dim to be seen. "No. Those are your Amar raiders. They must have fired some torches, though I don't see why they'd do that."

Drij touched her arm. "Look at the captives."

Aleytys leaned forward, looking past her at the little green males. They were bouncing along, taut with suppressed excitement. Their mobile pointed ears were quivering forward; they kept their heads down and their shoulders rounded, but Aleytys could read glee mixed with malice radiating from them. "They're reeking anticipation," she breathed. "They have to be planning something."

"They know the others are out there. Quale is a fool for fighting a primitive on his own ground. If he hadn't taken those captives, he wouldn't have lost so many men already. Not that they hadn't earned it." She scowled ahead into the mist. "I want to see it when they get him; God, do I want to see that."

"Drij, about tonight. . . ."

"Mmmh?" She was still focusing on the darkening grayness ahead of them, not listening to Aleytys.

"Drij!" Aleytys waited until she swung around, surprise widening her dark eyes. "You've made it quite obvious you don't believe me when I talk about my talents. I don't intend wasting time or energy trying to convince you, but this you can believe, I'm a damn good fighter. What about you?"

Drij smiled a little. "Best thing I can do is run like hell. You know I'm Indarishi?"

"Yes. But you're a field scientist. You must have had some training in self-defense."

Drij shook her head. "They tried to teach me, but I . . . well, I resisted learning. I had to pass a test, but managed to forget most of the material almost immediately. I've always found that patience and talking worked better for me." She pulled her brows together. "Until this year. And none of what I learned would have helped me much against so many anyway."

Aleytys nodded. "My temper has brought unnecessary trouble on my head," she said absently. "Drij, do you smell anything?"

"Those torches." Drij sniffed at the trails of mist blowing into her face. "The Amar are burning wet wood downwind of us. Drugs in the sap."

"No wonder our little green motor is prancing. We'll all be riding high in a little while if they keep this up. How long till it's too dark to move?" She looked around. The fog was gradually closing in. The sun's blur had nearly vanished and the muted colors of dusk had darkened to a hazy purple. Overhead the web of the Sink traced pulses of lighter areas through the murk, but it was already hard to see the ground that slid past beneath the wheels. The Scav circle had tightened until the men were trotting within a few feet of the carrier.

"Can't read Quale's mind," Drij muttered. She was swaying with the jerk and slide of the carrier, already succumbing to the drug in the smoke. Aleytys sighed, caught hold of her shoulders and eased her down on the bed-webbing. The smoke was strong around them now. Out in the mist she could see the fire-shine of the torches much more plainly; the Amar were moving closer. Drij began to snore. The Scavs closest to the carrier were beginning to stumble though they seemed unworried about it, unaware also of the crisp spicy aroma that overlay the ordinary odors of dampness and decay around them.

Yawning, Aleytys rubbed sore and heavy eyes, then stretched out on the carrier bed, shifting about until she was comfortable. The drug's seductive intrusion teased her toward sleep. She drifted for a short while, then struggled to sit up, alarms ringing in her head. She *reached* and the black water of her power river washed the drug from her body.

The walking men were plodding along, moving slower and slower. Out in the mist the Amar kept shifting about. Several of the red glows dimmed, went out, then were replaced by more fiercely burning lights as new torches were kindled in place of those that had burned out.

A red glow bloomed ahead of the carrier—another fire, this one stationary, entirely too big to be carried about. Quale was waiting for them by the fire, a dark demonic figure in the swirling mist that picked up the red of the flames and cast it back onto his face and hands. He was scowling as he watched the Scavs stumble into the space he'd selected as a camp, their eyes dull, their faces slack. The Tiks were a little less affected than the others, their hotter bodies burning away the effects of the drug more quickly, and, as they were nocturnals, the night was the time when they felt more comfortable and more alert. The Ortels were lumbering on four legs instead of two, bent over so that their mid-arms were serving as a second pair of legs. They chittered and creaked erratically, talking as much to mind-ghosts as to their companions. When they reached the fire, they lowered their center sections to the ground and stared at the leaping flames, ignoring everything going on around them.

Quale watched a moment, eyes narrowed. He'd escaped the effects of the drugged smoke, ranging too far ahead of the carrier to realize what was happening behind him. His scowl deepened as he scanned the dazed faces of the Scavs. He swung from man to man, roaring questions that got no answers and little other response. Then he staggered, fell hard

against the carrier, driving it ahead a good two feet. He
shook his head, shook it again, in an attempt to clear away
his sudden dizziness. Grim, he forced himself back onto his
feet, his eyes fixed on the shifting red glows. Cursing under
his breath, he unslung his rifle, steadied himself and squeezed
off a series of shots, sweeping his fire along the line of lights.

Aleytys watched his brief sharp struggle with the effects of
the drugged smoke and his quick assessment of the problem.
Once again she had to revise her opinion of him. His persistent stupidity about women was no excuse for an answering
stupidity on her part. His was a cultural blind-spot; hers had
no such excuse. She dropped her head onto her arms, turning
it sideways so she could see but close her eyes and pretend to
sleep with the slightest of warnings. If he found her awake
and unaffected by the smoke, he might start digging into that
vague sense of familiarity her name woke in him the first
time he'd heard it. She scanned the mist, saw the torches
falling, heard several howls. Her outreach touched the Amar,
counting ten of the twelve sparks. *Two dead*, she thought. *If
my first count was accurate.*

When all the torches were quenched, Quale slung his rifle
onto his shoulder, then started around the sandy clearing,
prodding the dozing, dazed men with his boot, cursing steadily as he moved from man to man finding all of them in no
shape to stand guard or fight off anything stronger than a bad
dream. Not too pleased at the need for it, he ordered the Tiks
to patrol the clearing, telling them to keep alert for greenies.
Now that it was dark, he really didn't expect any attack, but
he didn't want them taking chances. He watched them
waddle off on their short crooked legs, anger and disgust
twisting his face into an ugly grimace.

Aleytys lifted her head a little, sniffed at the air. The
breeze was strong now, blowing strings of mist thick around
them, cleaning the air of the drug-laden smoke. As Quale
prowled past the end of the carrier, she dropped her head
back on her arms, closed her eyes and began waiting.

THE HUNT

CHAPTER V   Roha

Roha crouched in the corner of her house, rubbing and rubbing at her hands unable to get the feel of Rihon's death off her skin. At intervals during the night she'd flung herself about the room, shrieking her rage, calling on her womb-mother Earth, sister night the dark twin for a hundred deaths to pay for this one death. Now there was only coldness, helplessness and loss.

As the morning crept inside the silent hut, the Wan climbed the ladder with a mug of loochee and a bowl of mush. He squatted beside her, set the mug and bowl by his feet and cupped his hand under her chin. She tried to pull away, but his gentle withered fingers were too strong for her as the weariness from the endless terrible night broke suddenly over her. Shaking, weeping, she pressed her face against his shoulder and clung to him.

He patted her back, then held her until the storm passed. When she drew in a long shuddering breath and stopped shaking, he eased her away, smiled down into her damp face. "Eat, Roha. There are things you'll have to do."

She looked down at the cooling mush and the still steaming loochee and felt her throat close. She swallowed, swallowed again, but the lump was still there. "I can't."

He lifted the mug and closed her fingers around it, holding them tight against the wood with his hand. His skin was warm and dry like a year-fallen leaf in the sun. He helped her lift the mug, held it to her lips until she took a sip. It warmed her mouth. The warmth spread. She drank more, then gulped down the loochee until the mug was empty.

When she set the mush bowl down empty, he smiled at her. "Sit and be, Roha." He edged back a little, and began rubbing at her feet.

Roha lay back on her sleeping leather, the tiredness her

115

grief had held off before creeping over her. With the warmth in her belly and the soothing seductive manipulation of her feet, she was finally able to let her grief drift away as if it were something apart from herself, outside her, like one of the floating ghosts. In a few minutes she was asleep.

It was late afternoon when she woke. She lay flat on the leather as memory brought back her grief, although food and sleep had taken the edge away. Already it seemed distant. But there was nothing distant about the cold anger that filled her whenever she thought about his death. She pushed onto her feet and walked stiffly to the low door, ducked through and stood a moment on the narrow ledge outside.

Women were bringing wood for Rihon's pyre. Angry, Roha backed rapidly down the ladder and plunged into the trees. Right now she couldn't bear to watch the women. She didn't want to talk to anyone. Restless and impatient, she ran beneath the trees with Rihon's ghost beside her. She could smell him, hear his feet pattering with hers. She pulled herself up on the air-roots of her womb tree, sat with her back pressed against the trunk but there was no peace for her even here. She fidgeted restlessly, trying to draw strength from the tree that had fed on her buried womb. It was her second self; she was bound to it, had brought her pains here and her joys, but Rihon had always been with her. Always. Without him the tree was cold. No pulse beat in it for her. "I'm dead too," she said, then winced at the empty sound of her voice. She shivered and climbed down from roots. Arms hugged tight across her chest, she stood on the path her feet and Rihon's had beat into the earth and tried to think. She couldn't make words stick together, then images of the demons filled her head. She started running.

As she circled the clearing she saw the demons throw one of their own over the wall, a dead one who splatted hard on the ground and lay tumbled half across a dead Amar. She glared at the wall with the heads moving up and down behind it, her claws extending and retracting. She stood without trying to hide herself even though the demons were using their flinging sticks to spit the small deadly pellets.

Churr caught her arm and pulled her into cover. "You shouldn't be here, Twin. Go back."

She saw his face change from irritation to uncertainty to

anger. "Not twin. Not any more." Turning away from him she focused on the wall. "What are the demons doing? Are they just sitting there?"

Churr knelt beside her, his strong scarred face wrinkled with his own anger. "We can hear them moving behind the walls. What they're doing. . . . ." He shook his head, then hissed as the gate in the wall swung open. He whistled urgently. An Amar ran from the trees, raised his bow. And was blown onto his back by a crackle from the spitting sticks.

Churr growled as the long thing rolled out, pulled by six Amar warriors, stumbling and rebelling, driven along by the whips in the hands of two demons.

Roha clutched at Churr's arm. "How . . . how . . . how . . ." she stuttered. She pressed herself against him, taking strength from him, not in a flood as from her brother but in a brief effusion like a windborne mist. She watched the strangers rattle closer, then Churr pulled free and whistled again. Yells sounded around the clearing then arrows flew from the trees striking here and there, dropping a few of the demons, skittering off others.

Churr lifted her, startling her into a sharp cry. He set her down several paces back from the clearing. "Go home," he said firmly. Before she could protest, he'd faded into the mist.

Roha listened to the noise of the combat as it retreated slowly until it was hardly louder than the wind whispering in the trees over her head. She walked slowly back to the clearing and stood watching the wall. The gate was closed and she could see a demon's head like a misshapen fruit sitting on top the wall. She turned to the west, pricked her ears forward, then started following the faint sounds that still reached her. Behind her she heard the crack of a flinging stick then felt a hot line of pain across her shoulder. She trotted faster, her hand pressed over the shallow groove in the muscle that padded the top of her arm. For the first time since Rihon's death she felt the Twin change within her. Her blood heated, turning the real landscape though the serial and simultaneous distortions familiar to her in her heightened state—flat lines and planes of black against white, white against black, crossed and recrossed with swooping and jagged shimmers of color that were the sounds she no longer heard, only saw.

She reached the edge of the mistlands as the rolling thing

tilted down the incline into the domes of mist. Churr caught
her as she started to follow.

She didn't struggle. Standing in the curve of his arms she
stared at the mist and wanted . . . wanted so many things
she couldn't name them all, wanted to go into the terrible
place and finish the thing she'd started, finish the demon egg,
wanted to destroy all the demons, even the Nafa now. All the
demons. Destroy them and heal the Womb-Mother of her
burning great wound. Flames danced on the fog before her
eyes. She saw the great gray egg burning. Burning. She
blinked and it was gone, only the billowing domes of mist left
as they rose from the floor of the basin far below.

Churr stepped back from her, but kept hold of her wrist as
he turned to face the ten Amar who stood around him.
"They have our brothers, those demons. They took them
there—you saw." He jerked his head toward the beginning of
the downslope where the flat stone crumbled away into a long
easy slant toward the basin floor. "Who comes?"

The ten shuffled their feet, exchanged measuring glances,
then, one by one, walked to Churr, set a hand on his extended fist, then stepped back. He nodded. "Good. Najin, you and
Pitic collect what arrows you can from the flat outside the
Nafa's wall. Take care; some demons stayed behind." He
scowled, touched his hand to the quiver angled across his
back. "We're all low and we got no time to make more. Rest
of you—fetch trail food, knives and some fresh poison-pots.
We could have a hard time getting our brothers back. Fulz,
you and Bayin get a couple firepots and some sinzi wood for
torches." He chuckled at their sudden grins. "A sleeping
demon's throat is easier to cut."

Pitic looked at Roha. "Before the burning?"

Churr shrugged. "Wan, Serk and Niong are enough for
honoring the Bright Twin. We got others to worry about."

Pitic glanced at Roha once more, nodded, then trotted after Najin. The others slid silently into the trails of mist,
loping slowly toward the village. Roha stood gazing at Churr,
saying nothing. "Go home," Churr said gruffly. "This is man's
work, Dark Twin."

She turned her head away. "No. . . ." Pulling free, she
went to the rock slope and sat facing into the billowing mist.
After an extended silence, she looked over her shoulder. He
was frowning past her as if she didn't exist. "Churr," she

called. He swung around to face her. "Churr, I'm going with you even if I have to follow by myself." She rose to her feet and took a step down the slope.

He caught her shoulder. He was only a head taller, but her frail body was no match for his wiry muscle. She didn't try to struggle. "You can stop me now. You can't stop me following."

"Roha. . . ." He broke off as she stood without moving or speaking, then he turned and walked away to stand waiting for the return of the warriors.

Roha watched him as he paced restlessly over the stone, moving in and out of tendrils of mist. She should have felt triumph but was empty inside. She sat again, waiting with him with a cold patience that changed her into stone to match the stone beneath her.

She heard shouts and confusion ahead of her as she picked her way down the loose rock on the slope, moving carefully around the scattered vegetation. Here on the fringes of the mistlands almost all that grew was dangerous. She heard a loud cry as one of the demons much farther down the slope tangled with a bush and went tumbling over and over as the center of a small avalanche. Sometime later she almost stumbled over his body; it was partially covered with small stones and prickly leaves. His flesh was bloated and puffy. She stood staring down at him, then lifted her head and laughed. "One," she cried.

There was more noise in front of her. The ten Amar with Churr were attacking the demons with stones, knocking them down and cutting their throats, driving them into the poison bushes. Roha stepped over and around more of them, feeling with each an upsurge of anger and triumph that quickly flattened with the realization that the blood of all the demons would never be enough to pay for Rihon. She circled the feet of the last and ran down the slope to rejoin Churr. *We'll send their ghosts to serve you, brother,* she thought. *One by one, we'll send them.*

THE HUNT

CHAPTER VI   Aleytys And Roha

ALEYTYS

In the dark the fog seemed thicker and warmer. The fire had burned down to a few flickering coals. Aleytys lifted her head, looked cautiously about, then sat up. After sniffing the air, she smiled. The mist was laced again with the drugged smoke. She narrowed her eyes and scanned the dark on the downwind side, searching for more glows that would mark the position of the torches. A dark, squat figure waddled past—a Tik on his rounds. She pushed wandering tendrils of hair back off her face then she felt about for the Amar, searching for the ten sparks of life out in the darkness.

They were gathered together, sitting quietly in one spot as far as she could tell. The torches were either out or smoldering so dimly she could see no sign of them. *How long will I have to wait?* she thought. *What are they waiting for?* She felt herself drifting, blinked heavy eyes, realizing she was more under the influence of the smoke than she'd thought. She washed the drug from her system, hesitated, then dropped her hand on Drij's shoulder, letting the black water flow into the sleeping woman and clean the smoke effects out of her. When Drij's body was free of drugging, Aleytys snapped the tie to the power river and shook her awake.

"Wha. . . ." Drij sat up, blinking uncertainly, tongue passing over dry lips. She scanned the dark lumps of the sleeping Scavs. "I wonder how many of them will be alive in the morning."

"Better not talk." Aleytys sniffed at the air blowing vigorously past her face; the spicy tang of smoke was nearly gone. "Relax. Nothing's happening."

"What about the Amar?" Drij made no attempt to keep her voice down. "Where are they? Do you know?"

120

Amused, Aleytys eyed her for a minute, then reached out for the life-sparks in the mist. "Didn't think you believed in this. Ah! They've started moving. Coming toward us."

"I don't know what I . . . you're sure?"

"Yes. Coming slow, perhaps because the Tiks are still on their feet."

"Where's Quale?"

"Asleep somewhere. Drij, I want to talk to the Amar. I need you to translate for me."

"Why? Let them come in and get their people. They don't need help."

"They're going to cut every throat they can reach, including ours, my friend. You know that. I need those Scavs, Drij. I want them alive."

"These . . . these bastards? Let the Amar have them." Drij's voice was low and filled with hate.

"No. Translate for me."

"I have no desire to die. Not to save a bunch of scum like those." She gestured. "Could you keep them from killing us? And don't give me nonsense about wild talents." She saw Aleytys grimace. "I thought so. Forget it."

The Amar settled to the ground as two of them edged close to Tiks. There was a soft flurry of sound and the life-fires of the sentries snuffed out. Aleytys jumped down. Looking up at Drij, she said, "They just got the sentries. If you don't help, I'm going to have to wake Quale."

"That's not fair." Drij sighed, slid down beside Aleytys. "Well, I'm ready. Keep me alive if you can. I'd appreciate it very much."

"I share the feeling." With Drij trailing close behind her, she moved toward the crouching captives. When she passed close to one of the sleepers, she knelt beside him and touched his cheek, then slapped him hard, her palm splatting loudly against his flaccid cheek. He was deep in a stupor, would take a lot of waking. Out in the fog the Amar huddled together. They could see her and Drij moving about, alert. She slipped his knife from the sheath at his side, hesitated a minute, then slipped the rifle off his shoulder and shrugged it onto hers. Knowing the Amar were watching, a little nervous about approaching the captives with a knife, she started toward the tethered natives.

Before she could take more than a few steps, small forms burst from the mist and came at her.

She wheeled, gathered light between her hands and threw it at them, then rushed toward the captives.

"Roha!" Drij shrieked. "Tenda-si! Tenda!"

ROHA

The flash burned in front of her. Roha felt a tingle but there was no pain, just the blinding light that made her eyes hurt. She blinked, saw nothing but the flare with black specks swimming in it. When her eyes cleared, the fire-haired demon was kneeling beside Daal, a knife at his throat. Whimpering, claws coming out, Roha started for her then stopped as the Nafa stepped in front of her.

"Roha," the Nafa said softly, her hands outstretched, empty.

The deep voice thrumming inside her, Roha drew back. "Demon," she cried desperately. "Stand aside." Snatching the knife from her belt, she raised it in threat.

ALEYTYS

"Tell her to stop." Aleytys winced, the translating part of her talents called into action, producing the thundering headache it always did. She screwed up her face, then relaxed as the worst of the ache went away. "I don't want to hurt her, but I won't let her kill me or the others."

Drij nodded. As she and Roha spat words at each other, Aleytys cut the captive free. She tapped him on the shoulder, pointed toward the mist. "Go!" she whispered, then gave him a light push. He got the idea and trotted off.

ROHA

Roha watched Daal trot to join Churr and the others. She looked around at the sleeping demons. "They have to die," she moaned. "They have to die, Nafa. For what they've done, they have to die. They killed Rihon. He's dead."

"Ahhh." The Nafa caught her hand. Roha tried to pull away, but the long slim fingers of the demon were too strong for her. "I didn't know, Roha," the demon said. "There are no words. If I could change things, I would."

Roha pressed the knife against her chest, taking some comfort in the coolness of the stone. "Why do you try to stop us?"

The Nafa nodded at the Fire-hair, who was busy cutting the rest of the captives loose. "Left to me, I wouldn't try. She says she needs them and won't let you kill them. Tell you this, young Roha, take the men when they're walking. You and your people can do that easy enough. She won't hurt you or yours unless you force her."

A third and fourth Amar were loping into the mist. There was only one captive to free. Roha watched the Fire-hair move quickly to him and bend to cut his ties. "She is a demon of great power."

"But one well-disposed to you. She knew when you killed the guards. She knew how many of you were running after us. She sees through the fog just as an Amar can see through clear water. She could have warned the sky-demons but she didn't. She is pretending to these men that they have captured her. When she is where she wants to be and has what she wants to have, these sky demons, the ones you haven't killed, Roha, they will find suddenly that they are the captives and she the captor." The Nafa stopped talking and looked around, saw Churr and the others watching. "Send your people away now. Look, the last of your brothers is free. Take your people into the mist and wait. Sleep. Eat. Gain strength. Tomorrow you can attack again, take the stragglers one by one. Roha, do you hear me?"

Roha nodded; she pulled her hand free and fled to Churr. "The demon will burn us if we touch the sleepers," she gasped. She drew strength from him, a weak flow that brought anguish with it, too powerful a reminder of what she'd lost, a part of herself gone. She looked at the Nafa, then at the Fire-hair. The pale face came at her at her at her, strength came from her, warmth came from her, comfort came from her, comfort she didn't want, wouldn't accept, tried to push away but was not strong enough, that quietly caressed her and would not go away. With a cry of anguish, Roha wheeled and ran from that terrible place into the mist and darkness that seemed more certain and far more familiar. Churr scowled, voiced a low command to the other Amar, then ran after her. They followed, glad to leave the demon-cursed place.

ALEYTYS

Aleytys stared into the mist. The tiny Amar girl reminded
her too much of herself a few years ago, both of them forced
to deal with people and things they had no way of understanding. She tossed the rifle aside, turned to Drij. "Thanks.
Here." She held out the knife. "Hide this where you can get
at it."

Drij shivered and clasped her hands behind her back. "I
could never use it."

"You let others do your killing for you and rejoice in the
corpses. What's the difference?"

"None." Drij shrugged. "But I won't—can't—use that
thing on anyone."

Aleytys looked down at the blade, shook her head, then
threw it among the scattered pieces of rope. "Just as well, I
suppose. You did a good job with the girl."

Drij sighed. "I just wanted to convince her to go away and
leave us alone."

"Whatever, you did it. I'm hungry enough to eat a boot
raw. There's half a dozen tab-cans of stew in one of those
cells. Been resting my head on it all day. A hot meal first,
then we'll get some sleep. We'll need it when we face Quale
in the morning." She grinned. "He'll have the grandaddy of
all hangovers. Since he's made a habit of cheering himself up
on your face, I'll see if I can head him off. Don't want him
to get ideas about me. Be damned if I stand for a busted
face." She pulled herself up onto the carrier's high bed and
reached down for Drij.

In the morning Quale surprised her again. The explosion
she'd expected never came. He kicked at the bits of rope,
then moved purposefully about the edge of the clearing, stripping the bodies of the Tiks and tossing their weapons onto
the carrier. He stopped by the two women, turned his back
on them to watch the men getting unsteadily to their feet.
"Throw down some of the food cells," he said abruptly, then
strode away, leaving Aleytys and Drij staring at each other.

After a breakfast of self-heating stew and copious drafts of
cha, the ten Scavs left lined up again, looking brighter and
meaner. Quale stood by the tongue watching them thought-

fully. Aleytys felt his anger rise, then the coolness of second
thought taking over, saw that he wasn't about to risk a re-
fusal by ordering any of the men to pull the carrier. He still
dominated them, but in their present short-tempered mood, it
would only take a spark to unite them against him. He stared
down at the tongue, lifted it, tugged at the carrier, measuring
the force required to move it. With a grunt of satisfaction, he
dropped the tongue and looked up. "You women. Get down
here and strap in."

They began moving along behind him as he led off into the
brightening mist. The sun was up, a greenish blur low in the
eastern sky. A brisk breeze whipped the fog about; moving
became difficult. One minute Aleytys could see a dozen feet
ahead, the next she was lucky to see where to put her feet.
With the harness taking part of the stress of her arms the carrier was easy enough to pull, but Aleytys was nervous about
the ground and vegetation ahead of her. She avoided bushes
as much as possible, kept her eyes on the ground, preferring
the patches of coarse sand and rubble to smooth stretches of
stone. *And I was complaining about just being along for the*
ride. *Bored!* she thought suddenly and chuckled. This brought
a startled stare from Drij but she didn't bother explaining
what had amused her.

The Amar were moving along with them. Aleytys glanced
at the men marching beside the carrier. They were jumpy,
ready to shoot at shadows. She hoped little Roha and her
warriors had the good sense to let the Scavs settle before they
tried anything.

An odd sensation brushed at the far edge of her outreach.
Hastily she scanned the ground ahead of her for dangers,
then closed her eyes and extended her probe. Out beyond the
Amar there was something else, life-sparks so dim she was
not sure they existed or were figments of an overheated imag-
ination. As she struggled with the limitations set on her talents by the interference of the Sink web, she cursed softly.
The touches were tentative and unclear and nothing she
could do would make them yield more information. To add
to her jumpiness, she grew slowly aware of a swarm of tiny
vibrations hovering about the carrier, radiating a greedy hunger but impossible to locate with any certainty. Another
vague threat. Aleytys groped about but found no center to
take hold of, only clouds of smoke that flowed away when-

ever she reached for them. As time passed she walked along in harness, muttering softly to herself, so intent on her outreach that she forgot everything else but the need to examine the ground ahead of her feet.

"Lee." Drij looked around to see if the Scavs were watching, then whispered, "Lee, what's wrong?"

Aleytys jerked her head up, smiled at the anxiety on Drij's face. "Nothing." She looked around, then back at the ground in front of her. "Nothing yet, anyway. Mmmh. Tell me, are there any larger forms of life here in the mistlands?"

Drij frowned. "Roha said something about Mistlanders but she seemed to think they were stories for children. Like the floating ghosts." She was silent a minute. "Why?" she said after a while. "Or should I ask?"

"I don't know. . . . ." Aleytys shrugged her shoulders. "Ever feel uncomfortable and turn around to see someone staring at you? That's how I feel now. Itchy. Tell you what, Drij. If I yell, you hit the ground fast."

THE HUNT

CHAPTER VII   Aleytys

Three more Scavs died before Quale brought them to camp on the second day in the mistlands. One had stopped to relieve himself and finished with a slashed throat. The other two fell behind a little and went down with arrows in arm and thigh. Aiming was difficult in the shifting mists but the poison was so strong that any hit meant a quick death to the victim. A Scav saw the last one fall, yelled a warning and began firing wildly into the mist until Quale kicked the rifle from his hands, cursing him for wasting ammunition. After that, the Scavs bunched close about the carrier, jumping at every shadow in the fog but not quite bold enough to risk Quale's anger by shooting.

When they stopped, Aleytys slipped the harness straps from her shoulders and stretched, groaning. "I wasn't meant to be a horse."

"Nor I." Drij rubbed at her shoulder; she looked very tired, years older than she had in the morning. There were tiny lines webbed over her pale brown skin, deeper lines around eyes, nose and mouth. Her hair hung lankly about her face, falling in oily strands from the knot at the back of her head. Sweat and the mist had washed away her cosmetics and she had none to replace them and no will to use them if she'd had them. She stepped away from the tongue and stood watching Quale as he bullied the tired men into setting up camp and gathering down-wood for a fire. After a long silence, she turned to Aleytys. "Is it worth all this, the thing you and Quale are after?"

"Yes." Aleytys dropped to the ground and sat with her back against one of the wheels. She waited until Drij was settled beside her, then went on. "A queen's ransom."

"What?"

"A Haestavaada Queen. They hired me to get her back. If

127

Quale gets her, he'll sell her to the highest bidder—Haestavaada or Tikh'asfour. For him, it's a prize bigger than anything even he ever dreamed of. For me, it's a world of vaada
who'll die if I don't bring their Queen back—and, I must admit, a very hefty fee."

"I see." She pushed wearily at the hair plastered to her
forehead. "In the end is there any difference between you and
Quale?"

"In the end. . . ." Aleytys sighed. "This maybe. I'm already bought, though not quite paid for." She turned her
head and met Drij's curious eyes with a smile. "I get my fee
when the Haestavaada get their Queen."

"Oh?"

"Keeps me honest."

They rested without speaking until Quale set them to serving food to the men. The Scavs huddled around the fire,
glancing continually over their shoulders, stuffing food in
their mouths as fast as they could. Quale climbed onto the
pile of supply cells and settled himself there, rifle on his
knees, Drij and Aleytys crouching at his feet.

Aleytys felt his satisfaction as he glanced over her, over the
men, around the camp. With the satisfaction was a touch of
self-mockery. *Besieged by tricky natives,* she thought. *Trek-
king toward a treasure. Standing guard while his men eat, his
women crouching at his feet. A Farou saga. Knowing it's
nonsense. Unable to resist the dream. Bloody murdering
bastard with a small boy lost somewhere inside him.*

Later Quale set up the shelter and crawled inside leaving
Aleytys and Drij to stretch out on the carrier. This night the
sentries were dug into pits looking out over banks of thrown-
up earth. The other Scavs were rolled up in blankets close
about the carrier, seeking at least the illusion of shelter. Drij
was asleep almost immediately, exhausted by her strenuous
day, but Aleytys lay staring up at the faintly glowing mist.

In the darkness within her skull Swardheld's black eyes
opened and his bearded face developed around them. "Bone-
head."

Aleytys grinned. "Me or Quale?" she murmured.

"Both of you. Way you're acting, you're going to waste all
these men before you get to the ship." His eyes shifted.
"What the hell are those things?"

Drifting overhead were small spheres of emptiness visible

now because of the night-thickening of the fog. As she watched, two of the spheres bumped together, merged into a larger emptiness, bumped again, continued to grow in erratic leaps. "I wonder," she whispered. "Drij said something about floating ghosts." Her lips twitched into a brief smile. "If anything ever deserved that name, those do."

The spheres bobbed about, moving in slow spirals over the camp. The largest ones hung about overhead. Aleytys watched with growing apprehension. Two of them were already larger than her head and they radiated hunger. Hanging beneath each sphere, translucent tendrils fine as silk threads grew longer and longer as their parent spheres merged. They circled above her, dipping lower and lower as they passed over her, rising as they moved away from the carrier, dipping again as they circled back.

She sat up. The largest ghost dropped quickly. Before she could avoid them, the dangling tendrils brushed across her face; she jerked away and bent to shake Drij awake.

After a minute she brushed at the air in front of her face, brushed again, looked up to see a bloated hollow drifting over her head. Her face and shoulders began to tingle. A pleasant warm lassitude spread through her.

"Lee!" Swardheld's yell broke through the warmth. She jerked back, falling flat onto the carrier bed, then slammed a powerful negation at the ghost, forgetting caution, forgetting also the distortion in her reach created by the web of the Sink. For a moment she glowed red-hot as power streamed from her, searing the ghost above her, leaping from it to others of the swarm, leaping again until the floating ghosts were linked in a red-gold webbing like that of the Sink.

Screaming silently, screaming their agony, the ghosts fragmented and swirled away through the fog, spraying outward in a desperate flight to escape the fire she was throwing at them.

Then the flare was gone. Swardheld was gone. Her head was locked in a band of pain. Her eyes blurred. Her head was stuffed with sand—dry, stifling sand—she was terrified—suddenly—diffusely—thoroughly—terrified. She crouched on the carrier bed, afraid—afraid—helpless before another attack of the ghosts as the sand slowly trickled from her head, as the bill was paid for the sudden enormous augmentation of her power.

She stretched out flat on the carrier, feeling limp and exhausted, aching in every joint. Uneasy, she scanned the clotted fog over her head; she relaxed when she saw nothing but the faint glow from the Sink invisible overhead.

The black eyes opened again. Looking startled and angry, Swardheld demanded, "What happened?"

"Floating ghosts." She yawned. "Did you catch any of that?"

"Sucking. Or fingers closing around me before I pulled back." He raised an eyebrow. "Rough ride there for a minute."

"Damn Sink." She yawned again; it was hard to keep focused on his image. He blurred and shifted like a figure in a dream.

"Go to sleep, freyka." Amusement and affection roughened his deep voice. He winked at her and was gone.

"Mmmh." She drifted away, too tired to talk or think any longer, too tired even to be afraid. In the first moments of her sleep, she dreamed that Swardheld stood beside her, his black beard and hair ruffled by the wind, beaded with moisture from the steamy mist. He was leaning on a long black sword, his hands placed one over the other on top of the hilt. Feeling safe and comforted, she sank easily into a deep and refreshing sleep.

At sundown on the third day, Aleytys and Drij circled a large group of purple-tinged bushes then stopped to stare at the stained, half-buried ship whose long gray curve vanished at both ends into steam and mist. Quale was standing on the gritty soil staring at the barricaded lock. By his feet lay the battered body of a vaad, the only sign of life in the desolate clearing. He swung around when he heard the scrape of feet as the remaining few Scavs moved warily past the circle of brush.

He glanced quickly at the carrier, then at the mist-shrouded bushes. The silence around them was oppressive. With a frown he waved Aleytys and Drij forward. Following his directions they worked the carrier around until it was parallel to the ship, the large wheels providing a measure of protection for the Scavs. When he was satisfied, he strode to the lock and pulled himself up into the opening. He tugged at the barricade. A dangling section of rod came off in his hand, but the tangled mass in front of him didn't move. "Hey!" His voice boomed into the cavernous blackness. There was no response. He brought his rod down on a section of the barricade, producing a reverberating clang that made him wince when the echo blasted back at him. He banged at the barricade again and again, yelling and cursing.

Stones came flying from the mist. A Scav lounging against one end of the carrier cursed and dropped his rifle to clutch at a broken arm, then went down as a second stone slammed against his temple. The other Scavs dropped behind the wheels and began to fire into the section of the mist the stones were coming from. Aleytys stripped off the harness, helped Drij fumble out of hers, pulled her behind the carrier.

When the stones stopped coming, Aleytys grimaced and stood. As Drij started to rise, Aleytys waved her back. She moved closer to the ship, glanced up at Quale, then cried, "Ksiyl the Hook. Maladra Shayl sent me to get you."

Quale dropped from the lock, caught hold of the knot of hair and pulled it. His face crimson with fury, he whispered, "Talk when I tell you, bitch." He jerked her head back, the pain bringing tears to her eyes. "You hear?"

"I hear," she gasped. "But. . . ."

"When I tell you." He forced her to her knees, stood glaring down at her.

Aleytys fought down her anger and lowered her eyes. "I hear," she said dully, flattening all expression from her voice.

"You know the bugs in there?" He stepped back, his boots crunching on the soil. A gust of wind blew sulphur-laden air past them. Quale choked, spat, cursed.

Aleytys focused on the stained and scuffed toes of his boots. "Yes."

Quale glanced at the barrier, then caught hold of her arm and jerked her to her feet. "Get them out here." He stuffed one hand behind the waist-band of her trousers, grabbed her thigh with the other and threw her up into the lock.

Breathing hard, shaking with rage, Aleytys clutched at a broken girder, felt the cold steel smooth and strong under her hands. For a moment she closed her eyes, then stared into the thick, pungent blackness visible through cracks in the barricade. She sucked in a breath, steadied herself, called, "Ksiyl the Hook!" She could hear the words bouncing about and breaking apart as her voice echoed about the interior. "Ksiyl the Hook," she called again, more loudly. "The Navigator reached Kavaakh." Again she waited until the echoes died. "Maladra Shayl valaad sent me here to bring the Queen away."

She began to wonder if Ksiyl was dead. The valaad was captain of the Queen's guard but the others had to understand interlingue; they wouldn't have been chosen otherwise. There was no way she could speak the clik-tongue of the Haestavaada. She couldn't make the sounds, couldn't even hear some of them. Edging her head around, she risked a glance at Quale. He was prowling about, dividing his attention between her and the mist-line. She could feel his impatience; it matched her own. She turned back to call again, then saw a valaad face staring at her through one of the small openings in the barricade. "Ksiyl?"

The four eyes stared at her, the mandibles moved slightly but produced no sound then the face shifted and the valaad was looking past her at Quale and the carrier. Still without making any attempt to communicate, it turned and vanished into the darkness. For a moment she could hear the soft scraping of its feet. Her fingers tightened on the metal. More waiting.

"I said get them out here." Quale's hand tightened painfully around her ankle. She looked down. He was scowling, but she didn't need that to read the nervous irritation building in him.

"One of the valaad came; it just left to get the guard captain," she said hastily, hoping what she said was true. She was beginning to feel like a sacrifice tied on a bulge in the earth waiting for the volcano below to explode beneath her. Out of the fog she could feel converging areas of hostility. Higher in the mist the floating ghosts were circling, remaining some distance from her, but gathering more thickly than ever. *I have to be careful,* she thought. *They're starting to forget what I did to them before.* She felt sick at the thought of those bulbous nightmares sucking out her life. It was getting dark. The glow from the setting sun was fading, the rings of color about it darkening to a greenish purple. She could hear the creak of the carrier as the men leaned on it. *Scavs,* she thought. *Five of them left out of the double dozen we started with. Little Roha, you're taking us out, you and your warriors. I wonder if we'll make it out of this nightmare.*

Quale jerked at her ankle. "Five minutes," he snarled. "Then we try smoking the bugs out." He didn't wait for an answer, but stalked to the carrier and sent three men toward the pile of dead brush near the tail of the ship.

A triple clang of metal against metal brought her head around. The valaad was back. She looked closer. *No*, she thought, *it's another one.* "Ksiyl?"

The valaad lifted its signing hands. WHO ARE YOU? Aleytys read.

She felt a sudden relief and closed her hands tightly over a broken strut until the shake was out of her legs. Then she stepped back and signed: HUNTER ALEYTYS, HUNTERS OF WOLFF. WE WERE HIRED TO FREE THE QUEEN. DOES SHE LIVE?

YES. WHO ARE THOSE MEN? YOURS?

Aleytys hesitated. Finally, she signed: NO. SCAVS. THEY THINK TO RANSOM THE QUEEN. I'M USING THEM TO GET US OUT SAFE. MANY DANGERS OUT THERE. She waved a hand at the mist that surrounded them.

USING THEM? If signs could be skeptical, these were.

I AM A HUNTER OF WOLFF, KSIYL THE HOOK. I AM NEVER DISARMED. THINK QUICKLY. THE BIG MAN IS IMPATIENT AND I DON'T WANT TO HAVE TO FIGHT HIM YET. She glanced at Quale, then made a quick, sharp gesture. YOU HAVE TWO CHOICES, KSIYL. YOU CAN SIT HERE AND ROT UNTIL THE TIKH'ASFOUR LAND AND ROOT YOU OUT. AND THEY WILL, THEY'RE OUT THERE, THREE PACKS OF THEM, WAITING FOR THIS WORLD TO EMERGE FROM THE SINK. OR YOU CAN COME WITH ME AND TAKE YOUR CHANCES THAT I'M NOT A FOOL OR A LIAR. She paused and waited.

The valaad stared at her for a long minute then backed away. She heard him moving off and sighed impatiently.

Quale came striding up. "Well?"

Aleytys pressed her back against the jagged outside of the barricade; he was a hair away from explosion. "I talked to the captain, sir." She spoke quickly, her voice soft, trying to catch the submissive rhythms of Drij's habitual response to him. "It went to get others to pull back the barricade." Keeping her eyes down, hoping what she'd said was the truth, she waited, ready to use the stunner implants on him though she hoped it wouldn't be necessary.

With a quick powerful leap he came up into the lock

beside her. He grasped a protruding bar and tried to shake
the barricade loose. The effort made it rattle a little and
squeal loudly; more important, it drained off some of his
pent-up irritation. He peered into the darkness, then glared
down at her. "That bug don't come back quick, I'll kick this
thing apart, waste every bug I get my hands on and drag the
Queen out myself."

About to protest that they needed the vaada and valaada,
Aleytys bit down on her lip and swallowed the words; he had
to know that and wouldn't appreciate her reminding him, interfering with him, he'd call it, sticking her nose in where it
had no business. She watched him shake the barricade again,
then jump down and start a pair of Scavs tumbling the remaining supply cells to the ground between the carrier and
the ship. Behind her, she heard a scratching, squealing, scraping. She turned.

Through the openings in the barricade she saw bits of
vaada bodies. She touched the barricade and felt it move.
"Quale," she called. "They're clearing the lock."

He straightened, triumph in his wide, flashing grin. He
grabbed the shoulder of the man beside him. "Gebe, get that
thing . . ." he jabbed a thumb at the carrier. ". . . ready to
roll inside soon's the junk's hauled out of the way."

The barricade slid back intact, moving very slowly but
steadily until the lock was cleared and the way opened to the
inside of the ship. The darkness inside was broken as a vaad
came toward them holding a smoking torch in a hand, its
mid-arm pincers pressed tight against its thorax. It stood back
and lifted the torch above its head, ignoring the spattering
bits of hot sap that fell about it.

Aleytys started to move inside, then stopped and stood
aside for Quale. He swung up into the lock and strode past
her. He moved to the junction of the wide corridors, paced
the distance, then beckoned to Aleytys. When she reached
him, he pointed to Ksiyl standing like a shadow figure in the
flickering, uncertain light. "What's that bug saying?"

Aleytys frowned. The hand talk was widespread, used ex-
tensively between species with non-compatible speech forms.
She suspected that Quale knew it well enough to catch most
of what was being said. She stepped a little in front of him,
risking a short, emphatic warning, cutting Ksiyl off before it
could call her Hunter.

Ksiyl's signing hands faltered, then moved into a formal greeting.

"It welcomes us. If we follow, it'll take us to the Queen."

"Tell the bug to get on with it."

"It understands you, sir," she murmured. She pointed to Ksiyl who was snapping its mandibles and producing a rapid string of sounds. The vaad with the torch edged past Aleytys and moved with awkward rapidity along the echoing corridor that ran down the center of the ship. Ksiyl signed a formal request for them to follow, then swung around and moved off down the cluttered corridor with the sliding lurch of great weariness.

The ship was far more broken up inside than Aleytys had expected after seeing the nearly intact skin. The inner walls were ripped, twisted and crumpled, with debris spilling from what had been separate rooms; she found herself stepping over desiccated pieces of long dead vaada, kicking a round object that wobbled off, a vaad head. The acrid, pungent smell of unhealthy vaada was thick enough to cut, intensified by the fumes from the torch carried ahead of them. They passed several still living vaada standing in openings, dull-eyed and indifferent, their carapaces mucky and scratched, their top arms dangling limply in front of their tilted thoraxes, their mid-arms tucked up tight. Their breathing echoed in the heavy air, shrilling through the spiracles along their sides.

Aleytys trudged behind Quale, trying to fight off the despair coming from the weary vaada—weary to the point of death but they were not allowed to die—a despair that was thicker than the stench that was choking her. She remembered her briefings. No zesh pairs left.

The pairing between the neuter Haestavaada was a non-sexual but intense bond formed at the onset of maturity. The capacity to form such bonds was the mark of maturity in the neuters as puberty was for the sexed Haestavaada. The pairings were made for life. If one of the pair died, the remaining vaad usually lived less than a year, fading from life like a dried-up leaf. These vaada only lived because the Queen needed them—the Queen and the Queen's guard who were valaada, their natural leaders. If Ksiyl was any example, the valaada were in far better shape than the miserable vaada.

In the heart of the ship the vaad with the torch stopped in

front of a massive door-iris. Ksiyl halted, tilted forward until
its pincers touched the floor, then straightened and turned to
face Quale and Aleytys. TURN YOUR BACKS, it signed.

When Aleytys translated this, Quale scowled, then shrugged
and turned his back. Behind them they heard a long thrumming then felt a flooding of hot air and saw the light
around them intensify. Ksiyl touched Aleytys on the arm. She
turned and saw him stepping carefully into the dimly lit room
beyond the partly unfolded iris. Eyes glittering with greed,
Quale ducked through the small opening and straightened, his
eyes fixed on the casket that took up much of the space.
Aleytys came through behind him.

The Queen's transport room was spherical, the inner skin
able to revolve freely, a sphere inside a sphere. The Queen's
casket was suspended in the center of the room, cradled in a
nest of webbing. Two of the six guards were sitting atop the
casket, working levers that kept the air and liquids flowing
through the tubes inside. Around the room small torches were
burning in improvised holders, heating the air until the room
was like an oven. There was light enough to show the larger
details of the forms that sat beneath the casket. Three of
them. They wore ceremonial swords and energy weapons in
black leather holders on the same leather belts that held the
swords. Their armored eyes had a deep glow. They looked a
bit worn but otherwise in excellent shape. The valaad on the
end had an extra belt looped over its legs. Ksiyl touched the
top-arm fingers with this one, then took the belt and fastened
it around the lower part of its thorax.

Quale jabbed a finger at the casket. "Queen?"

Ksiyl signed: YES.

"Alive?"

YES.

After a last look at the smoky hot chamber, Quale caught
hold of Aleytys's arm. "Watch them." He pushed her away,
then disappeared into the long corridor. Aleytys heard his
heels coming down hard on the torn rubber sheathing. She
ducked out and saw with relief that he really was leaving; his
powerful body was almost lost in the shadows, but she could
feel the exultation exploding in him. He was nearly running,
so eager was he to get the Queen on the carrier and start her on
her way to the hold of his ship.

Aleytys ducked back into the room. HE'S GONE, she signed. FOR THE CARRIER.

WILL IT TAKE THE WEIGHT?

KSIYL, FRIEND. VALAADA HELPED DESIGN IT.

Ksiyl signed an apology, added a quick twist of chagrin.

Aleytys waved the apology away. THOUGH HE'LL LOAD THE QUEEN TONIGHT, HE'LL WAIT TILL MORNING TO START BACK. YOU CAN USE THE NIGHT TO GET READY ANYTHING YOU WANT TO TAKE WITH YOU. HE WON'T OBJECT TO ANYTHING THAT DOESN'T REQUIRE TOO MUCH ROOM. ONE THING. HE'S PROBA-BLY GOING TO USE YOU AS BUFFERS AGAINST NATIVE ATTACK. THERE ARE TWO GROUPS OF NATIVES OUT IN THE FOG. WE LOST OVER FIFTEEN MEN TO THEM ON THE WAY IN. She paused. THREE DAYS. IT WILL TAKE THAT LONG TO REACH THE SCAV SHIPS.

YOUR SHIP? The valaad glanced at the Queen's casket then at Aleytys.

TO CATCH THE TIKH'ASFOUR PACK OFF GUARD, I DROPPED IN A SPECIAL CAPSULE. HUNTERS KNEW THE SCAVS WERE HERE SO I PLANNED TO TAKE A SCAV SHIP OUT OF HERE.

YOU ARE ONE AGAINST MANY. The valaad took her hands, looked down at the soft flesh. It dropped them and stepped back. HOW WILL YOU TAKE A SHIP FROM THAT MAN? The last words were staccato gestures that expressed its agitation and growing distrust.

KSIYL, I DID NOT NEED TO ASK YOUR HELP. I COULD HAVE COMMANDED IT. She snapped the signs out briskly. The heat in the room, the heavy still air thick with the acrid smell of the valaada, the knowledge that Quale was due back in minutes, these irritations ate away at her temper until she was on the point of exploding, scrapping her plan and taking con-trol into her own hands; only an uneasy suspicion that con-trolling so many through the treacheries of the mistlands was more than she could take on held her back from acting im-pulsively. I AM HUNTER AND HALF-VRYHH, KSIYL. AND NOT A FOOL! MY LIFE IS AT RISK HERE TOO.

Its four eyes were fixed on her for several minutes. She couldn't read its expressionless immobile face, but caught snatches of curiosity, then a sudden flash of understanding. Its signing hands lifted, hung still, then moved through quick signs. YOU WERE THE HUNTER ON THE HAREWORLD?

YES. YOU KNOW OF THAT?

THE VALAADA HAVE HEARD.

SAY NOTHING OF THIS TO THE MAN. She hesitated, then began signing slowly, extending her gestures to add weight to her words. THE WAY IS PREPARED, KSIYL. WALK IT WITH ME.

The valaad performed a bow of honoring. WE WILL FOLLOW YOUR PATH, it signed. It turned away and went to talk with the other valaada. When they heard the rattle of the carrier, two of the valaada moved to the entrance and used their eight arms to muscle a wheel around, dialing the opening large enough to bring the carrier in—and out with the casket.

Quale strode through, noted the change. He stood beside Aleytys and watched the shambling vaada work the carrier in place under the casket, then lower it, the two valaada on top imperturbably continuing to work the life-support. When it was settled, he walked over to it and laid his hand possessively on the smooth golden metal, a great black beast claiming his prey, for the moment draining color and force from the others in the room by the suffocating power of rage and desire held in a precarious control—black beast and shimmering golden casket in the uncertain light from the torches.

The valaada were caught for a moment in the spell, then Quale grinned and with the grin lost his dominance, shrinking abruptly from demiurge to merely human. Ksiyl moved, then stilled as Aleytys flashed it a warning sign. With the torchlight glittering in its bulging eyes, it moved its head in a quick circle, clicking out a command to the guards to back against the curving wall. Quale patted the casket a last time, then strolled back to Aleytys and took her arm, his fingers tightening until he drew a murmur of protest from her.

Satisfied, he hauled her into the thick blackness of the corridor. She went with him without further protest, wondering if he still needed her enough to offset his growing irritation. No light at all came back this far from outside but he surged ahead, his feet scuffing and thumping on the rubbery compound that sheathed the passage. She could hear her own breath coming harsh and too quickly in the stillness around them that was as thick and unnerving as the stench of the disintegrating vaada hanging about everywhere.

The blackness grayed a little as she turned the corner and moved toward the lock. Near the opening he jerked her to a stop. She rubbed at her arm where his fingers had left bruises; watching him take a stance in the pale circle of light with one arm extended, hand closed around the rim, the other hand fisted on his hip, she wondered what he was up to and, with a bit more apprehension, what he was planning for her. Moving as quietly as she could, she edged closer to the lock.

The pile of supply cells was a white blotch in the swirling mist that had closed in tight about the ship. The Scavs were dark smudges fading in and out of view as the fog between them and the ship bunched and thinned. A faint glow came through the mist from the Sinkweb but it was dimmer than ever. *Not much time left,* she thought. *We're coming out of the Sink.*

A stone arced through the mist and whanged against the metal close to Quale's hand. He cursed but didn't move. More stones splatted down around the crouching Scavs. Two didn't seem to notice; the other three began firing blindly at the point where the stones were coming from. After a moment more of this, as if by mutual consent, the stone bombardment and the shooting stopped.

"Stinking greenies."

Aleytys glanced up at Quale. The rock throwers weren't Amar. She considered telling him, then the thought of what his reaction would be to unasked-for comment from her started her laughing. She choked down the giggles, her breath coming in little snorts.

Quale cursed again, dropped his hand and strode back into the corridor beyond the lock. He paced back and forth, muttering, his nostrils flaring with disgust at the stench. Abruptly he was beside her, his hands closing around her waist; the urge to laugh left her and she tensed. Before she could do more, he lifted her and dropped her to the ground outside.

Off balance when she landed, she staggered forward a few steps, nearly kicking into the supply cells. She wheeled to face him as he jumped down, starting the muscle-jerk sequence that would activate the stunner implants in her left hand.

He nodded at the supply cells. "Haul those inside. Stinking hole, but it'll keep the greenies off our backs." Without waiting for an answer, dismissing her attack crouch as a cover of fear, he walked toward the Scavs.

Uncertain as to whether she was more annoyed or relieved, Aleytys relaxed her hands. She hefted one of the cells then

stood watching the Scavs. Gollez had lost his chance in the
lottery about midday when he'd stepped on a patch of grass
and was sucked under too fast for the nearest man to haul
him out. Szor went next, then the Scav who'd mocked at
Herz, then two of the Ortels—falling to another hidden hot
spring under a skin of rock, to a bush with attendant fliers
who swarmed over one of the Ortels, penetrating to his
flesh in spite of the armor of chitin plates, to single arrows
coming from the mist. Five left. One man had his arm in an
improvised sling and a garish bruise on his forehead. He was
sullen, responding to Quale's prodding with angry grunts. The
remaining Ortel crouched apart, staring at the ground, ignored by the others as profoundly as he ignored them.

Drij came out of the mist. "What's happening, Lee?"

I forgot about her, Aleytys thought guiltily. "Help me get
the cells inside." She started for the lock. "He wants us to
spend the night inside. In the morning we'll be heading back
with the Queen and the vaada and valaada still alive." She
tossed the cell into the lock and turned back. "With a little
luck we'll be out of this hell soon."

"I'll believe that when I'm standing in front of the shelter
gate." Drij picked up two of the smaller cells and stood
watching Aleytys come back for another load. "They trusted
you, the guards?"

"I had the right words." Aleytys chuckled, then frowned as
she tried to balance three cells that were just too large for
comfortable holding. She started slowly for the lock with Drij
pacing beside her. "And Ksiyl knew my name."

Aleytys moved stiffly into the opening and stood, stretching
and yawning, trying to revive sufficiently to face the emerging
day. The sun was a greenish blur on the eastern horizon; the
morning was already hot and steamy. She pulled at her tunic
to coax a bit of breeze against her skin. A small stone
whooshed into the opening, skimmed past her knee and
landed with a muted thumping on the resilient mat just beyond the lock. She probed the mist, finding a single life-spark
retreating without haste or concern. *Saying good morning*,
she thought, smiling. The smile faded. The two sets of enemies were waiting out in the mist, one to the east, the other
to the west, waiting for the demons to emerge. Overhead the
floating ghosts drifted about, attracted to her but still wary.

Out in the clearing the head of the vaad-body moved suddenly, staring at her out of vacant holes where its eyes had been. She started, then swore. The body was moving in tiny rapid jerks; lines of large flat insects were burrowing into the rotting flesh through breaks in the chitin. She shivered. This was the natural ecology of life and death but it was too strong a reminder of the fragility of her own body.

Hearing movement behind her, she jumped down to watch as a number of vaad appeared in the lock, carrying long strips of a light-metal wall boarding. They maneuvered the strips out the lock and let the ends fall to make a ramp of sorts. They piled more of the strips on top until they had a fairly sturdy incline from the lip of the lock to the ground.

Quale came out, stomped on the ramp, moved down it, stood looking back up. Finally he nodded. "Right. Kelling, get the bug and send the thing down. Move it fast. That ramp won't hold long."

The Scav acknowledged the order and disappeared inside. The nose of the carrier appeared beyond the lock. The tongue was tied up, the nose shifting about as if sniffing for the ramp. More and more of the carrier emerged until it finally tilted down, the front wheels finding the metal strips. The ramp groaned beneath the weight, began to creak and sag. Quale jumped closer, yelled, "Faster. It's breaking up."

The carrier came hissing down the ramp, the front several wheels reaching the ground before the ramp collapsed. The axles groaned and the carrier bed bounced sluggishly, nearly unseating the two guards still working the life-support on top of the casket.

Standing a little apart, watching the valaada move about the carrier and the vaada carry from the ship a number of curved sections of metal—shields to fend off the stones that came unopposed and at unpredictable intervals—Aleytys saw Drij move slowly into the lock. She stood watching the flurry of movement past her and around the carrier, her shoulders sagging a little. She looked weary and afraid. All of this was none of her business, she'd been dragged into it and forced to abandon the work which was the center of her life. There was no way the Amar would accept her if she stayed. Without Aleytys's help she'd even have to abandon her notes and collection of artifacts. Aleytys edged through the shambling

vaada and stopped by the lock, waiting until Drij noticed her.
Meeting the dark, tired eyes, she said, "It'll be over soon."

Drij shrugged, squatted. She started to speak, then winced
as several stones came from the mist, damaging two of the
vaada because they were too clumsy to move fast enough to
avoid them and because their chitin was brittle and thin after
months of slow dying. As he'd done before, Quale dispatched
them with a shot through the head, giving them even less
time and attention than he had spared the wounded men. He
waved six of the strongest vaada to the front of the carrier
and saw them buckled into the harness. Drij stared at the
sprawled bodies, wiping nervously at her mouth. "That's what
he's going to do with us."

Aleytys closed her hand over Drij's shoulder, feeling partly
sympathetic and partly annoyed with her. *Too many things
coming at her*, she thought. *What can I say? Nothing, I suppose*. She stood beside Drij, watching Quale as he got the
procession organized, spreading the Scavs around in a thin
circle with the one-armed man in front, saw that they all
hefted the shields and got them settled as comfortably as possible, with a stone or two from the mist to underline his instructions. The Queen's guard arranged themselves two on
each side of the casket. Quale checked the casket, shoving at
it and watching it rock slightly on the webbing. It was stable
enough, its weight pressing the webbing down into the brac-
ing struts, lowering the center of gravity so the carrier rode
more easily than before. He ran his hand along the finish
then stepped back. "Move out."

The multiple wheels biting at the coarse earth, the carrier
started smoothly forward as the six vaada leaned into the
harness, set moving by a clicked command from Ksiyl. Quale
watched a minute, then called Aleytys and Drij to him with
an impatient snap. He stabbed a finger at the rear of the carrier. "Follow if you want. Don't get in the way." Dismissing
them, he turned and loped for the front of the carrier as it
began threading past the ragged brush at the edge of the
clearing.

Drij stared gloomily at her boots. "I told you. He's through
with us."

"So?" Aleytys began pulling her after the carrier. "Does
that mean we curl up and die?" She edged through the plodding vaada and came up behind the carrier. "I have surprises

left, friend." She considered telling Drij what she intended. *She wouldn't believe me. Her creed is rationalism. Everything is explainable eventually, even things that seem to defy known rules. A year from now she'll have all this settled to her satisfaction. Wonder where I'll be a year from now? A ship. Head will have the Haestavaada tied tight. If I get the Queen to them, I'll have my ship. Drij has been a good friend. I've paid for my sanctuary but there's a lot she did she didn't have to. Gray's had to put up with a mountain of idiocy from me. A year from now. . . .* A flare of hate in the mist gave her a moment's warning. She saw the stone flying at her head and jerked aside, almost grateful for being aroused from her confusion. She tugged Drij around to the far side of the casket where they'd have a little protection from the stones. The shields provided by the valaada began clanging musically under the bombardment. Aleytys sneaked a look around the casket. The stones were targeted at the dangerous ones, the Scavs and the Queen's guard, though a few fell among the uneven lines of trudging vaada, leaving two of them curled up on the stony soil, the others stepping dully over them. Abruptly the attack was over. Protected by the shields, none of the Scavs had bothered to fire back so the halt to the bombardment was as inexplicable as the beginning of it was unpredictable.

Trudging once more behind the carrier, Aleytys faced the unpalatable realization that she could very easily be killed by a rock she didn't see coming. *Absurd to survive so much and fall to a stupid rock.* She glanced at Drij. *Do something . . . has to be something I can do. I refuse to be killed by a rock.* She giggled at the thought then sobered. *Nowhere did existence or chance or whatever it was that directed lives promise dignified endings. What are they doing now? Wonder if I can scare them off?* She searched the mist for the rock-throwers, touched them, touched a seething mass of fear and hatred. She jerked away then forced her outreach back and began to explore the tantalizing bits of information she teased from beneath the suffocating passions that nearly obscured everything else about them. There was a suggestion that they were more animal than man, yet there was purpose in what they did, a purpose beyond merely the drive of instinct. And her probing began to make them uneasy; she felt the individual sparks moving closer, almost merging as she pressed them, trying to discover what they would do if she caught hold of and amplified their fear. *Flee or fight?* The wrong trigger would bring hell down on them all. She focused more and more intently on her probing until she failed to notice a coiling root that caught her boot toe and brought her flailing to the earth, confused and disoriented for a moment.

"Lee! What. . . ." Drij knelt beside her, anxiously.

"Help me up." Still a little shaken, Aleytys lifted her face from the dirt and, with Drij's assistance, got back on her feet. She leaned on the dark woman as the vaada split around them, paying no more attention to them than they would to any obstruction that had to be circled and left behind.

Aleytys brushed at the grit clinging to her palms, bleeding at small cuts from the sharp gravel she'd plunged into. She rubbed her hands together to get the last of the gravel from the wounds, suppressing an urge to gasp with the pain of it. She *reached* and the black power-water flowed into her, knitting the flesh into a smooth whole again. With a small satisfied sigh, she began dusting the sand and debris off her clothing.

Drij caught hold of Aleytys's left hand, turned it palm up, and ran her own fingertips over the unmarked flesh, scratching with the nail of her forefinger at traces of blood from wounds that no longer existed.

Aleytys grinned at her. "Seeing things?"

Drij dropped the left hand and inspected the right. With a shake of her head she stepped back. "I think so." She glanced at the carrier disappearing into shifting mists that had already swallowed the Scavs and the Guard, then looked nervously at half-seen bushes and jutting outcroppings of rock. "We have to catch up." With Aleytys striding beside her, she moved at an anxious trot toward the illusory safety ahead.

When they were walking more comfortably at the slow pace of the carrier, Drij touched Aleytys's arm. "What were you trying to do?"

Aleytys rubbed at her nose. "Survive. It hadn't really occurred to me before that one of those damn rocks could kill me. Hurt I don't mind. I can fix that easy enough." She chuckled at the expression on Drij's face, a compound of distress, disbelief, and reluctant acknowledgment that she had seen something she couldn't explain. "Lend me your arm a while to see I don't walk into anything?"

With Drij mystified but complying, Aleytys *reached* again for the mistlanders. They were moving closer, spread out in a long line that her outreach saw like a procession of torches bobbing nearer and nearer. She started probing again, throwing snatches of fear at them in quick light touches.

The life-sparks bunched together. She tried a stronger projection, taking their own fear and amplifying it and sending back. As the thrust touched the life-sparks, they flared back and started racing toward her, radiating triumph and rage. Hastily Aleytys dropped that projection, assembled a combination of negation and anger and hurled that at them.

The life-sparks dimmed like gale-blown torches, huddled together, radiating uncertainty and pain.

Trembling with fatigue, Aleytys leaned heavily on Drij and tried to reach for her healing water, but the draining effect of the Sink that still affected her capriciously—never giving warning that her accommodation with it was about to be breached—left her with a profound lassitude that made the least effort more than she could endure. Drij seemed to sense this; she supported Aleytys with her arm, taking most of her weight for several minutes until Aleytys regained her strength. Again Drij realized what was happening almost as soon as the change took place in Aleytys. She pulled away, glanced repeatedly at Aleytys as she trudged beside her through the shifting veils of mist, trying to understand what she was seeing.

As the morning slid away, the mistlanders and the Amar drifted along at the edge of her outreach, keeping even with the carrier but hanging back. Her touches fed her a sense of confusion and dissensions among the Amar and a rising anger in the mistlanders. At times they started to converge on the carrier, she would tense, then they'd back off. They kept her nervously alert the whole day until her temper was cocked to explode at a word or a touch.

Quale kept them going until the light was gone, then bullied the staggering vaada into digging trenches and throwing up banks of earth. Prowling about unable to stand still, nervous and tense, he snapped his fingers at two of the Scavs and set them to putting up the shelter. Cursing, stopping now and then to stare into the fog, appearing and disappearing as he moved about, he passed Aleytys and Drij several times without seeming to see them.

"I'm hungry," Aleytys said abruptly and started for the pyramid of supply cells at the front end of the carrier. "There are some packets of food for the vaada there."

Drij caught her arm. "Don't. Lee, he'll. . . ."

Aleytys jerked free. "Let him try," she snapped. She left Drij a silent reproachful figure in the mist and started digging among the cells, feeling for the marks that identified the Haestavaada food. She found one, threw it to the valaad standing quietly beside the carrier and continued rummaging about, scattering the cells carelessly as she hunted. She heard a roar behind her and turned to face Quale. He grabbed for her and she ducked away then stumbled to a stop, gaping, as a horde of silent, grimacing beasts—six-legged, horrendously fanged, covered with stiff gray-white hair—exploded from the mists. Quale wheeled, his rifle snapping up. He got off a few shots before the knob end of a long club came down first on his arm, then, as he leaped at the mistlander, on his head. Aleytys backed against one of the wheels, frowned and tried to assemble a negation, but she wasn't ready and it took too long. She grabbed for Quale's rifle. A thrown club whistled past her head. With a startled yelp she dropped to the ground and started crawling toward Quale. A gray-white mistlander leaped at her. She rolled onto her back and slammed her boot into his belly, sending him arcing over her to crash into the ground. Before she heard the thud, she had wriggled back onto her stomach and was reaching out for the rifle.

The knob crashed down on her head, there was an instant of shock—then nothing.

THE HUNT

CHAPTER VIII   Aleytys

Aleytys came drifting up out of blackness with a grinding pain in her head and stubs jabbing into her back. She became dimly aware she was tied to something. As her head cleared, she pulled at the ropes, throwing her body from side to side. Almost immediately she was aware of another body tied with her to the knobby pole. Relaxing as much as she could, she eased her head around.

Broad shoulders and fine black hair with a white streak, a section of scarred cheek. Quale. And they were tied to the roughly stripped trunk of a dead tree, a tree far larger than any of the spindly growths she could see around them, with a stone-hard wood she couldn't dent even with boot heels. She leaned her head against the wood and closed her eyes. Drawing in a breath, she started to reach for her power-water, but a gentle tickling drifted across her face and neck, drawing away the pain, leaving behind a pleasant lassitude. She sagged against the ropes.

"Lee!" The soundless call roared through her head. "Freyka! Get it together!"

Aleytys struggled to focus on the angry black eyes, the shouting that was bouncing around inside her head. A scowling scarred face came together around the eyes. Then the tickling trailed over her again and she lost interest.

"Freyka, dammit, floating ghost. . . ." Abruptly the image faded.

A darkness dropped over her, a vast *hungry* darkness that held her immobile and woke in her a terror that grew as she felt Quale wake, felt *his* shock and horror. The misty sphere held them both, a floating ghost bigger than any she'd seen before. Abruptly it pulsed, sucked at them both. Swardheld was jarred loose. She felt him drawn from her, tried to cry out her anguish, tried to reach out and draw him back. The

147

ghost pulsed again. A pattern of forces frozen into being by the power of the diadem, the weaponsmaster started to dissipate then shelled over, fighting assimilation successfully for the moment. Then Aleytys was fighting too; angry and afraid, she rooted her being in her body, struggled to close a shell about herself as Swardheld had done. Pulsing and radiating a great frustration, the ghost abandoned them for the moment—though the darkness stayed clamped around her head and shoulders—and peeled Quale from his body; she felt the flush of new strength in the beast, heard Quale's silent dying scream. Then the pressure was back.

She burned with rage, lunged with her mind for her black river, her power source she'd never understood but used anyway. The water poured into her, filled her and she directed the force at the ghost.

With the ghost distracted, Swardheld broke free and dived into the handiest receptacle—Quale's empty moribund body.

Freed from worry about him, Aleytys struck harder at the ghost, slamming a thundering negation at it, pouring power into it until she was burning red-hot.

The floating ghost was blasted into shards small as buckshot, spraying out in all directions. With a thousand tiny screams they fled, bobbing through the mist, radiating pain and terror, tongues of foam racing from the creature who terrified them.

Drained by that blast, Aleytys sagged against the ropes, her chin dropping onto her chest. Her headache was gone, but her wrists still hurt. Closing her eyes, she hung limp until the ropes started cutting into her, then she straightened and let her head fall against the dead tree. Finally, she *reached* and called at the same time, "Swardheld?" She waited a moment. "You all right?"

Her reach touched coldness. Driven by a sudden fear she probed deeper, gasped with horror. The Quale/Swardheld entity was dying. She snatched back the power, pooled it within her, wriggled about until she could press the fingers of one hand against his wrist, then let the power pool stream out of her into the cooling body, let the black water drain through her, expending her power recklessly. She didn't try to direct it; she had no idea how to heal that strange amalgam tied to the post with her, simply let the deep instinct work, sinking, as it did so, into a mindless contemplation of the ground around her feet.

Slowly she felt the tension and electricity of life come back to the flesh beneath her fingertips. The wrist moved. Wearily she loosed the power and waited.

Swardheld moved Quale's body, cleared Quale's throat. He fit uneasily into the man, though the diadem had given him some practice in controlling strange bodies; slowly and warily he was extending his control.

Aleytys was happy suddenly without knowing quite why. Not simply because Swardheld lived. No, not simply that; there was more, a complex feeling that she was too tired to examine just now. Pressing her back against the pole to take some of the weight off her trembling knees, she closed her eyes; she could forget about Quale with her eyes closed. "Swardheld?"

With warmth flooding her body, she heard a rusty, tentative chuckle. He cleared his throat again, then spoke slowly, forming the sounds with unready lips so that the words slurred a little, but his amusement and astonishment came through. "You do bring us these little surprises, Lee."

Forgetting entirely about their precarious position, she laughed happily. "Are you all right, my friend? Are you really all right? How do you feel?"

"Startled."

"Do you mind too much?"

"Suddenly acquiring mortality? At least you got me a good body." He straightened, pulled tentatively at the ropes. "It takes some getting used to, the idea of growing old after so many years. . . ." He fell silent a moment, sucking in lungfuls of the pungent steamy air. "To smell things again, to feel and taste . . . to go where I want and when . . . ah!" He laughed. "Right now, freyka-min, it's a damn good feeling, even if I am tied to some damn post in the middle of a stinking volcanic swamp."

"Is there anything of him left?" As she listened with some trepidation for the answer, she began wriggling about trying to reach one of the knots.

"No." The curt negative cut off any further exploration of that question. "What are you doing?"

"Knots."

"Getting anywhere?"

She twisted as far as she could, then relaxed, breathing hard. "No. Damn."

Swardheld started moving. She could hear the soft rasp of the ropes over his clothing, then a grunt of interest. "They got the belt knife but looks like zippers don't mean much to them. There's something in the side pocket of this jacket. The tab's close to your fingers. Think you could get it open? Stylus maybe. Just about anything could help."

"Right." While he worked as close to her fingers as he could, Aleytys scraped her back across the stubs and won an inch of play in the ropes wound around her torso. She strained toward the tab, caught it between her fingers, then eased it down. "Got the pocket. Now . . ." When she worked her fingers in past the scratchy tracks of the zipper, she just managed to touch a long cool object that nestled in the bottom of the pocket. Holding her breath, she struggled for the additional half inch she needed—and failed to get it. Trembling with the effort, she eased back on the ropes so she could catch her breath and let some of the pain fade. "Swardheld."

"What?"

"I'm a half inch short."

He said nothing. After a moment she heard and felt him moving. The trunk they were tied to grew gradually smaller in circumference as it rose from the ground. Aleytys had already taken advantage of this as much as she could, stopped by the jutting stub of a low branch that at present was poking painfully into her hip. Swardheld edged closer until he too was stopped by that stub. "Try again."

This time she had no difficulty fishing the object from the pocket. Stretching her neck she managed to see it. She grinned. "Luck's changing, old growler. Dainty little pocket knife. Relax while I start sawing at these damn ropes."

He rested his head against the trunk. "Don't want to worry you, Lee, but I got a feeling there's more coming at us."

"Ummh." She looked about. The mist had closed in thick around them; although there was enough light from the Sink-web to make out things close at hand, the darkness a few feet out was impenetrable. A brisk wind blew a medley of smells past her; the sweet-sour stench of the mistlanders was unmistakable, mingling with a smell that was similar but different enough to be disturbing. "Right."

Working with careful small movements, Aleytys managed

to get the knife unfolded. The blade proved to be irritatingly dull and the ropes tougher than they looked, but she managed to cut through the rope around Swardheld's wrists, then began using the point to pick at one of the loops around her hips. Intent on what she was doing, she missed at first the increasing pungency of the air and a low murmur that gradually became a melange of whistles, squeals and a pattering like a heavy rain. When the noise became too loud to ignore, she lifted her head and stared into the mist.

The mistlander was a vague shape that grew sharper in outline as he came closer. He held a bundle tucked into the curve of a mid-arm that he dipped into again and again, dropping gobbets of bloody meat to the ground behind him. Mouth gaping in silent panting laughter, he dropped the rest of the bloody bundle at Aleytys's feet, then loped off. Aleytys sniffed at the breeze, then started sawing frantically at the rope, her hands shaking, horror mounting sour in her throat.

"What is it?" His hands free, Swardheld had been fumbling awkwardly at the ropes, making little progress since he wasn't solidly in command of the body he wore. "Calm down, Lee, or you'll lose the knife."

"No time." Her voice was strained. "The mistlander. Baiting a swarm here. Kinya-kin-kin. Remember them?'" She glanced up. "My god, I can see the scouts." She slashed at the rope, missed, hit the stub by her hip. Her fingers flew open and the knife sailed into the mist.

THE HUNT

CHAPTER IX   Roha

"Kill them." Roha paced beside Churr, shoulders slumping, as she tried without much hope to stir him into action. She felt the tiredness in the men moving silently behind her, a tiredness that was more in the will than in their bodies. The turning of the demons back toward the outside, the presence of the mistlanders and their attacks on the demons that were surrogates for Amar activities, these things drained them of their resolution. There was no need for them here. What they had come to do was being done without them. This sense of futility touched Roha too. More and more she found herself thinking of the sun shining on the water, the trees, of the children running through the stilts that held the houses up to the wandering breezes, of the tree that was her sister, of the sticky acrid sap that sent her spirit winging, of the Wan's smiles and stories, of the smells and sounds and sights that had filled her life until this time when things fell apart. The poison in the Mother was spreading farther and farther, rotting the world as she knew it until everything familiar was melting away from her. Her center was gone. Rihon was dead. But she had to force herself to remember this—that he was dead, that the demons had killed him. She had to scourge her spirit over and over to raise her anger from her grief.

When Churr set the others to making camp, Roha watched a while, then left, moving cautiously through the mist, slowly at first, then more quickly, driven to recklessness by an anguish that choked her, born of the wall growing between her and the warriors. She left slowly because she'd expected someone to call out to her or try to stop her—at least Churr. She couldn't understand how his care for her had eroded so completely. But no one called. She was outside their circle now, a reminder of death and defeat. Her place was gone.

Pain shot through her leg as a strangle vine lurched out of

152

the mist and coiled about her ankle. She crashed to her knees, dazed for a moment, then she was thrashing wildly about, trying to tear free as the vine sank hollow thorns into her flesh. Panting and afraid, she crawled away as far as she could, but she wasn't strong enough to pull free. She whipped around, stone knife in hand, and slashed at the tough writhing vine. The blade slid futilely over the slick surface, mangling a few side tendrils but doing little more damage. She grabbed the stem and tried to pull it loose, but it was too strong. Finally she tried pushing at it using both hands and her other foot. Inch by inch, she forced it down over her foot, then scrambled frantically away as it lashed out for her.

She limped on, moving more carefully now, exhausted by the struggle and the itching poison from the vine, drained of emotion, driven forward by inertia and a lingering curiosity. Having nothing to go back to it was easier simply to keep going toward the demons.

She heard them when she was still too far to see them, talking and working, busy about setting up their own camp. She crept up the far side of an upthrust of moss-slimed rock and eased her head cautiously over the top.

Through the thickening darkening strands of mist blown across the rocky clearing she watched the big demon move from point to point. Absently she curled up, scratching now and then at the small stinging cuts on her ankles, watching the demons from the Egg casting up banks of rock and earth, watching the Nafa and the Fire-hair talking, quarrelling, she thought, watching the Fire-hair break away and start digging through the thick-skinned eggs on the long rolling thing, watching as the sky-killer came roaring after her.

When the mistlanders came out of the mists to attack, she crouched lower on the rock, watching with a touch of agony as her brother's killer went down under a mistlander's club. She pressed her hand against her mouth, teeth clamping down on her forefinger to keep her pain inside, as the mistlanders picked up the body of the sky-killer and trotted off with it, followed by others carrying the Fire-hair on their backs. The fight broke off and all the mistlanders melted into the darkness.

In the shattered camp the survivors began coming out, standing up and looking around with a dazed disbelief. Dead demons lay at ·their feet like discarded husks. The Nafa

walked slowly from one of the dead to another, looking at
them, touching them. All the demons from the Nafa's house,
all the sky-killers but the one carried off by the mistlanders,
they were dead. The smaller demons from the Egg sat about
among their own dead, many dead, more than half. The taller demons that stayed near the long rolling thing held the
sky-killers' spitting sticks. Roha sniffed at the breeze and
thought she could smell pride and strength boiling off from
them. She scratched at her ankle again as the Nafa walked to
them and began signing to them. *If Churr and the warriors
were here,* she thought, *they could kill all the demons. And
Mother Earth could be free and whole. And things could be
the same again.* She closed her eyes and bit down on her
forefinger to stifle the wail of desire and grief that swelled in
her throat. Swallowing and swallowing, she slid down the
rock not caring that her kilt tore and was stained by the slick
green moss, not caring that the slime clung in long ragged
streaks to her skin. She couldn't bear to look at the demons
any longer.

On the ground, she stood brushing at her torso wondering
what she should do. Hunger was an ache in her stomach but
she felt sicker when she thought of going back to Churr. She
stroked her fingers up and down the leather-wound bone hilt
of her knife and thought of the sky-killer. *I will kill him,* she
thought. *Churr doesn't matter any more. I will kill him.* This
was a new thought and startled her a little. Fighting and killing were men's work; she closed her fingers tight around the
hilt, shivering with a fearful excitement as she stepped onto
tabooed ground in her mind. "I will kill him," she said aloud.
Saying the words made the thought real, not a fever-dream.
She began to circle the clearing, casting about for the lingering stench of the mistlanders, repeating over and over under
her breath, "I will, I will, I will, I will. . . ."

A width of trampled earth marked their passage, as easy to
follow as the bed of a dry stream. She ran along it, eager to
find the brotherkiller, her blood throbbing in her ears, the
words beating in her mind though she no longer said them: *I
will kill him. My brother, I will send his ghost to you.* The
fog darkened around her. She slowed, trotted along, stooped
over so she could see their traces, slowed further until she
moved in a crouch. She was almost on the trussedup pair in
the clearing before she saw them.

She backed off a few steps. The Fire-hair and the brother-killer were tied to a dead tree trunk, a tree that, alive, must have towered even through the mists. She couldn't have reached around it with the full span of her arms. Feeling cold and unready, her passion in ashes, Roha fingered the knife, trying to gain strength to draw it out. Now that she was here and he was in front of her, what seemed such a simple answer to her need suddenly was not so simple after all. She backed away another two steps, listened, then fled to the shelter of a thin line of brush.

Three dark shadows loomed ominously in the mists, awkward and misshapen because they were walking on midarms and legs. Roha pressed herself harder against the earth as she saw the huge floating ghost they were driving before them. She gaped at it. The empty sphere was as tall as she was. The mistlanders pushed it at the demons, watched as it settled over their heads, then lallopped off with that curious lumbering four-legged gait.

Shuddering with cold fear, furious with herself for not doing what she'd come to do, Roha forced herself to her feet and across the clearing until she was standing in front of the brotherkiller. He stirred. Through the watery transparency of the ghost she saw his eyes open, his face twist in horror then go blank. His body slumped against the ropes. For a moment, she felt a glorious exultation, then she was empty, her triumph shriveled to nothing. No matter what, Rihon was still dead. No matter what, the Amar warriors wouldn't speak to her. She stared at the demon's limp body for a long time, then blinked.

The ghost was convulsing, throbbing. Roha ran to the other side of the tree. The Fire-hair was glowing in a red-gold aura, her face ugly with strain, her body taut with her struggle.

The ghost exploded. Fled. Roha shrieked and fled the clearing as the force reached out from the Fire-hair and brought unbearable pain; she was burning. . . .

She ran until she slammed into a spindly tree. For some minutes she stood shuddering, gradually realizing that she was by some miracle still alive. She slid her hands over her arms and torso. The pain was gone. Her skin was smooth. She rubbed and rubbed at her arms, then turned and went slowly back to the clearing.

The Fire-hair was working frantically with a small knife,

trying to cut the ropes that bound her to the tree. Roha stood hidden in the mist, fury building in her again as she saw the brotherkiller moving and alive again. She didn't understand it, but she knew what she was seeing. And hearing. She swung her head and saw the kin scouts scurrying toward the demon. Beyond them she could hear the squeak-punctuated grumble of the swarm. The Fire-hair gave a despairing cry. Roha swung back to see the demon's hands falling, her eyes fixed on ground where the small knife appeared and disappeared as the Web-light touched it through shifting knots of the mist. Roha sucked in her breath, feeling a fierce satisfaction. Then she saw the brother-killer's hands at the ropes that bound him to the trunk. Horrified, she saw one strand snap, heard the demon's grunting release of tension. He worked one arm loose. She saw him start to strain again then turned away. The Fire-hair was still staring at the knife, her brows drawn together, her face taut with effort. As Roha watched, shaking with a growing rage and frustration, she saw a circlet of flowers shimmer into solidity around her head, the jewel centers chiming with strong pure notes. *Rihon,* Roha thought. *They'll get away. They'll get away. . . .* Her claws tapped against the leather winding of her knife hilt. *No. I won't. . . .* She gasped. The Fire-hair had twisted around, opening out her bound hands, the fingers extending like flower petals. The little shiny knife shot upward and slapped into the cup of her hands. The demon closed her fingers around the handle and began sawing again at the ropes. "No!" Roha plunged at the sky-killer, her own knife in her hands, throwing herself on the bearded demon. He brought an elbow up and smashed it into her chest, shoving her violently away. As she struggled to catch herself, she stepped on a rounded stone, turned her ankle and fell awkwardly with her foot twisted under her. She felt and heard a small crack like a twig breaking. When she tried to stand, her leg buckled under her.

The shrieking and crunching of the Kinya-kin-kin was loud and close. The soldier kin came running across the open space and threw themselves on the Fire-hair. Most of these first slid off again, defeated by the toughness of her clothing and boots. A few found purchase enough to cling; these were working slowly up her struggling body, moving toward the soft flesh of her neck and face. Then the whole swarm was there, kin climbing on top of kin, leaping higher and higher, snapping in air inches from vulnerable hands and head.

The sky-killer worked with awkward strength, tearing at the weakened ropes. Cursing and staggering, he at last came away from the trunk. Kicking at the swarming kin, tearing them off him, knocking them aside as they jumped at him, he started on the Fire-hair's ropes.

Roha gasped as teeth sank into her leg. Ignoring the agony in her ankle, she began crawling away, crying out as the kin bit into her, ground their teeth in her flesh. She was dead, but she refused to lie down. She wouldn't die here, not in the same place with the demons.

Hands struck aside some of the kin. Strong arms lifted her, carried her at a jolting run from the horde. The kin with their teeth sunk in her flesh were still gnawing at her, working deeper and deeper into her body. The pain was beyond anything she'd ever experienced; it was a totality blocking out everything else—she didn't even wonder who or what was carrying her.

She was laid on the ground. One by one the kin were taken off her. She could feel searing touches as if they were burned off. Her blood was dripping from her. She grew weaker. Her eyelids were too heavy to lift though tears slid from the corners of her eyes and ran down the sides of her face into her ears. Hands were laid on her. Gentle and warm, they hurt terribly, pulling a whining cry from her as she felt them on her stomach and chest.

Warmth flowed from them, washing away the pain until it was a distant thing like someone calling to her from a great distance whose words she couldn't make out. For the first time since this string of odd events had begun, she could consider her dying, could decide she didn't want to die, not as uselessly as this, not with so much left unfinished.

Anguish in her voice as much from despair as it was from remembered pain, she cried out and opened her eyes. The Fire-hair was bent over her, her hair falling in shining wings on either side of a face lit by the glow from a golden circlet of delicate blooms that sang in a series of faint notes like drops of water falling. Strength flowed into Roha with the warmth from the hands pressing down on her. She lifted her head a little and stared down the length of her body, then gasped, blinked, lay back in confusion staring at the softly

shining trails of mist drifting by overhead. The holes gnawed
in her by the kin were closing rapidly; even the short time
she'd watched she'd seen the flesh growing together. She was
beginning to itch; she twitched about then scratched at the
worst spots.

The brother-killer came and caught her hands, held them
down at her sides. She couldn't endure having him touch her.
Crying out, she struggled to wrench herself free but the man
held her so easily she lay back and wept her fury and frustration, not even noticing when the itching went away. Then the
Fire-hair said something to the other demon and he stepped
back until he was a blur in the mists.

The circle of flowers fading quickly into nothing, the Fire-
hair bent over Roha. Though she smiled and her hands were
still very gentle as she touched the faint markings on Roha's
smooth torso, she looked desperately tired. She'd been bitten
too, there were a number of small wounds on her hands. Satisfied with her examination, she settled back on her heels and
watched calmly as Roha sat up. "Go home, child," she said.

Roha stared. "You know Amar speech?" The Fire-hair
smiled mockingly as if to say she was a holder of power with
nothing beyond her. Roha nodded. *It is true*, she thought.
Then the demon's face changed again. After a moment, she
reached out to touch the center of Roha's chest. "Go home,
little Roha. You don't know what you're mixing in here."
The sense of power held in check was gone; her smile and
voice were gentle and caring. Roha whimpered and rolled
away, angry, confused and afraid. She jumped to her feet,
glanced from the squatting Fire-hair to the nebulous darkness
that was the mist-shrouded brother-killer sky-demon. Back
and forth her eyes moved until she was dizzy. Forgetting the
need for caution in this world of hidden threat, she darted
away a few steps without bothering where she put her feet,
stopped, wheeled and looked back.

The sky-killer was holding out a hand to the Fire-hair,
helping her to her feet. Roha passed her hands over the chest
that was whole again because of what the demon had done.
She looked at the woman standing with her hand on the
killer's arm smiling up at him and hated her more passionately than even the man. She had upset everything, was
undercutting everything Roha knew to be true, mixing good

and bad in Roha's head until she was sick with it. She stared at the Fire-hair a minute longer, then ran into the darkness, heedless again of the dangers that lay there to trap her feet, trying to run away from these things she couldn't cope with.

THE HUNT

CHAPTER X   Aleytys

Leaning against Swardheld, forgetting already that the body warm and strong behind her had once been Quale, Aleytys watched the tiny figure disappear. She turned her head, rested her cheek against his chest, listening to the strong beat of his heart, then looked up at him, briefly disconcerted to see Quale's face where she'd unconsciously expected to see the image she knew from Swardheld's materializations in her mind. Feeling strange, she reached up and touched the scarred cheek.

Quale's eyes narrowed in amusement and Swardheld looked out at her. He laughed at the expression on her face, hugged her vigorously, then held her at arm's length. "I'm not ready to cope with you yet, freyka-min-miel." The ends of his moustache twitched up as he drew the fingers of his right hand down the side of her face, then returned the hand to her shoulder.

Warmth spreading through her, she rested her hands on his arms, feeling happy and relaxed for the first time in days. "I need time too," she murmured. "To get used to your new look." For a long moment they stood together, then both stepped away. Aleytys wiped away some of the moisture condensing on her face. "I suppose we'd better try finding the carrier."

He raised an eyebrow. "If it's still in one piece." Taking her hand, he stood looking down at her. After a minute, he went on. "The Queen could be dead. What I remember. . . ."

"I know." Holding tight to the strong hand closed about hers, apprehensive and reluctant, she *reached*, searching for the familiar feels of Drij and the Haestavaada. When she found them, she leaned against Swardheld, weak with relief.

"What's wrong?" He pulled her close.

160

"Nothing." She smiled up at him through a haze of tears. "Nothing at all. They're alive, my friend. They're still alive." She sniffed and widened her grin. "I got the direction of the carrier."

Swardheld glanced over her shoulder toward the clearing where the Kinya-kin-kin swarm was still passing. "Not that way, I hope."

With a laugh she lightly kissed his hand and moved away. "You lose, I'm afraid. We ran the wrong way."

"Looks like. What do you want to do? Try going around?"

"I don't know. They seem to be settled calmly enough. Madar, I'm tired." She looked vaguely around then dropped to the ground, sitting crosslegged on the rocky soil. "I'm tired and dirty and sick with all this dying. They promised me a ship, Swardheld. I keep trying to remember that."

"And the vaada on Duvaks."

"There is that." She sighed. "When things get too bad, I tell myself about the dying vaada. All those dying vaada." She rubbed at her eyes. "Think the swarm has passed?"

"I'll see." Long loping strides carried him into the mist.

Aleytys watched him go. *I can't afford this*, she thought. For several minutes she rested, drifting close to sleep, relaxing until she was floating. Her *reach* expanded effortlessly, going out and out. And out. She started tensing as she wondered if she'd used up the power she had access to; that had happened once before—in her last hunt on the Hareworld she'd expended the power so recklessly only wisps and dregs of it were left to her. She began to wonder if the river winding around the stars was really a good image of it—a series of small pools might be more accurate. Pushing away that unwelcome suspicion she cast about until she finally touched a frail transparent shadow of her river and drew from it a trickle of the power-water, washing the fatigue poisons out of her system. When Swardheld came back, she was on her feet waiting for him.

The Kinya-kin-kin had moved on; she could hear the swarm chewing its way across the basin floor but even the stragglers had disappeared into the mist and darkness. She stopped by the dead trunk, touched the smooth hard wood, then looked up at Swardheld who stood a few steps away, a dark outline with glints of white as he moved his eyes about.

The body was beginning to change in subtle ways that nevertheless added up to a physical expression of the change in personality. Her hand still on the wood, she asked, "Is it going to work?"

He didn't pretend to misunderstand. "I don't know, Lee." Coming closer he touched her shoulder. "Time will show. Where now? We both need rest."

She pointed then moved across the clearing, picking her way among the bodies of dead kin.

She almost stepped on an Amar snug on his stomach and near invisible as he lay in a hollow in the earth, watching the silent camp. He hissed, then was up and away, vanishing into the mist. Aleytys jerked back as an arrow skimmed her shoulder and rustled through the leaves of a small tree just behind her. She heard Swardheld drop to the ground behind her, wheeled, then went down as he grabbed her ankle.

"Dammit, Lee," he growled, his voice constrained to a taut whisper. "You know better."

She eased onto her stomach and lay rubbing at an aching buttock. "Don't do that again or I'll kick you where it hurts, friend," she hissed back at him angrily, but she grew depressed as she examined the camp. The dead lay strewn about, crumpled or splayed out as they'd fallen, where they'd fallen, vaada and Scav alike. She eased closer until she could see more than the shadowy outline of the carrier and the Queen's casket.

The two valaada were still perched on top of the casket, working the life-support. Two guards were with them, holding the curved shields, their bulging eyes sweeping repeatedly over the severely limited field of vision. More of the shields were set up just outside the wheels of the carrier.

Swardheld moved up by her. She looked around. "The rest of them under there?" He nodded at the carrier then moved his head close to hers for her answer.

"Right."

"Crowded."

"No . . ." She sighed and moved restlessly. Swardheld took her hand. He said nothing, but there was no need for words between them. After a minute he moved his hand away, again saying nothing.

Aleytys stared stiffly at the line of shields without seeing them, abruptly aware that he knew her too well for her comfort. Six years. More. Living inside her head. Inside her body. Knowing her thoughts. Hearing what she heard. Seeing, feeling. . . . She turned her head and stared at him.

His eyes met hers. "Lee. . . ."

She slid away, stared a moment longer, then scrambled to her feet. "Drij!" she cried. "Ksiyl. Don't shoot." She started running toward the carrier, hearing Swardheld curse and come after her, hearing the clacking of the valaada, the soft flurried tones of Drij's voice. Between the shields she caught glimpses of dark forms, moving shadows, unidentifiable.

Behind her, she heard a grunt then the sound of a body falling, a blasting of pain against her nerves. She wheeled. Swardheld sprawled on his face, an arrow in the calf of his right leg. Aleytys gasped. "Harskari, help me. Time. Oh madar, I need time." She threw herself down beside Swardheld and began *reaching* frantically.

"Calmly, Lee. Relax, let us take it a moment." Amber and purple eyes shone in the darkness of her head. The diadem was lighting the mist, the chimes ringing softly, then the sounds slowed, deepened, dipped below her hearing range. She felt the air stiffen; even the mists froze in place. Moving with some effort against the resistance of the air, she pushed the arrowhead through his leg, broke it off and pulled the shaft from the wound. There was no blood, but she didn't expect any. She pushed the pieces of arrow aside and pressed her hands around the small puncture. There was a whisper in her head. "Hurry. Lee. The Sink. . . ." She sighed and *reached* again.

The black water trickled into her from a thin and filmy river. She choked down a fluttering panic and let the power gather within her before she tried to wash the poison out of him, remembering too vividly the effect of the poison on her. The air began to stir against her face; she heard the chimes surging up from a basso murmur to a singing ripple, heard the clatter of the arrow pieces against the stones, as Harskari and Shadith loosed the compulsion and she dropped into normal time. She poured the power into him, driving out the poison, healing the nerve damage. The rigidity passed from Swardheld's flesh. His eyes opened and he smiled at her as the burning under her hands cooled. The diadem was reflected in those gray-green eyes, painted highlights on his sweating face. She shut off the flow, holding the remainder of the power-pool in reserve, took her hands from him. "That was close."

He sat up, rubbed thoughtfully at his calf. "Hurts like hell, that poison. You look tired."

"Worn to a nub." Her uneasiness was back; she felt uncomfortable with him and angry at herself for reactions she couldn't escape. She risked a glance at him, met his eyes, turned away from the flash of sudden anger in them. She got up heavily. "I've got to get some sleep." Without waiting for him, she strode to the line of shields, banged her fist against one of them. "Drij!"

As Swardheld came toward her, two of the shields tilted apart and Drij crawled out. Aleytys was shocked out of her preoccupation with her own problems when she saw the deterioration in the woman. At first Drij stayed in a crouch, looking fearfully at the blowing mists and the dark figure of Swardheld. Her eyes were sunk in dark circles; lines of strain were carved deep in her face. She reached up and caught hold of the carrier's bed and pulled herself to her feet. Hesitantly she stepped beyond the shields. "We thought they killed you." Her eyes flicked past Aleytys to the man she knew as Quale. She started to speak, then shrieked in terror and went scrambling back under the carrier as another arrow sped from the mist and skimmed past her.

Aleytys wheeled, screamed, "Amar, Rus-sis. K'pa apa mah tok!" *Get the hell out of here, leave us alone.* She flung out her arms, gathered the remnant of her power pool, excited the air around her until she was a radiant golden figure in a sphere of red-gold light, her hair rippling out from her head, burning crimson, the diadem bright around her head, a circlet of gold-thread flowers with jewel hearts. She caught light in her hands and flung it at the mists, hurling with it a pall of repulsion and fear, swinging around in a circle, the black fear spiraling out from her, spreading over the Amar crouched in the fog watching her. She held the display until the reserve power-pool was exhausted and the natives were vanishing life-sparks fleeing through the mist. Her knees trembling, she retreated until the curve of her back was pressing against the bed of the carrier, stood there too tired to move.

Strong arms closed around her. Swardheld lifted her then sank to his knees and eased her into a space left open under the carrier. She lay against his chest, too weary to bother about the things that had troubled her only minutes before, happy for the moment to feel warm and cosseted, dimly aware of the long oval of Drij's face, pale and featureless in the gloom, of crowded dark figures huddling silently at the far end of the space under the carrier, of the strong acrid scent of the vaada and valaada. Pressing her fàce against Swardheld's shoulder, she closed her eyes and slept.

When she woke, she was alone under the carrier in the grayed-green morning light. A little way away, Drij and Swardheld were talking, the vaada were moving about and there was a scrabbling above her as the valaad guards changed shifts. She stretched and yawned, grimaced as she remembered the night's strains. "Harskari," she whispered. "Talk to me."

The amber eyes opened. "Lee."

Aleytys closed her eyes and saw the thin dark face framed with the shining silver hair. "What a night that was."

"Surprising." Heavy black brows met over the dark gold eyes. "Interesting. He seems to be settling comfortably enough in that body."

"You saw what happened?"

"If I read what you're asking, Lee, yes, I could reproduce what occurred."

"Would you want a body?"

The amber eyes closed abruptly and the image of the ancient sorceress was as abruptly not there. Startled, Aleytys sat up. "Harskari?"

The image returned, a look of pain in narrowed eyes. She spoke with a restrained passion that seared the words into Aleytys's mind. "I want to come out. Yes, I want a body." She stared at nothing, her eyes widening, suddenly misted with tears. "I want a body."

Sitting crosslegged under the carrier, Aleytys felt alone and disturbed; the anguish suddenly visible in the ordinarily controlled and cool being was like acid on her skin, transferring the pain and mixing it with fear. "But you'll die. When that body dies, you'll die."

"I'm tired." Harskari sighed. "I am . . . too old."

"But . . ."

"Lee, my people believed that what they called the soul—

whatever that is, perhaps this collection of forces that constitutes my present being—that this soul passes on and is reborn and never wholly ceases to exist, that it gains in awareness and in wisdom as the ages pass and the bodies change, in the end becoming something beyond man's comprehension, a part of the wholeness of things, encompassing within itself that wholeness as it is encompassed within it. I don't know. I exist this way. Perhaps the true death is just that—a ceasing to exist. Therrol denied me my chance to discover this truth when he fashioned the diadem and sentenced me to ages beyond number of. . . ." She laughed. "Of boredom, Lee." Her broad smile radiated affection and humor. "Though you have certainly livened up my existence."

Shadith was suddenly with them, her purple eyes sparking with excitement. She laughed and the sound filled Aleytys's head, tickled her into laughter in return. She sat in the misty morning light beneath the Queen's carrier, surrounded by the discarded dead, rocking with laughter.

The poet-singer lifted her imaged harp and played an inaudible music. "I salute the society of ghouls," she sang. "Newly formed and casting greedy eyes on walking shapes."

Aleytys wiped at her eyes, weak from laughter, thoroughly relaxed and suddenly content. "Only the best bodies," she murmured.

Harskari smiled, then shook her head. "Gently, friend. We must not think of displacing the living. That's one thing. Another—we should wait to see how Swardheld does. I have no desire to dissipate myself needlessly."

Her red-gold curls bobbing vigorously as she nodded, Shadith said, "I plan to enjoy my new body thoroughly and for as long a time as possible before I try merging with the infinite." She turned to Harskari and giggled.

Aleytys lay back down, her eyes fixed on the underside of the carrier bed. "You know, there's one thing I don't understand. If it's this easy to shift to a body, why didn't you do it before?"

"Easy!" Shadith grimaced. "You don't know how close Swardheld came, Lee. Without you he couldn't have taken that body and held it, he simply didn't have the strength. He needed the support of the power you control, Lee. Not that we knew that before." She shook her head, her violet eyes shining with amusement. "You will understand it wasn't a thing we really could experiment with. Too final if something didn't work. Now . . . dammit, Lee, get this Hunt moving. I want to start visiting morgues."

"All right." Aleytys sat up. "All right. Go away so I can think." She crawled from beneath the carrier.

Swardheld was nowhere in sight. The valaada and vaada were eating from the supply cells and Drij sat alone by the end of the carrier, knees drawn up, her head resting on her arms. An unopened tab-can sat beside her foot.

After brushing off clinging sand, leaves and small rocks, Aleytys walked over to the silent woman, squatted beside her and pulled the tab on the can. She touched Drij's arm, waited until she looked up, then held out the can. "You need to eat."

Drij pushed at the can, grimacing as if the smell rising from it nauseated her. "What are you?"

"Not who?"

Drij said nothing.

Aleytys sighed, pulled the spoon loose from the side and began to dig into the hot stew. The first mouthful reminded her that she hadn't eaten for a very long time. She emptied the can and wondered if she was hungry enough to finish off another, then jumped to her feet. After fumbling through the cartons, she ripped one open, then came back to Drij with a film-wrapped food bar in her hand. "Eat this. And that's not a request, my friend. Eat or I'll feed it to you."

Drij took the bar in shaking fingers. Without looking at Aleytys, she broke off a piece of the concentrate, hesitated, then lifted it to her mouth.

Swardheld came out of the mist refastening his belt. He raised a hand in greeting, moved to the front of the carrier and came back with an open cell of tab cans tucked under his arm. "Eaten yet?"

"Some." She held out a hand. "Still hungry though, that was one busy night."

"Tell me about it." He laughed. "I was there, remember?"

She took the can from him, opened it, and dropped to her knees. As soon as he was settled beside her, she stopped eating and examined his face and hands. "How are you?"

"Fitting in easier as time passes. You decided yet that I won't bite?"

Her fingers tightened about the can. "You know too much about me." She fixed her eyes on the stirring vaada. They

were closing up the cells around the discarded husks of their
own food. Three got heavily to their feet and began moving
around the clearing, ignoring the bodies but picking up the
other debris. "It makes me uncomfortable," she said. "Whenever I think about it." She spooned up more of the stew, sat
chewing in silence for a moment, risked a glance at him. He
was frowning. "Harskari and Shadith want out too," she said.

"I'm not surprised." Hesitantly, he held out a hand, smiling
when Aleytys took it. "Lee, be glad for us." Then he laughed.
"And think what fine times the four of us will have."

The day was a struggle, tedious and exhausting, as the
stolid vaada dragged the carrier around the stinking pools of
sulphurous boiling water, over layered runnels of hardened
lava where broken bubbles had knife-sharp edges, edging cautiously away from the innocently lethal bushes. The two sets
of natives stayed far away, beyond the range of Aleytys's
outreach—as did the floating ghosts, twice burned and doubly
wary. Swardheld and Aleytys ranged out ahead, using their
experience during the butchery of the inward trek to lead the
carrier through potential dangers. Without the stimulation of
possible attack the passage of the carrier—the passage of
them all—through the steamy claustrophobic mists, moving
with slogging effort in a room whose walls moved with them,
a room they never broke out of, this passage became a march
into nowhere, a march without end through a place that
never changed, as if they paced on a treadmill. The coming
of darkness stopped them, closing the walls of mist in so tight
around them they moved not in a common room but in their
individual cocoons.

The next day was a continuation without change or hope
of change. Drij plodded behind the carrier, her head down,
following more because there was nothing else to do than because she cared where she was going. From time to time she
caught hold of the carrier bed and let it pull her along for a
few steps.

Late in the afternoon the land began to ease upward.
Aleytys missed the creak and groan of the carrier and
stopped to look back. For a time—too long a time—all she
saw were the knots and trails of the mist then a darkness
took shape and the first pair of vaada came into view, bent
over until the pincers on the mid-arms, if extended, would

trail along the earth. They weren't meant to be draft animals, they had too little mass—their flesh was frail and the chitin lighter than bone—and they were awkwardly built for such work. Already the slight rise was slowing them; another degree and they might not be able to move at all. Swardheld came back and stood beside her. He watched as the vaada struggled closer then looked down at her. "Natives?"

"None about."

"Any rope?"

The front pair of vaada were almost even with them. "Better. A winch with a spider-silk cable, stronger than rope—if I understand you." The vaada didn't look at them or stop to see what they waited for, simply plodded on, the clawed feet digging into the coarse soil, throwing up bits of small rock that struck the ones behind who ignored them as they ignored everything but the need to throw their weight such as it was against the crossbars and dig their feet in, taking step after step, pulling the Queen out of the hell around them to the ship that would take her to her kin on Davaks. No questions, no doubts—all available energy thrown into keeping the carrier moving. Aleytys looked up. The sun was a shimmer low in the west and the Sink-glow overhead close to non-existent. "Time's starting to pinch out. The Tikh'asfour will be crowding closer." The end of the carrier rolled past with Drij walking dull-eyed and alone behind it. "Another casualty, that." She glanced at the sky again. "I don't want to spend another night here."

"We'll have to winch the carrier up the last hundred yards, maybe more." He started walking, circling wide about a dart bush then around another with abrasive leaves that brought blisters to the skin, blisters that broke and let in poison dust, jumping over a humping stranglevine, moving around a small geyser. Aleytys hurried after him.

In a darkness thick with the scent of a dozen spices, about an hour after sundown, Aleytys stumbled and fell heavily against the crossbar as the carrier nosed over the rim of the basin. It creaked to a stop as Swardheld straightened from the winch. The vaada around her took several more steps then stumbled themselves as their feet kicked against the drooping cable. Aleytys stretched, rubbed at her back, sighed. A cool breeze came sweeping through the scattered trees, a clean dry breeze that felt like new life flowing over her sweat-sticky skin. She sighed with pleasure at the touch of coolness.

The vaada around her crouched in harness, their pairs of arms folded inward, the air fluting in and out of the spiracles on the sides of their thoraxes. She felt the tongue jerk as Swardheld jumped from the bed and moved with long loping strides to the anchor tree. She watched him bend to unhook the chain, then toss it impatiently back toward the weary vaada. *He's as antsy as I am. I wish this was over.* Arms crossed over her breasts, she stared up at the ragged webbing of light that obscured less than half the sky until the scrape of boots on the rock brought her head around.

He glanced briefly at the sky. "How soon you think we can fire up one of the ships?"

Abruptly irritated at him, then more irritated at herself, she said, "I don't know. Tomorrow maybe." She dropped her hands to the crossbar, stared down at them. "Let's get moving. I want a bath."

Chuckling, he swung up on the bed and began rewinding the cable. Hastily, Aleytys moved her feet as the chain at the end of the cable snaked past, clanking, jerking, scraping over the rock. Behind her, she heard the clatter as Swardheld slapped the hook on its rod; in front of her the vaada straightened thin stubby legs and threw their weight against the crossbars. The tongue jumped again as Swardheld swung down, his weight shift rocking the bed slightly, the pendulum swing continuing even after the weight was gone, imparted to the tongue so that it too twisted uncomfortably.

Slowly, painfully, the carrier began to creep forward, its silent valaad guards pacing beside it, as unobtrusive as if they were mechanical appendages joined to it by the mid-arm pincers they kept closed over the edge of the bed. The guards on the casket continued all the while with their endless work, keeping the life-support going for the Queen held dormant within the thick metal skin. Groaning and creaking, with Drij and the last of the vaada stumbling behind it, the carrier rolled past the trees over uneven stony ground, ground that began softening as they moved away from the rim of the basin, and among trees that grew higher and closer together, ignoring patches of brush that they didn't have to shun as they would the growths in the mistlands.

As the carrier nosed into the shelter clearing, Swardheld

came up to Aleytys, touched her shoulder. "Stay ready."
When she nodded, he smiled, then started loping across the
clearing, his boots hitting the stone with a surprising loudness
in a silence that hung oppressively over the shelter. It looked
deserted but the gate was still closed, evidence that someone
lurked inside. Swardheld kicked at the gate, waking dull
booms that fell dead almost as soon as they sounded.
"Blaur!"

Aleytys absently stripped off the harness and stepped away
from the tongue. Tired and nervous, she moved past the
silent, patient vaada to stand in front of them, as a dark
round came slowly over the top of the wall.

"Quale?" There was little welcome in the hoarse voice.
Blaur eased a bit higher, resting his rifle on the wall. "Took
your time." He looked past Swardheld toward the carrier still
in the shadow of the trees at the edge of the clearing. "You
got her?"

Swardheld grunted and kicked at the gate. "Move ass,
man."

Blaur rubbed at his nose. "Give me a reason."

Swardheld smiled. "Think you got an edge, huh? You find
ship's keys? Want to spend the rest of your days on this stinking world?"

Blaur swiped a rough palm over his scarred head, the
sound rasping loud enough in the heavy air to reach Aleytys.
Even across the clearing, she could feel the resentment, anger
and reluctant fear boiling in him. His days alone had engen-
dered hopes in him; away from Quale, he'd forgotten Quale's
strength, remembering instead his bluster and occasional
blind spots—now he was reluctant to let go of his dreams,
but even more reluctant to provoke the man in front of him,
though he could have no idea that the personality that wore
the body was more dangerous than the original had ever
been. Aleytys *reached*, tapping into her power, ready to act if
the man lifted the rifle. For a long moment the tableau held,
then she relaxed as Blaur jumped down and started yelling at
invisible Scavs, his voice harsh with the anger he didn't dare
express. Her knees trembling a little from relief, she signed to
the vaada to start moving.

When the carrier rolled through the gate with vaada and
valaada and Drij trailing behind but none of the Scavs, Blaur
scowled at Swardheld Quale. "What happened?"

"Natives, the land and the shitheads' own stupidity," he said impatiently, then moved away from the burly glowering man toward Aleytys, fishing in his pocket for the key to the shelter. Handing the key to her, he muttered, "Feel like I'm walking on eggs. Get her down fast as you can."

She looked at the bit of scrolled metal lying in the palm of her hand. "Be careful."

"Tell me. Hunh. I'm going to yell a few more orders at them, then duck under cover fast." He grinned at her. "Don't take too long at that bath, Lee. One thing I forgot is how strong a week's sweat can smell." He caught her shoulder and pushed her toward Drij who was crouching dispiritedly by one of the carrier wheels. "Move."

Aleytys coaxed Drij to her feet and led her, dull-eyed and shambling, to the low hutch in the center of the walled space while Swardheld yelled and slapped the Scavs away from the valaada when they wanted to disarm them. Her hands firm on Drij's wrists, she talked her onto the ladder, watching as she moved hesitantly from rung to rung, stopping at times as if she forgot where she was, staring at the wall behind the ladder until Aleytys called her back from whatever limbo she hung in and started her moving down again. Out in the court, Swardheld wasn't standing about waiting for questions, but shouting and signing orders until he got the carrier into a corner, the armed valaada surrounding it, the Scavs backed into an opposite corner. The men were morose and demoralized, hungry because they'd eaten up the supplies left to them when the expedition set out. As Aleytys started down the ladder, he was using the vaada to transport the few remaining food cells to the hutch, watching with a brooding anger by the crouching Scavs. When she reached bottom, Drij was nowhere in sight and Swardheld was a dark shape in the hatch opening. "Catch," he called down, then dropped one of the food cells.

Aleytys caught it, sent it rolling down the little side hall. "Fool," she called then had to catch another cell. He pitched all but two of them down, stood on the rim and threw these last cells to the Scavs, then stepped onto the ladder, reaching up to pull the hatch closed as he moved down the rungs.

"Don't." Aleytys came back from the inner room. "Wait till I can get one of the lamps lit." There wasn't much light coming down from the fading Sink-web but there would be a lot less with the hatch closed. She waited until he grimaced, nodded and steadied himself. "Matches in the kitchen. Opposite the door to the bedroom, remember?"

"Right. Remember yourself where you were at the time." Chuckling, she groped her way through the workroom into the kitchen. Bringing the wooden mug with the matches back with her, she moved into the workroom again and stood looking about. A trickle of light came down the ventilation shafts, enough to show her vague blotches where the chair and table stood and smudges against the walls where the lamps were hanging. She lifted down the tubular flame-shield and wound up the wick, checking to see if there was oil left in the reservoir. She lit a match and held it to the wick. There was a flare of smoke-capped light, then the flame cleared and she wound the wick down until she had a bright clean flame. She fit the cover back in place, turned to light the second lamp, halted before striking the match.

Drij was crouched in a corner, staring at nothing, trembling at times, at times still as a lump of clay. Aleytys had hoped that the familiar surroundings of the shelter would halt her growing withdrawal, but so far that wasn't happening. *Time*, she thought. *There hasn't been time yet for her to realize where she is.* Sighing, she lit the second lamp. *That's enough for the moment*, she thought. Thrusting her head through the arch, she yelled, "Come on down. We're in business."

He came in while she was lighting the rest of the lamps. "Got through that all right." He grinned, but the grin faded as he walked over to Drij and stood looking down at her; shaking his head, he walked back to Aleytys. "Not so good. Seems to be accelerating downhill. Anything you can do?"

"I don't know." She pushed oily hair back off her face. "If it was just her body. . . ." She shook her head. "I'm afraid to touch her. . . . afraid I'd make things worse. Damn, I wish. . . . I'll get her cleaned up and out of those filthy clothes. Maybe if she feels better about herself . . . she hasn't been eating, maybe if I get some food down her. . . ." She grimaced and patted her stomach. "Talking about food, I could eat half a dozen cans of that stew. You hungry too? Better keep out of her way." She nodded at Drij. "Quale started her trouble."

Swardheld rubbed a hand across his short beard. "Get a

move on then. Sooner you get her fed and tucked into bed, sooner we can clean up." He touched her face. "And do the talking we need to do."

She stepped away from him, shut her eyes until her breathing steadied. When she opened them again, he was gone and the tapestry that hid the arch to the kitchen was still swinging a little. With a sigh, she crossed to Drij, bent down and took her arm. "Come on, Drij. You'll feel better if you have a bath."

With no resistance and no sign of understanding in her eyes, Drij came to her feet and walked beside Aleytys, moving like an outsize Placon Doll, letting Aleytys prod her through the bedroom into the bathroom. Even the coughing roar as the water exploded from the faucet drew no response from her. With an exasperated sigh, Aleytys pushed on her shoulders and sat her down with her back against the tub's side. She contemplated the woman for a minute, then shook her head and went out through the curtained arch into the bedroom where she began rummaging through the deep drawers set into the stone wall, working more by touch than sight since little light came down the ventilation shafts, stopping repeatedly by the curtains over the arch to look through into the bathroom and make sure Drij wasn't doing some inadvertent harm to herself. She found sheets, threw them onto the bed, found spare blankets and some towels and what felt to be a clean dress cloth. After glancing in at Drij again she went back into the workroom and fetched the cup of matches.

Carrying towels with her, she brushed past the arch curtain, dropped the towels on the dressing table and lit the lamp. After checking the temperature of the water and shutting off its flow, she stopped in front of Drij. "Stand up," she said firmly and a little hopelessly, sighing again when Drij seemed not to hear her. "Just being stubborn, aren't you." She bent down and caught hold of Drij's arm. "On your feet now. Worse than having a child."

With some difficulty she got Drij undressed, throwing the soiled and sweat-stiffened clothing into a pile in the corner of the room, tossing the boots on top the pile. Coils of steam rose from the hot water in the tub into air too saturated to absorb more moisture. Fragments of words dropped down the ventilation shafts as the Scavs wrangled desultorily in the enclosure above, a reminder Aleytys didn't need of the effort morning would demand as she tried to gather in the loose threads and bring the Hunt to a successful close.

After more wrestling with Drij's inert but unresisting body, wrestling that left her sweaty and very wet, Aleytys got her into the huge bathtub. Words no longer seemed to have meaning for her; she ignored scoldings and pleadings alike. Cursing softly, Aleytys stripped and got into the tub with her.

Swardheld was sitting at the worktable looking through Drij's field notes when Aleytys came padding into the workroom, blankets under one arm, holding a towel around herself with her other hand, her hair damp and tangled. At the rattle of the curtain rings he swung around. "How's Drij?"

"In bed."

"Asleep?"

She shrugged. "I shut her eyes for her and she left them shut for what that's worth."

Swardheld pushed the chair back a few more inches, then stood. "My turn at the bathtub." At the arch, he turned, his hand on the tapestry. "Make us some cha, will you?" Without waiting for an answer he pushed past the heavy cloth and disappeared into the darkness beyond. Aleytys grimaced and padded into the kitchen.

When he came back looking cool, clean, and a great deal refreshed, she was setting a tray on the worktable. She glanced at him then began pouring the streaming brown-amber cha into two large mugs. "Feels good, doesn't it."

He collected a mug and food from her then moved away and settled himself cross-legged on the floor with his back braced comfortably against the wall. He waited until Aleytys was down beside him, then snapped off the cover of one of the self-heating cans. For several minutes neither spoke, content to eat and drink in a companionable silence.

The night noises drifted to them, broken and jumbled together, falling down the shafts with the shifting light of the Sink-web. The tension between the two sitting in the flicker-flutter light of the lamps gradually increased until both set aside the remnants of their food and sipped at refilled mugs of cha, each carefully not looking at the other. Swardheld took a large gulp of the cooling liquid then stared down into its slow swirl that he kept moving by moving the cup. He looked up. "There's a problem."

Aleytys's hand tightened on her mug. "Which one?" She set the mug down and tucked the towel higher over her breasts. "I can think of a dozen without trying."

He made an abrupt, impatient gesture, as if brushing aside a flight of gnats. "Ships' keys," he said. "Quale took his memories with him. He didn't take the keys."

Aleytys rose and wandered along the walls, upending native bowls, baskets and other artifacts scattered along shelves incised in the stone, shifting books to look behind them, pulling out and shaking loose-leaf notebooks, not a serious search, more a way of using up nervous energy. She looked back at Swardheld. "You know as much about Quale as I do. What do you think? Where would you hide them if you were him? He *did* lock this place." She moved on, handling but not examining the objects on the shelves.

"Locked." He snorted disgust. "How long would it take you to tickle that thing open?"

"Still, with the Amar nosing about outside. . . ." She put the scraped horn down and ran her fingers over a fragile bit of wooden lace in the shape of a bird. "If a greenie found the keys and carried them off, they'd be lost with no hope in hell of getting them back."

"Point to you." Swardheld let his head fall back against the wall and sat grinning at her. "If *he* took the point."

"He had reason enough to be wary of them." She moved restlessly on, glancing now and then at him. His eyes were drooping, shut into slits, his powerful torso pale against the darker russet and gray stone, the damp towel loose about his hips. He yawned, scratched along his jawline. "You could help," she said. She winced, ashamed of her own fretful irritability.

"I'm tired." He yawned again, opened one eye. "Sit down, Lee."

"In a minute." Her head beginning to ache, she crossed to extinguish the lamp. With great deliberation she wound down the wicks until the last red glows disappeared. She set the last shield carefully in place then moved to the lamps on the wall Swardheld leaned against. When she was finished, the only light in the room came from twin rows of pale green squares marching across the ceiling, the outlets of the ventilation shafts. With the light came the sound of voices, the soft whisper of falling air, the eerie call of a night bird. Aleytys went to kneel by Swardheld's feet. "I'm afraid," she said, and reached for his hands.

Aleytys stirred, sighed. She sat up carefully, listening to Swardheld's steady breathing. Her head had been lying on his outstretched arm. She moved the arm gently across his chest, letting her hand rest a moment on his warm flesh, still astonished at the totality of her response to him, profoundly disturbed by the shattering of her sense of self—by the intensity of her need—by her hunger—by the . . . god knows what . . . that had seized her without her willing it and without any possibility of controlling it. *Me and him*, she thought. *Him too. He felt it too.*

She took her hand away, her knees drawn up as a kind of barrier between them. His eyes moved rapidly, darting back and forth under the closed eyelids; his moustache amplified the twists of his working mouth. There was a sheen of sweat on his face. *No pleasant dream*, she thought. *Oh god, I can't go through this again.* She sat staring into the darkness trying to sort out the complications in her life. *We need space between us for a while. Until we can be comfortable . . . comfortable! A few more days*, she thought. *Just get through the next few days. The Haestavaada will have their Queen back and I'll have a ship. Was there ever a time when I was sure that was all it'd take to straighten out my life? A ship.* She looked down at Swardheld, still moving, caught in a dream or nightmare, she couldn't tell which. *I want to wake you now, I can taste the need, remember. . . . No, I can't . . . I won't surrender myself again, abrogate me, but oh god, the glory and the terror of it.* With a groan she dropped her head on her arms. *And there's Gray. What am I going to do about Gray? I can't just dump him. I don't want to dump him. We've hurt each other a lot, one way or another—but out there in the Wild, out there we found something. . . . I don't want to lose that.* She lifted her head and ran her fingers through her hair, absently pleased with the soft clean feel of it. *I can try finding my mother now*, she thought. *If her instructions are still good. Not yet, no, I can't face her yet, not till I've sorted things out, she can't help me with that, no one can. Still, I'm half Vryhh; I need to know what they're like, my Vrya kin. Not just crazy Kell. The normal ones, if any of them are normal.* She bit on her lip as she saw again Kell's

face as she'd seen it on Sunguralingu, saw him looking hate
at her out of greenstone eyes. Thinking of Kell reminded her
of his threat to her son, the boy she hadn't seen for more
than five years. It was an old hurt, but the pain was still
strong enough to make her want to avoid thinking about him,
though she had to wonder if he remembered her at all and if
he did, what he thought of her. *I hated my mother when I
found out she'd gone off without me.* "Damn!"

"Damn what? Swardheld looked up at her, his pale eyes a
surprise whenever she saw them. The link between them was
still extraordinarily intense and she knew he was as unwilling
as she to repeat what had happened before.

"Counting my complications. It's not so soothing as sheep."
She turned toward him. "What now?"

He laced his hands behind his head. "I won't be going back
to Wolff with you."

"You'll be back? After a while?"

"After a while; you're carrying around some friends of
mine." He yawned, smiled sleepily at her. "Stop fussing, Lee.
Get some rest. No complications till tomorrow."

THE HUNT

CHAPTER XI   Roha

Roha stopped running and began picking her way more cautiously through the mist, confused and unhappy—unhappy because she found her world picture challenged by, of all things, a demon, a fire-haired demon who was supposed to be wholly evil, whose actions were close to incomprehensible. "Stupid. She's stupid," Roha whispered over and over to herself, trying to shut away the memory of the warmth and gentleness of the demon's hands. She rubbed her hands down over her flat narrow chest where lines of blood still clung to her skin. She heard the bubbling of a small spring and edged around bushes that were little more than shadows in the dark and mist until she found a small round hole in the stone where water was bubbling up, spilling over to pool again in a hollow years had carved in the rock. Away from the source, the water was cooler, enough so she could dip her hands in it. She splashed water over her trembling body, washing away the last of the blood stains and the old, dried smears of slime-moss.

As her taut muscles began to relax under the influence of the heat, fatigue washed over her. She closed her eyes and knelt beside the spring, breathing in the hot wet air until she was nearly asleep, her mind drifting in chaotic images. After several minutes she stirred, rubbed at her eyes, then forced herself on her feet. Overhead in the mist the floating ghosts were gathering, starting to merge, and in the surrounding mist she could hear rustlings and scrapings as the night runners began their foraging.

Desolate, her emotions and her mind pulling her apart, she turned toward her own kind, seeking blindly for the comfort their presence would give her; she trotted warily through the mists, experience and a sharpening night sight taking her

safely through the traps of the land until she saw a blurred
spot of red and yellow light flickering ahead of her.

She dropped beside Churr, reaching out to touch his leg,
the hard, cool flesh a reassurance of reality, her hand on him
an assertion of her claim to kinship in the tribe. He pulled
away and walked to the fire leaving her afraid in a way she'd
not known so strongly before, though she'd had tremors of it.
He came back with a sharpened stick skewered through
chunks of meat. Silently he handed it to her then moved
away to join the ring about the fire, his back to her as if he
closed a door in her face. She stared down at the charred
flesh. After a while she started eating. *I'm not sakawa yet*,
she thought. *At least he gives me food.*

Sakawa. It was a hard thought. When a demon seized a
Rum and drove him to commit acts no Rum could possibly
do, the tribe drove him out. The kin-slayer, the man who
killed by magic cursing a Rum to death, the woman who
abandoned her hatchling, the Rum who fell to the earth
foaming at the mouth when Mambila was not in the sky, the
child who could not stop destroying things no matter how he
was punished—these were drummed from the village. Sakawa. No village would take him in. No one would speak to
him or feed him or clothe him or even stay in his sight. Sakawa. Outcast. Demon driven. *If the Amar cast me out*, she
thought, *I'll know my luck was lost when Rihon died. I'm not
a demon's vessel but he surely must think I am. The Wan
won't let them do it, he can't, he'll have to know I haven't
changed, I'm still Roha the dark Twin. The demons from the
sky, they're the ones who did this, they have to die. All of
them. All! Then everything will be all right again.* She stared
at Churr's unyielding back, afraid to say anything. Whatever
she said, he'd discount as demon's talk. She looked down at
the congealing meat on the stick and wanted to throw it at
him, but she forced herself to finish it, unwilling to anger him
in any way.

Abruptly Churr jumped to his feet. "Time," he growled.
The warriors cast aside what was left of the meat, kicked dirt
over the fire and followed him into the mist, leaving Roha
gaping after them. She stood, tossed the skewer aside, hesitated, wondering if she dared follow them, then knew she
couldn't bear to be alone and started after them as silently as
she could. The way seemed familiar; she stepped over the

crumpled dying leaves she'd slashed from the stranglevine and knew the Amar were heading for the demon camp. She wanted to shout her triumph; instead, she closed her eyes and stood swaying until she could contain her excitement, then she trotted on, her breathing rough, her eyes glittering.

She reached the edge of the clearing in time to see the brother-killer go down with an Amar arrow in his leg. Hissing, her claws out, Roha flung her arms wide in a great triumph. This time the brother-killer was dead, properly killed by an Amar arrow. Then the Fire-hair turned, cried out incomprehensible words and the triumph was washed out of Roha. She watched the demon run to the brother-killer, then the air seemed to thicken in a great blurr around the two of them, the Fire-hair and the brother-killer. Something was happening, she couldn't see what. Then the blur was gone and the Fire-hair was bending over the brother-killer, her hands pressed around the wound in his legs, the arrow was out and fallen by her side, and the circlet of shimmering golden blooms was shining around her head. Roha remembered the touch of those long firm hands, the touch, the warmth coming from them, remembered her flesh closing over the gaping wounds in her body. She watched without surprise as the brother-killer sat up then strolled with the Fire-hair to the long thing, watched the Nafa come out and dive for cover as one of the Amar sent an arrow at the three of them, watched the Fire-hair start to shine, the flower circle back on her head.

Then the terror struck. Roha moaned and dropped down to claw at the damp earth. Not far from her Churr gasped and struck at his head. His eyes bulged. Around the two of them, the Amar howled in mindless fear. Casting their bows aside, the warriors fled blindly into the mist, terror nosing after them like a bawa pack racing through the forest after a bounding happa. Churr was the last to break, but break he did, fleeing from the demon with a great cry of shame and fear.

Clutching desperately at the earth, the Mother of them all, the holder of her womb, the only mother she knew, Roha shuddered and suffered but rode out the fear as she'd learned through much practice to ride the tumult of her mind in the drug dreams that were a major part of her life. She watched as the Fire-hair turned in slow circles, shining like a daughter

of the sun as she poured out fear and terror. Then the glow
faded, the glory was gone and the demon sagged in the arms
of the brother-killer who took her out of sight under the long
thing.

Exhausted by her ordeal, cold with despair from seeing the
brother-killer escape death again, sick with her failure and
the failure of the Amar, she stumbled away after Churr, too
driven to stop and rest, too tired to do more than put one
foot in front of the other. After an interminable groping
through the darkness, she halted, brought her ears out and
up. Somewhere to her right a voice was calling for help. She
hesitated, then turned slowly in the direction of the sounds.

In his unthinking flight Churr had run into a bog. Still carrying his bow, he'd managed to slip the end over a small nub
of rock. It wouldn't take his weight but it was enough to keep
his arms and shoulders above the slime. When he saw Roha,
his hands jerked. The bow slid over the hump of rock and he
started sinking. Hastily Roha caught hold of the bow and
tried to pull the warrior free, but his weight was too much
for her strength. Already exhausted, she spent so much of
herself trying to free him that her fingers began trembling
and threatened to open without her willing it. She stared
down at Churr, unable even to think for the moment, then
she thrust her arm between the string and the wood, hoping
the string was caught tight enough in the groove so that it
wouldn't come loose. She found a purchase for her feet in the
knob of rock that had saved Churr's life and small wiry
poisonbush. She sat, braced her feet, then looked wearily at
Churr. "Work yourself out," she murmured.

The bowstring cut painfully into her flesh as Churr pulled
himself slowly from the choking muck; the pain seemed to go
on forever. Then he was rolling onto the solid ground. He lay
there shaking, twitching in every limb, plastered over with the
slimy mud, sucking in great gulps of the thick night air. Roha
took her foot from the poison bush; her leg from the knee
down was covered by large blisters. She sat staring at them,
too tired to do more. Dimly she heard Churr curse, then he
was slathering handfuls of the muck from the bog over her
skin and scrubbing it off again with handfuls of the soft green
grass that grew over the slime. He smoothed on more of the
mud. This time he left it and sat down beside her, his body
shaking as he drew in great lungfuls of air again and expelled

them in loud snorts. Roha lay back, staring up into the swirling mists with their faint Mambila glow, watching as floating ghosts no larger than her thumbtip swarmed over night bugs and wide-winged moths, dropping their bodies like rain around and on her.

With a quick almost hostile glance at Roha, Churr jumped to his feet and whistled a summons into the mist, calling to him such of the Amar as still lived. After repeated whistlings and scattered answers, nine shaken warriors came stumbling from the mist, relieved to find they were not alone in this hell. Roha lay very still, searching face after face, feeling a chill growing in her in spite of the steamy heat of the night. They were beaten. The spirit had gone out of them. They couldn't take any more of this moving about in eerie isolation within moving walls of fog. In their bodies, in their faces, in their eyes she read another thing. Blame. They cast on her the blame for what they felt. She sat up and fixed her eyes on the slowly drying mud smeared on her blistered leg. *There's nothing I can do,* she thought.

With one man left awake to keep the ghosts from merging, the Amar stamped the biters out of the roots of the scattered grass patches, curled up and slept heavily. Roha sat watching them, feeling colder and stiffer as the moments passed. In spite of her exhaustion she couldn't follow them into sleep. *My time is done,* she thought. The floating ghosts started swarming over the sleeping men until Dahor came by, waved a long stick through them and drove them off again. Roha shivered and closed her eyes, deliberately recalling happy memories from before—chasing with Rihon through the trees, sitting with the other children listening to Gawer Hith chant the story songs, stuffing herself with nuggar meat at Karrams, laughing and giggling with other girls at the great Feast that celebrated the emergence of Mother Earth from Mambila's belly, feasts when a truce was declared and half a dozen tribes met to dance and boast and eat. In this retreat from the horrors of the present, she found some of the comfort she needed and finally drifted into sleep.

When she woke, Churr and the warriors were gone and the sun was high in the east. She sat up, rubbed at her eyes. In the crushed spots the warriors had left behind even now the grass stems were slowly straightening. Morning sounds cycled

around her, a rustling, hissing, chirping and squeaking that
only underlined the absence of Amar voices. She knew she'd
been finally abandoned, that she was already sakawa though
the Serk had not yet proclaimed her so. *Not yet*, she thought.
If I could talk to the Wan. . . .

The wind strengthened as it blew past her, carrying scents
of all the small animals that rooted about among the bushes
and grass, odors of crushed leaves and warm wet green
things. She thought of the cool and dry air of her own
forests, of the trees and the tart fruit smells. The wind shifted
a little, carrying to her the sour musty smell of mistlanders.
She gasped, started running then settled to a steady lope,
heading home as fast as her small legs would take her.

She kept moving all day, not stopping to eat, only to drink
and that only when her body forced the decision on her. As
the sun settled in a greenish blur on the western rim of the
basin she stumbled and fell. For a moment she lay stunned,
then she sat up, slumped over, trembling, a hollow in her
middle, realizing that she needed food before she could go
farther. She raised her head and looked around, sniffing the
air, hoping for a familiar smell.

Everything looked washed-out, small, spindly—and barren,
at least those bushes she dared touch. She got heavily to her
feet and forced herself to move on, looking constantly for
something she could eat. It was almost dark when she came
on a short almost leafless bush that would have been a small
tree up in her forest. Cascades of dark fruit hung on racemes.
She crushed one between thumb and forefinger, sniffed at the
dark red juice that looked like blood but smelled sweeter,
touched her tongue quickly, lightly, to one of the juice runnels. Even that small taste sent her head floating. She hesitated. The fruits were smaller and more potent than those
above, but she needed the energy they'd give her although
she'd pay for it later.

With the drug singing in her blood, she trotted up the increasing slant; the one idea she could hold onto was the
thought of getting home, of the Wan comforting her and protecting her. Home. She ran through patterns of black and
white, then through white on white, then there were no patterns, through shifting melting colors, across stone that
seemed to melt before and behind her until at times she was

running unconcerned on air following a line that unreeled before her like purple-blue threads.

Exhausted and disoriented, she stumbled from the mistlands long after the sun had left the sky. For the first time in days she could see the Mambila web and even through her drug-haze she was astonished at how thin and ragged it had grown. There were great holes in the reticulated glow and a great black arc in the west showed Earth Mother moving for Mambila's mouth. The cool air blew against her face through twisting patterns that grew as frail and ghostly as the dissolving web. Still focused on reaching home, she found herself able to think of other things. The stench of the Egg-demons was strong on the ground. *They got out*, she thought. She forced herself to keep walking, in a dull, automatic progress that brought her eventually to the Nafa's clearing.

The gate was closed, the shelter walls deserted, but she heard the sounds of voices inside and felt a surge of hate, a dull heating of her body only dimly felt through waves of fatigue. There was nothing she could do. Nothing. She circled the clearing and crept painfully along a trail she and Rihon had run many times. She didn't dare stop moving, not even to cling to one of the trees and rest a while, fearing that if she did stop, she'd never get her aching body moving again. She passed one of the garden patches. It was deserted but the women didn't always leave guards to chase away intrusive nuggar. She began to smell smoke. At first she was only aware of a rough tang in the air blowing past her face, then slowly and fearfully she stopped and sniffed. Smoke. Hanging in the air like mist in the mistlands. She almost turned away, afraid to face what she knew she had to see when she stepped into the village clearing. She took one step, then another and another.

The houses were piles of ash and blackened poles rising at steep angles or lying flat on the ground. Charred bodies lay scattered about, bones here and there glinting white in the Web-light. "Rum Fieyl," she whispered. She moved slowly toward the Ghost House, her feet stirring the gray ash until she walked in a cloud. She stopped a moment when she saw other prints, scrapes and sprays in the ash. "Churr," she breathed then coughed as ash got into her nose and throat. "And the warriors. Oh Bright Twin, if only they'd come in time. It might—might—might have made a difference."

In the center of the village the Ghost House had three headless bodies tumbled in its ash. One was female. "Serk," she murmured. A scarred and battered male. "Niong." She touched his body with her toe. "You were right, we should have attacked the Fieyl. I. . . ." She moved on to stand over a slight gnarled figure. "Wan." She dropped to her knees beside him, touched his burned and torn flesh, tears gathering in her eyes. Numbed by weariness and too many shocks, she couldn't feel this loss deeply now; in her mind she knew the pain would come but her body refused it. She stood and brushed the ash off her legs, vaguely troubled when she saw the gray powder falling on the Wan's body. Turning in a slow circle, she took a last look at the village then walked away from it.

When she reached the garden plot, she pulled open the gate and walked into the enclosure. Behind her she could hear the drone and snort of nuggar hidden in the darkness. When she stepped aside, the nuggar noises grew louder and more disturbed. She knelt, wrapped shaking fingers around the thick tough vine that webbed the earth; closing her eyes she concentrated on keeping her fingers hooked, trying to work the tuber loose. Three nuggar pattered through the opening and started clawing and rooting at the earth, their six clawed feet creating rapid destruction in the plot. With a sound almost like a sigh, the tuber Roha was pulling at came from the earth. She broke it from the stem, glanced at the growing numbers of nuggar digging, squealing, nipping at each other as they scrambled for the food they craved. She stood, clutching the dirt-crusted tuber, watching the writhing backs of the nuggar among the whipping leaves. *I should open all the gates for them*, she thought. *Better the nuggar should have the work of the women than that the Fieyl should.* She brushed absently at the hairy tuber. *Tomorrow. There's no hurry now. Tomorrow.* Avoiding the nuggar, she sidled through the gate, then moved slowly along the familiar path.

She stopped at the stream to wash the dirt from the tuber and to drink, the crisp coolness of the water shocking her awake. Not bothering to remove her ragged kilt, she slid her body into the water and sat in the rapid flow, breaking and eating the tuber; her knife was gone, left behind to be trampled into the earth by the Kinya-kin-kin, but she didn't need it, ripping the tough rind away with her claws, chewing the stringy, tart orange-yellow flesh into a paste, washing the paste down with gulps of cold water.

When she was finished, she washed her hands and mouth, then pulled herself reluctantly from the stream.

There was little to see. The scatter of stars and the rags of Mambila provided just enough light through the vault of leaves to make trunks visible as darker blacks against the grayed-black of the night air. As the first flush of new energy from the food and water began to fade, she stood on the path, wondering where to go, what to do, finally understanding there was only one refuge left to her—her womb tree.

When she reached the mat-akuat, she hadn't the strength to climb into the lower branches. She pushed through the tangle of aerial roots and nestled on the thick leaf-mold next to the trunk. As she lay in the darkness, her body aching, too tired to sleep, she drifted in and out of consciousness, surrounded by the sharp familiar scent of the dream-sap; sometimes she talked with Rihon who was warm and strong beside her one minute and gone the next. Other times she knew with terrible clarity the ruin of her life and was filled with a corrosive hatred for the demons, a hatred she knew was futile even when she suffered it. In between she was troubled, wondering what to do with herself in the morning, whether she had any right or need to keep living. Finally her exhausted body overcame her suffering mind and she slept.

She woke to great noises and beams of light walking across the sky.

THE END OF THE HUNT

CHAPTER XII   Aleytys

She woke to the clink of glass against metal and a foggy gray light that bleached the color out of things. Impatiently she kicked away her blanket, watched with interest as Swardheld slipped one of the lamps back into its bracket and moved along the wall to the next. "Hunting?"

"Had a thought." After he lifted the lamp down, he glanced over his shoulder at her. "I hoped to be done with this before you woke." He eased the oil reservoir free, shook it vigorously, grimaced, reassembled the lamp and replaced it. "A dud would be embarrassing."

With narrowed eyes, he contemplated the lamp hanging over the worktable, one Aleytys hadn't been able to reach. As Swardheld rubbed thoughtfully at his beard, Aleytys sat up. "You've tried all the others?"

"Saved the best till last." He took a deep breath then lifted the heavy table smoothly away from the wall, walked around it and lifted down the lamp. After dismantling it, he shook the reservoir with small absurdly gentle jerks. Aleytys met his laughing eyes as they both heard a muted scratching noise. "Now that's gratifying," he murmured.

"Stop gloating and see if you've really found something." She jumped to her feet and stood beside him, looking down at the base of the lamp.

Swardheld applied a slow pressure to the oil reservoir's cap. "Get some kind of container from the kitchen," he said absently, increasing the force he was using on the cap as it stubbornly refused to turn. "I don't want to spill this oil over me."

"Oh yes, master." Aleytys grinned as he looked up, startled then she trotted into the kitchen. She returned as he was easing the cap free, set a small metal bowl down as he breathed

188

his relief. She watched anxiously as he tilted the reservoir and poured out a few ounces of oil.

Something heavy flopped against the opening, too large to fall through it. Swardheld fished into the hole with two fingers and eased a bulky object through. He thrust the reservoir at Aleytys, his eyes fixed on the thing he was holding, a package wrapped in multiple layers of foil.

When the foil was peeled away, three flat discs—each a little larger than a mid-sized coin—lay in the palm of his hand. He laughed and closed his fingers over them. "Bonanza." He piled them on the table as they had been packaged, one on top of the other. "Three ships to choose from, Lee."

Aleytys flipped the top disc off the pile, listening as it rang on the table. "So little and bland-looking to be so important."

He tugged at his moustache, eyes glinting with triumph. "You'd have had a hell of a time getting in if we hadn't found them."

"If you hadn't found them, you mean." She ran her eyes over him. "Go put some clothes on, you peacock, and try not to prance when you walk. It's unbecoming."

Grinning unrepentantly, he walked away from her with an exaggerated swagger that made her giggle. At the arch he turned, winked at her. "Take your own advice, freyka-miella." She threw the lamp reservoir at him but he ducked behind the curtain in time to avoid it. It rattled to the floor, hidden as the curtain dropped back in place. Aleytys went into the kitchen to make a pot of cha.

Swardheld stopped the carrier while it was still under the trees around the burned-off shelf where the three Scav ships sat in debris from months of idleness. There were symbols smeared on the metal—dried clays that were flaking off or had run in long smears during rainstorms—dots and jags and staring eyes along with streaks of carbon from the fires that had been set around the landing gear. He glanced up, then around. "Light-web's cleared off. What do you think?"

She shrugged. "Won't know till we try." Stepping past him, she looked up into a hazy sky, the cool, spice-laden wind blowing her hair, "We'd better be ready to move fast. The Tikh'asfour Packs will surely be edging in as close as they dare. Soon as I announce that we're sitting here, they'll be on us." She examined the three ships. "Which one?"

Swardheld raised his brows. "What do I know you don't?" When she just looked at him, he laughed. "All right. Number one is a Spinkseri yacht. Fast. But too complicated. Needs a lot of maintenance, which it might not get in the hands of a bunch of Scavs. Showy but takes too much fuel for me to like it." He glanced at her, got no response. "Right. Number two. The big one. Eschelle Destroyer. God knows how he got hold of that. Damn uncomfortable. Fast and fuel-hungry with a good-sized hold. If the original weapons are in place, it's a damn dangerous machine. Given a guess, I'd say that one was Quale's. Needs next to no maintenance so it's probably in fairly good shape. Number three's a Farsan troopship. Looks like it's been in one too many wars. Well?"

She chuckled. "Seems to me you've made your choice."

"My choice?"

"The Haestavaada have promised me a ship. I see no reason why you shouldn't have one also." She gestured at the ships. "Especially when we have three to choose from. Who's going to contest your right?" She glanced at him, smiled at the suppressed eagerness she felt in him. "If you can fly the damn thing."

"Could you?" He looked amused.

"Yes. Why?"

"And where was I when you were learning?"

"God knows." She smiled, shook her head. "All right. Let's move."

While Swardheld shepherded the carrier, Scavs, vaada, valaada, and Drij through the trees and brush, then over the rocks and ash to the center ship, Aleytys went swiftly up the line of toe- and handholds to the lock. She had to try all three discs before she found the one that started the lock cycling open. The fact that it did open was a good enough indication that *Nowhere* was far enough out of the sink to let complicated electronic devices function as they were meant to. She looked down, waved to Swardheld, then swung into the lock. Until her foot touched the floor inside the lock, the ship was dark and dead. As she moved inward, it woke around her. Light strips set into the sides of the corridors gradually came on, lighting her way to the bridge. The air freshened perceptibly as she drew close to a point in the ship just above the center of gravity. She stopped at the entrance to the bridge and looked around, felt the ship breathing around her. *Like a waking animal*, she thought.

She moved briskly across the small chamber and settled herself in a command chair adjusted to Quale's reach—which made things a bit difficult since her arms were half a foot shorter than his. Rubbing her hands slowly together, she inspected the rows of touch sensors. "Good, good," she murmured. "Got it."

Sliding forward to the edge of the seat, she touched a few sensors, then moved her fingers over the board, coding more surely as the moments passed—opening the hold, unfolding the crane and lowering the slings, powering the hold so that valaad guards could finally rest after they plugged in the life-support for the Queen. She hesitated a moment, frowned, then settled back in the chair, her eyes on the great screen as small swiveling owl eyes fed images from the ground and the inside of the hold. She watched as Swardheld and Ksiyl got the casket loaded then turned abruptly on the five remaining Scavs and got their rifles away, leaving them with futile scowls and a great deal of surprise. She slid forward again, shut the hold doors, teetered on the edge of the seat, watching as Swardheld eased Drij off the carrier and led her toward the exit.

She was standing when he came in. "What'd you do with Drij?"

"You didn't watch?" When she shook her head, he said, "In the navigator's quarters. We don't lack room. I strapped her in, by the way. Have you squirted out the signal to the Haestavaada?"

"No." She walked beside him and stood with her hand resting lightly on the back curve of the chair as he settled himself in and began examining the controls as she had done before him. "I've coded the signal into the computer," she said quietly. "All that remains is to push the button and send it out. I wanted to be sure we were ready to jump before I pinpointed us."

"Mm." His long fingers tapped gently over several sensor plates, touching the ship-beast into a greater alertness. She felt as well as heard the flow of energy as the engines began mumbling through the warm-up necessitated by the down-months. His eyes fixed on the readouts, Swardheld mur-

mured, "Get settled, Lee. Don't want you to worry about."
He continued to play his hands over the board. "No breaks,
steady flow of power." His eyes scanned the screen.
"Tikh'asfour at extreme range, coming fast. Move, Lee!"

Aleytys slipped into the navigator's chair and fastened the
crash-web over her body, pulling it as taut as she could. Like
the command chair, this one was too big for her, but the web
was a membrane designed to adapt closely to the forms of
the body and absorb energy from its movements. She touched
the sensor squares by her fingertips and activated her own
screen. Three very faint blotches were visible in the upper
corner. *The Packs*, she thought. As she watched, the blurs
sharpened rapidly into clusters of pinpoint lights. *Coming fast
is right.* She glanced at Swardheld, saw him punch the button
that would send the signal squealing in compact bursts to the
Haesatavaada fleet that was supposed to be standing by.
Queen rising, She thought. *It's what you wanted. Queen rising. You got the signal. Stir yourselves, Haestavaada.* Smiling
nervously, she watched the dots grow larger. *Let's get out of
here,* she thought.

Power shuddered into the engines. The ship rose in a sharp
curve, then went tumbling, gyrating, falling in a wild sprawl
around the world as the nearest Pack hurried too soon into
attack, their beams lancing around the ship, robbed of power
by distance and the diffusing effect of the atmosphere. Riding
a howling hurricane that left behind a churned, ravaged land,
a destruction doubled by the off-shunt of beams that glanced
from the shields, Swardheld completed the circuit with all
three packs coming down after him, interfering with each
other in their eagerness to take the prize. Mouth set in a grim
smile, Swardheld sent the ship abruptly up and out, taking
the Packs by surprise as he wove dangerously through the
ragged tendrils of the Sink and gaining a large bite of lead
time as Pack ships tried to sort themselves out and follow.

"Where the hell are the Haestavaada!" Glaring at a screen
that showed the packs stringing out behind and nothing at all
waiting in front, Swardheld squeezed as much speed as he
could out of the ship. There was no way he could fight the
ship, not without a trained, skilled crew as backup. He could
fly it for a while on his own; with Aleytys as navigator and
relief pilot he could keep it going near top speed for a little
longer—the Destroyer had been designed for a small crew—

but for the day-to-day survival of himself and his ship, he'd need a couple of men to take care of the engines, two or three more to handle the weapons and general maintenance, a navigator, and, for the comfort of everyone, a cook. Not having most of these, he concentrated on putting as much distance between himself and the pursuing Packs as he could while he kept an eye watching for the promised fleet. The Destroyer was just a little faster than the pack ships; bit by agonizing bit Swardheld began to pull away from them. He glanced across at Aleytys. "I think we've got them beat. What happened to your Haestavaada?"

Aleytys scowled at her stubbornly empty screen. "Don't ask me. Tell you this, my friend. When we get back I'm going to yell loud and long. We could have needed them bad. I know they're supposed to be no damn good at attacking but they promised me a double-dozen ships to distract the Packs . . . what's that?" A diffused blur slid slowly into the upper right quadrant of her screen. "If that's them . . . what're you doing?"

Swardheld turned the ship away from the blur though as a result he started losing ground to the pursuing Packs. "Until we reach split-speed. . . . ah! thought so. Two fives. Tikh'asfour. Probably chased off your distraction. You'll have to try that trick we thought up when we looked over the Tikh'asfour schematics."

"Mmph. That was a wild-chance thing." She eyed the ominously enlarging dots. "I don't know if I can *reach* far enough to give me the time I'll need to locate the pinch point."

"Stop arguing, freyka, and start reaching. Wild chance or not, it's damn well the only chance." He stopped talking and began concentrating on the computer whisper in his ear and the lighted touchplates in front of him, trying to coax a bit more speed from the sub-light engines.

Aleytys re-settled herself in her chair, closed her eyes and fashioned a probe which she sent searching for a ship she could enter, reaching out and out until it grew tenuous and she began to grow afraid; then there was a nibbling sensation as something flicked past the sensors dimmed to vagueness at the end-point of the probe. Several somethings, moving too fast for her to seize on. She chased after them but they kept slipping away. *Too slow, dammit, too slow*, she thought. With

great reluctance she began to draw more power from her
river, afraid of exhausting her source by expending herself
too recklessly—becoming more and more aware of the limitations of the power she could call on.

The tickle came again and she dived after it, got a brief
hold inside, lost it. She went after the ship again, tightened
her hold and began expanding her awareness, fighting a
growing urge to scramble desperately for her goal since in the
scramble she would lose everything. When the ship shuddered around her she knew—peripherally at least, since her
attention was focused so passionately through the probe—that
they were under attack.

As she fought to hold onto what she'd gained and to work
her probe into the engine room, the Destroyer faltered, then
squirted away, corkscrewing, dipping, slipping off heatbeams
and vibros, ducking flights of missiles whose proximity trig-
gers set them off to add silent shudders of flying shards to the
tormented area around the ships. Swardheld was crouched intently at the board, his crash-web rolled to one side, lightly
strapped in, his fingers dancing more surely over the sensors
as he learned the ship, his face growing grimmer as the
Tikh'asfour sting-ships swarmed more thickly around and the
Destroyer's shields—powerful as they were with all the energy he could spare from the engines channeled into them—
were reaching the limits of what they could absorb.

Aleytys felt her way through the sting-ship, gaining more
facility in holding the working end of the probe within that
ship no matter how it turned or twisted as it sought to attack
the Destroyer. She found the pinch-point on the anti-matter
bottle buried behind layers of shielding, invulnerable to ordinary attack. Feverish with triumph she fashioned a hot loop
and drew it through the pinch, loosing the power within, letting it expand until it reduced the Tikh'asfour and their ship
to their constituent atoms.

Having pulled away in that hovering instant before the
destruction began, Aleytys started looking for another ship,
socking in the probe and opening up the bottle almost as
soon as she felt the familiar tickle. Again and again she
dipped into the storm outside the embattled Destroyer, whif-
fing away ship after ship until she *reached* a last time and
found nothing. Weary, dispirited at the number of deaths it
had taken to break the attack, feeling the inevitable letdown

after a long period of exhaustive effort, she opened her eyes, unhitched the crash-web, stretched cramped legs and arms, finally looked up at the screen to see a diminishing blur as a few Tikh'asfour ships fled the carnage. She watched them fade, sighed, turned to meet Swardheld's eyes. "This time. . . ."

He stretched and grinned at her. "This time." He refocused the main screen on the view inside the hold.

The valaada of the Queen's guard looked a bit battered; two of them were holding rifles on sullen, muttering Scavs as the rest moved about the Queen's casket. Two Scavs lay dead among curled-up vaada who were scattered haphazardly about the floor like discarded husks, having relinquished such hold as they had on life now that they were no longer needed to protect the Queen. Aleytys and Swardheld watched a few more minutes, then Swardheld switched the screen back to the outside. "Split jump coming up." He settled back in the chair. "The computer can handle the ship now."

Together they swung around until they were facing each other, smiling both, uneasy both, now that the distractions of their fight to stay alive were no longer there to protect them from the unresolved tensions that hung between them. "It's a good ship," Aleytys said, choosing words almost at random to break the silence and give her back some control over what was happening.

"Tough and rough." He closed his eyes as the screen flickered and transfer was made into the intersplit, the glitter of the stars altering through shimmering whorls into a sprinkle of black dust in a gray fog. Aleytys watched him, worried, wondering if the distorting, twisting, sickening, mercifully brief transition between states had loosened the Swardheld personality from Quale's body. As the ship steadied and the faint sense of oppression lingered in the background, as it would the length of the trip, Swardheld opened his eyes and smiled at her.

"What are you going to do?" She wanted to ask him how he was but the words wouldn't come—as if she and he had built a wall between them that would pass commonplaces but screened out anything of a personal nature. "The Haestavaada will repair and refuel the ship for you. They owe me, dammit, after leaving us dangling like they did." She looked around as if answers lay hidden in paneling and banks of sensor plates and readouts. At his silence, she glanced back at his face.

His eyes were closed then opened slowly and focused somewhere over her shoulder. "Keep on as a Scavenger, I suppose. For a while anyway. No papers required. A little smuggling, maybe some informal freighting. Might hunt up Arel, your smuggler friend. Start checking out what Quale's got in the computer. Five days before we touch down on Duvaks. Time enough to make plans when I've got more information."

Five days, she thought with a touch of horror generated as much by the parting that waited for them as by the prospect of enforced togetherness, limited as they were by the narrow confines of the ship. In the midst of her preoccupation amber eyes opened in her head. She turned her attention inward, grateful for the distraction. "Ask him how he's fitting in that body," Harskari said, ignoring in her turn the turbulence around her. Aleytys could feel the restiveness in the words with their controlled passion; the voice crackled with energy and the face forming around the eyes was lined and hungry. Aleytys was torn briefly between satisfaction at seeing another being sharing her disturbance and shame at the satisfaction, then she shoved both aside. "Harskari wants to know if you're having any problems with the body," she told Swardheld.

He raised an eyebrow. "It's mine." After a short silence he swung away to contemplate the arrays of sensor plates, then added, "A few months and I can say this is not just mine but myself. Quale's gone, only some lingering muscle memories tucked away that can be surprising." The last words were clipped, final. He pulled the computer interface over his head and began listening with an intensity that built the wall between them again, this time with no openings for even the most innocuous of questions.

Aleytys closed her eyes. "Well?"

Harskari blinked slowly; Shadith materialized and both of them seemed to move about impatiently. *Like fleas in my head,* Aleytys thought, smiling when Harskari looked annoyed. The sorceress pinched her generous lips together, then smiled reluctantly. "It's hard to be patient. All these years, millennia, all the ways I've learned for coping—they don't apply any more. Yet I must be patient—Ah! I want a body,

Lee. A young woman's body, strong and healthy. How and where? I don't know. I don't know. A young woman newly dead and dead by accident—how can I pray for that and how can I help praying?"

Shadith sighed. "I know. If you find me a tone-deaf body, Lee, I'll come back and haunt you."

"You're shoving a lot on my shoulders, the two of you."

"We know," Shadith said, glancing at Harskari who was brooding quietly, still visible but nebulous as she struggled to cope with more emotion than she was accustomed to handling. "Chance—that's what will bring us what we want. As it did for Swardheld. But you can be listening, can't you, ready to take advantage of that chance? That's really all we ask, Lee. Keep watching."

Five long difficult days crawled past. Aleytys tended Drij who now spent her hours curled up in fetal position, uncurling her so she could eat, washing her, talking to her though she never got an answer, forcing her to walk around and around the small cabin. When she wasn't with Drij, she made her way back to the hold and spent some time signing with Ksiyl. Swardheld spoke little to her, immersing himself in the computer as a refuge from confrontation. She would have spent more time in the hold than she did, enjoying the happiness of the Queen's guard—for they were quietly content, their chitin glowing with health—but the Scavs depressed her; they were as close to mindless animals as sentient beings could get and remain alive, dangerous as rogue animals driven to act outside the confines of instinct by some fault in their brains, crouching against the hold wall half-swallowed by shadows, shadows themselves with eyes that followed her, followed every move she made, eyes that hated her and desired her, eyes of men that disturbed her because she'd written them off, used them to buffer herself from the dangers of the mistlands without thinking of them as men, caring even less that they died than she'd cared about the Tikh'asfour in the ships she'd exploded.

On the fifth day the Destroyer slipped from the intersplit and Swardheld sent the prescribed warning ahead to Duvaks so the defenses would be turned aside for them. Aleytys watched the navigator's screen as he brought the ship down, marveling at the great crowd gathered about the field, a

faceless mass, an intensity of yearning so strong she caught
hints of it a mile from the ground. Her hands lay restlessly
on the chair arms. The Hunt was done. The tightrope was
crossed once more. She had a moment's repose before she
had to walk it again. The Queen was delivered and the vaada
of this world were saved from a lingering death. She watched
the vaada and wondered if they even knew how the war got
started. *A habit of hatred,* she thought. *Why do they keep
on? Only out of habit? They hired Hunters' Inc. to get their
Queen back. We find things, why can't we mend things as
well?* She knew what Head would say. *Don't get involved
with the natives. We have a limited mandate, Lee. What right
do we have to impose our values on other worlds? Let them
alone, Lee, or you'll do more harm than you realize. We've
learned the hard way through bitter mistakes that cost us
fees—yes, money. Money that meant the difference between
living and dying for some of our people. So strangle that
temptation to step in and fix things, Lee. Nothing is ever as
simple as it looks.* She glanced at Swardheld's intent face.
Nothing is ever as simple as it looks, she thought.

When the ship was settled, Swardheld kept his eyes fixed
on the screen, watching a ragged group of valaada coming
across the metacrete field toward them. Then he swung
around, startling her. "Handle this, Lee. I'd rather stay up
here, keep out of this as much as I can."

She nodded. "Good enough. Open the hold, I'll meet them
there."

The Duvaks valaada moved into a respectful circle as the
portals cycled open and the crane lowered the Queen's casket
to the metacrete, the carrier left behind in the hold. They
waited in taut silence as the Guard took their places around
the casket and Ksiyl began the process of loosing the Queen.
Unnoticed in the portal, Aleytys watched, some of her
flatness slipping away as she was drawn into the tidal expectation surging from vaada and valaada. Standing above them
she could look down into the casket as it opened, could see
the Queen resting in the cavity shaped to her body, that
golden body veiled by miles of tubing, tubing that was being
withdrawn and stored in the sides of the casket.

The Queen stirred. Beyond the woven fence, Aleytys could
sense another great stirring, an unbearable heightening of tension.

The Queen stirred again, reached out long golden arms, closed top-hands and mid-pincers on the sides of the casket and pulled herself up until she was crouching in the cavity. Her crumpled wings moved, swayed a little through air still as on a summer morning before a storm, streaks of gold, shimmers of azure, glimmers of emerald and ruby playing among the shadows in the deep crooked folds. Her swollen abdomen began to shrink as the fluid stored there flowed into the veins that wove through the translucent wings, straightening the wings, spreading them wider and wider until they caught the sun in sheets of color slipping over the flattening planes. Long gilded cords fell away from the gilded harness that fit over her thorax, resting in loops on the metacrete, ending in clips snapped onto the ceremonial belts of the Queen's guard.

Air whistling through her spiracles, the Queen lurched to her feet. She was a great glowing golden creature with gossamer wings spreading twenty feet on either side. The wings moved, beat together behind her then stroked down, continued to move until the strokes were continuous and steady and she was rising and settling with them. Slowly, ponderously, the Queen rose into the air, each foot gained clearly easier for her than the one before, until she flew high over the field, her tethering cords stretching beneath her as she moved.

Except for Maladra Shayl, who waited for Aleytys beside a landing foot, the valaada who'd come to meet the ship marched off with the Queen's guard, tugging the Queen with them toward the domed hall where she'd spend the rest of her short life with her wing muscles cut, the glory of her flight forgotten. Not really intelligent, she would placidly endure her confinement, producing eggs by the thousands.

Aleytys watched a moment longer, tears drawn from her by the sheer beauty of the flight, then she swung down to join the Haestavaada representative. YOU PROMISED ME A FLEET TO DISTRACT THE TIKH'ASFOUR, she signed, snapping her hands angrily through the movements.

THE FLEET WAS SENT, BUT THE TIKH'ASFOUR DISCOVERED THEM TOO SOON AND THEY WERE FORCED TO WITHDRAW. The valaad's small top-hand hung a moment in front of its thorax, then began moving again, exhibiting a touch of petulance. YOU DID NOT REQUIRE THEM. THAT IS OBVIOUS.

WE HAD LUCK, SHAYL VALAAD—AND OTHER RESOURCES

THAT MIGHT NOT HAVE BEEN ENOUGH HAD THINGS BEEN A
LITTLE DIFFERENT. I WANT THIS SHIP REPAIRED AND FUELED—
THE DAMAGE WAS TAKEN IN YOUR SERVICE BECAUSE THE
FLEET WASN'T WHERE YOU PROMISED IT WOULD BE, THE
FUEL SPENT FOR THE SAME REASON. I WILL NEED TRANSPORT
TO WOLFF. THIS SHIP'S MASTER AND I WILL BE PARTING HERE.
She glanced upward, shivered with a sudden chill as she re-
alized loneliness and loss began now, not sometime in the fu-
ture. The impatient clacking of the valaad's mandibles called
her back.

Is that all? it signed.

YES . . . NO! *Drij*, she thought. *I've got to do something
about her. I forgot her.* I NEED PASSAGE FOR ANOTHER PERSON
TO WOLFF. THIS YOU CAN CHARGE TO ME SINCE IT IS NOT
YOUR BUSINESS.

IS THAT ALL?

YES. FOR NOW—THAT'S ALL. Still a little angry and more
than a little disturbed by the fact that she was walking away
from Swardheld, she moved with the prim and disapproving
valaad toward the domed building where the Queen had vanished and the valaada had their offices, knowing this valaad
was already reluctant to give her the ship they'd promised—
in spite of the contract they'd signed and their eagerness to
get her services, knowing she'd have to fight to get them to
do anything about Swardheld's ship, knowing she was going
to have to sweat out the ruling of the arbiters on Helvetia
who would decide if she'd earned her fee, if the Haestavaada
were bound by their promise of a bonus, a ship. *Nothing is
ever as simple as it looks,* she thought.

ROHA

Roha huddled against the tree trunk, her arms pressed over
ears, her eyes clamped shut as the light and noise shook the
world around her, going on and on until she was battered
with light and noise into an unthinking daze, clinging to the
tree, her claws sunk into the soft bark and wood, smelling
stone burning, wood burning, the air reeking with drug-saps
released by the fires, swinging in and out of reality, opening
her eyes and squeezing them shut again as the forest wavered
and melted around her, flattened into patterns that shattered,

reformed, melted again. The noise went on and on and the world broke apart around her.

Then it was gone. The noise was gone. The roaring winds dropped to a whisper of air. She lifted her head, rubbed absently at her flat chest, then at her eyes, crawled from the cage of aerial roots and stood, dazed, on a small patch of beaten earth staring around with disbelief. Trees were down, their trunks woven in a tangle by the great wind. A whimpering pudsi, its broad wings broken, blood a thread of red lining the working beak, lay by her feet, its feathers tickling her as it shuddered to a painful death. She shivered and stepped away.

Picking her way through the shattered trees, walking over their broken backs, drawn reluctantly but helplessly to the shelf where the sky-seeds sat, she came to the end of the trees and stood gazing at the destruction before her, appalled that such power should be given to demons. Great gouges sliced through the mother stone, the bones of earth herself. In places it was melted and still bubbling. Two of the seeds were crumpled and charred and pierced with ragged terrible holes like the wounds a hunting spear would make in a man's belly.

The third seed was gone. She looked up but saw nothing, only the sun still low on the eastern horizon, but she knew with a cold certainty that the Fire-hair was gone, taking the Nafa and the brother-killer with her; even without going to the Nafa's house and finding it empty she knew this. That terrible burning disturbing demon was gone. Gone. Roha gasped, wheeled and ran from the shelf, wanting desperately the comfort of her own kind, heading blindly for the burned-out village and the traces of the captive women. The Rum Fieyl had taken the Amar women. Perhaps they would take her too. She could creep among the women; they would slap and scold her then set her to work and she'd have a place again. The demons were gone. Gone and the world had to change.

She circled the village and found the trail of the captured women. She drank from the stream and ate some of the fruit still hanging from a mat-amat, then started off along the trail. All the day she trotted and walked after the women, passing after a while into land that was strange to her. The wandering breeze blew the leaves about over her head while the sun painted shifting dappled shadows on the dark moist soil under her feet. Around her she heard the soft rustles of life as the small ones frightened into hiding by the morning's terror crept out, forgetting what had driven them to shelter in the immediate hungers that clutched their small bellies, blessing Roha with a little of their forgetfulness as she drew pleasure from sounds and smells she'd known all her life. She sniffed at the air, felt the sun rippling across her skin, took pleasure in the play of light and shadow, the cool earth beneath her feet.

She reached the Fieyl village at sunset when the shadows were long on the earth and the last wisps of Mambila a tracing of light on the horizon. The village was lit by the feast-fires. The smell of roast nuggar was strong, reminding her that she was very hungry. She picked her way past the roasting pits and moved through the outer ring of the stilt houses, close to weeping with the familiarity of it all, the rattle of a Gawer's drum and the Fieyl Gawer's chanting of the Battle Triumph, the people answering with whoops and beating their cupped palms on their chests, children running about chasing each other, wrestling, their bodies slick with nuggar grease.

A small boychild saw her standing at the rim of shadows and shouted to his father. Some adults looked around. The dismay spread through the crowd until they all knew who was standing there. Her pleasure melting before their stares, Roha clutched at hope and waited for the men to come and put her with the other Amar women.

The crowd parted silently in front of the Fieyl Serk who strode up to Roha and stopped before her, a tall old woman with a lined, powerful face. Jabbing a finger at Roha's chest, not quite touching her, she said, "Sakawa. Go."

Roha saw the woman's fear and the accompanying cold hatred and saw with it the death of her hopes. There was nothing left for her, nothing at all. She turned away and walked from the village, leaving silence behind and a blighted celebration. Even when she reached the forest she kept walking, wanting to lose wholly the sight and smell of the village. Finally she climbed into the lower branches of a mat-akuat like her womb tree, folded small branches and wove them together to make a sleeping pad in the crotch of two larger branches, curled up and drifted into a dream-haunted sleep.

She dreamed of flames leaping around the gray demon-egg, consuming it, dreamed of flames rising around her, burning her free of her curse so she could return clean to the arms of her cousin the Dark Twin who had created the world from her womb and held the spirits of the dead within her until they were born again in the womb of the world. When the dream was over she dropped into a deep sleep beyond dream, beyond pain and loss, cradled in a nothingness that gave rest to both her exhausted body and tormented soul.

When she woke, she felt a sense of purpose growing within her, a thing that puzzled her until she remembered the dream. Dropping to the springy tops of the aerial roots, she pressed her face against the trunk. "Be blessed, Dark Cousin," she murmured. "Be blessed for showing me the way."

She reached her village clearing late in the day. Ignoring the rotting bodies and the ash, she ran through the shards of what had once been her home and turned in to one of the abandoned garden patches. Though the nuggar had cleaned out most of the tubers, she found enough and tied the hard knobby roots into a bundle using vine fiber then knotted a sling for them from that same fiber and slipped it over her shoulder. The sun was going down by the time she finished, but she started anyway for the mistlands.

She moved with some caution down the long treacherous slope then loped along until she could no longer move, re-tracing a path her feet seemed to know without difficulty though the night was darker than before, much darker, with Mambila no longer in the sky. A few floating ghosts bobbed over her head as she moved but she ignored them until she settled in a patch of grass beside a small spring whose water was hot but still drinkable if it was dipped out and left to cool a while. She whipped a branch through the ghosts, driving them off, than ate two of the tubers, drank, curled up to sleep, indifferent to possible dangers, knowing in her depths that, no matter what, she would live to reach the Egg.

When dawn lightened the mist, she woke to the touch of trailing fibers as the ghost prepared to take her. Crying out with disgust, she churned her arm through the ghost, breaking it apart, sending the small parts fleeing. She dipped water to cool without taking her eyes from the swarm of small thumbtip-sized ghosts, then dropped a tuber into the hot water to cook.

All that day she kept moving, loping when she could, walking when she was too weary to move faster. She kept her mind fixed on the Egg, the burning Egg, and felt strength coming to her from the earth each time her feet touched down. At intervals she felt Rihon running with her in the mist; she could hear his breathing, could feel the flow of strength and support from him.

When the sun was gone and the mist was dark and closing in around her, she sniffed out water and began making a second camp. Overhead, the ghosts swarmed and began to merge, stalking her as she moved around, the tendrils reaching for her. She dodged about, caught up handfuls of gravel and sprayed them with it. They were more persistent than before, reforming quickly when the stones broke them apart. She scooped out water and left it to cool, swished a tuber clean of dirt, then retreated beneath a squat thorny bush to eat and fend off the ghosts. Thought they couldn't merge and still reach her, the small nodules filtered through the matted thorns to suck tiny bits of energy from her until she prickled all over and felt a languor possessing her that almost enticed her out from the bush until hunger stirred in her. She backed further under the bush and bit down angrily on the stringy yellow flesh of the tuber, moving constantly as she did so in an attempt to keep the ghosts off, slapping at head and neck, brushing her hands and forearms now and then against the bush, acquiring scratches that burned and itched whenever she moved.

Before trying to sleep, she drank and gathered piles of small stones around the bush. Between snatches of fitful sleep, she drove the ghosts back with showers of rock, only to have them return and drain more strength from her.

She started out again as soon as light crept through the mist, the diffused shadowless light of early morning. After flinging more stones at the hovering ghosts, she trotted on toward the demon Egg, a short switch broken painfully from the thornbush carried in one hand, used to fend off the ghosts, slapping viciously through them when they came close enough for her to reach them. Before noon she was close to exhaustion, beginning to wonder if she'd ever reach the Egg, reminding herself again and again of the dream, the cleansing fire. Walking heavily, the branch dragging against her leg, too tired to feel any pain from the thorns, she grew careless about where she was putting her feet.

Stone cracked apart under her. Startled out of her lethargy, she threw herself to one side, tearing her skin, driving the air from her lungs as she crashed against the earth. Dazed, she lifted her arms to fend off the ghosts.

She stared. The ghosts were holding back, avoiding the steam rising from the hidden spring she'd opened to the air. "So you don't like heat." She sat up and started pounding with her heel against the stone, breaking away all she could, exposing more of the water until the stone was solid enough to hold her body. She curled up beside the spring, the warmth under her combining with her weariness and a newborn sense of safety to send her into a deep and dreamless sleep.

When she woke, it was late afternoon. She cooked two tubers in the boiling water, ate, then started off again, moving at a slow trot, still a little stiff and sore from her nap and her painful tumble before the nap. For some time the ghosts left her alone, then came drifting back until they swarmed over her again. Having recovered her switch, she kept them off and kept herself moving as quickly as she could through the dreary dripping land. When she saw the hard gray bulge of the Egg, she felt a great relief and almost an affection for it.

The clearing around the Egg was scattered with fragments of the demon's hard skin, the softer inside part eaten away. She lay beneath the leafless brush at the edge of the open space, scratching at small cuts on her shoulders from the brush she'd wiggled through, accepting the pain in return for protection from the ghosts, rubbing too at insect bites, gazing at the Egg, at the round hole in it, at the plumes of steam rising behind it like smoke. "Burn," she whispered, smiling warmly at the Egg. "Burn with me."

She gathered herself, then burst from the brush in a crouching run. When the ghosts began converging on her, she slashed at them with the thorn branch, whipping it through and through the swarm, sending them skittering away. Swishing the branch desperately and clumsily back and forth over her head, she stumbled across the clearing and threw herself into the hole in the side of the Egg.

Frightened and reluctant, she moved along the burrow in the Egg, looking back continually at the pale gray round of the opening, the last light, the only light. The inside smelled of mistlanders, their musty stench overlaying the pungent odor of the demons. Before she wanted to, she reached the end of the burrow and looked a very short way down another burrow, seeing little more than that it was there. She crouched at the crossing of the burrows, unable to force herself deeper into the stinking blackness, unable to break away from the only light. She crouched there until the smell made her feel sick, until she knew she had to move on or leave and she couldn't bear to leave. Trembling and nauseated, she straightened and began feeling her way into the lightless burrow, stumbling over things she couldn't see, bits of the Egg. It was broken badly inside; she hadn't realized that before, but her hand slipped over torn and crumpled edges and her feet knocked into bits of things on the springy floor. Her fingers slipped on a smooth thing, rather like water-polished rock. It was cool under her fingers, something pleasant, so she stroked it, then gasped as long strips of something smooth began to shine around her, like a flake of white translucent stone she'd found once in the bed of the stream high up on the mountain. Hesitantly she touched the shining thing, and it too was cool under her fingers. She could see many more of the strips. Some of them—most of them—were still dead but others lit the burrow for her.

For some time she wandered through the Egg; as she gained confidence she began to touch things, especially the smooth rounds like the first one that had brought the shining things alive; gradually she became aware of a low hum that shivered through the Egg, a hum that grew louder as she kept touching the smooth rounds. Sometimes other things lit up, sometimes not, sometimes she heard creaking or crashing noises, sometimes parts of the wall slid aside, sometimes chimes rang. The Egg was coming to life around her in a way that both frightened and fascinated her, at the same time reassuring her because she felt that it wanted the same thing she did, that its time was done as hers was done, that it lay abandoned just as she walked its burrows abandoned.

She found her way finally to the Egg's heart, where things she couldn't understand murmured to themselves behind thick walls of that hardness that was greater than stone, like the beating of her own heart within the walls of her flesh. She felt the Egg's life strong here, so strong it was hard to breathe. Panting, the sweat rolling down the sides of her head, the Dark Twin powerful in her, laughing her triumph, feeling the Egg's life enter into her and laugh its triumph with her, she ran along the walls touching all the smooth rounds she could reach, laughing more as they glowed to her touch and the glow danced on her face and along her arms. As she moved, the humming sound grew louder and louder until it was thrumming in her ears, until it filled her head, then another sound overlaid the humming as if the Egg tried to speak to her, a loud and rapid clicking like the sounds the demons made to each other. She finished her circuit of the walls and went to stand as close to the center of the room as she could, close to the things buzzing now like insects trapped in a buiba's spit. "Burn," she called to the Egg. "Burn with me."

The floor trembled under her feet. She felt it lift. A sound of agony came from the humming things, a clamoring beat as if they fought against each other. The whole Egg shuddered and shifted, throwing Roha down as the floor tilted under her. She sat up, pulled her knees to her chest and wrapped her arms around them. "Burn," she told the humming things, her voice calm now as she was calm within, understanding that the time was come for the ending, though the Egg still struggled as if it didn't understand this at all, struggled like a trapped beast for free running.

Heat flowed around her, coming from the humming things, coming into the air around her, into the skin of the Egg around and beneath her; her body burned where it touched the Egg, hotter and hotter; she struggled to keep her calm, to wait the final burning, the burning that would release her from the pain, but the pain went on and on, her skin blistering where it touched the Egg, the air itself blistering her inside. It wasn't like this in the dream, not this slow cooking, where was the fire, the swift, cleansing, freeing fire? She tried to run over the buckling floor to the burrow that had brought her here. She fell again.

Then the heart of the Egg unfolded before her, in one terrible, wonderful moment the humming things broke open and she saw their great glowing hearts. The glow like the fire of the sun touched her and there was no more pain, only the nothing she had desired.

In the mistlands the Haestavaada ship exploded, triggering a massive shock that gave birth to a hundred young volcanoes, whose ash-laden breath darkened the sky for days and terrified the Rum of all the clans. The slave women of the Fieyl, however, whispered among themselves that this was the passing of the cursed Twin, the Dark One who had brought proud Amar down. Gawer Hith watched the spreading darkness and began making for herself and the other women the Song of Roha. Later, while they worked in the garden patches of the Fieyl, the Amar slaves sang the slow sad song to make the hours pass more quickly.